PLAYING WITH DESIRE

MCKENZIE BROTHERS #4

LEXI BUCHANAN

HFCA Publishing House
Ireland

www.lexibuchanan.net

First Published 2014
This Edition 2024

Copyright © 2013 by Lexi Buchanan

Cover Design: Alison Chaffin Higson
Editor: Sirena Van Schaik
BETA Readers: Emma Clifton, Heidy Bendana, Kristy Louise Garbutt, Jamie Grant and Nadine Winningham

Alison Higson asserts the moral right to be identified as the author of this work

This novel is entirely a work of fiction.

The names, characters and incidents portrayed in it are the work of the author's imagination. Any resemblance to actual persons, living or dead, events or localities is entirely coincidental.

SYNOPSIS

Ruben McKenzie, owner of Kenza Nightclub, can have any woman he wants, but he only wants Rosie, his sweet, innocent employee who is eleven years his junior. Despite his inner struggle, Ruben knows he must keep his feelings in check in order to maintain a professional relationship with Rosie. But the growing tension between them becomes harder to ignore as their interactions become more intense.

Rosie has a lot of life experience, but she knows nothing about hot-blooded, sexy men like Ruben McKenzie. She knows she'll be badly hurt if she takes Ruben into her heart and he moves on to the next woman who catches his eye.

Neither of them can keep their distance for long. The tension in Kenza is finally boiling over, and when Rosie is caught in the crossfire, how far will Ruben go to protect her?

PROLOGUE
RUBEN

ALL I WANTED WAS TO ENJOY THE DAY, BUT FOR SOME reason 'Little Miss. Know-It-All' is driving me crazy. Let me rephrase that. She's driving me crazier than usual, and I damn well blame Michael. It was, of course, Lily's idea for the waitresses to wear pink uniforms and the waiters, pale blue shirts with black pants, but I sure as hell wasn't going to blame my gorgeous sister-in-law. I blame my brother, a much easier target. But my frustration wasn't completely because of him. It was because of a sexy little wait-ress, Rosie, who looks hot as fucking hell in pink with her dark hair and curvy body.

In fact, she's been driving me crazy since Simon, my club manager at Kenza, hired her about nine months ago.

Her looks are amazing but that wasn't what drew me to her originally. It was her sassy mouth and the fact that she doesn't give a damn who she uses it on, which has gotten her into trouble a few times at Kenza. Keith, head of security, has had to intervene several times.

And now, not five minutes ago from me asking her to help Jayne refill the empty platters, she's disappearing toward the barn.

Fuck a brick!

Turning to go after her, I collide with Lily's friend, Sabrina. "Sorry babe, are you okay?" I reach out to steady her.

"I'm fine." She laughs. "I'm sorry too. I wasn't looking where I was going."

"I don't mind. It's not every day I get a beautiful woman falling into my arms." I wink at her.

And she is beautiful, which my brother Lucien has noticed. I hope he sees us right now, and gets jealous because he needs a good kick up the ass or something to go after her. He's been looking at her often enough. If you want my opinion, he's an idiot and needs to get over his hang-up from the accident before someone else snaps her up.

I turn back to the woman in front of me who rolls

her eyes, which makes me roar with laughter, setting her off.

"I'll see you later...*Romeo.*"

I grin as I watch her retreat before turning back to go and find Rosie.

Rosie

He's an ass. Nine months of 'Rosie do this' or 'Rosie do that.' Argh! Yes, he's the big boss and I'm the 'little slave,' but fuck, he really has been on my case since I started working at the club.

I love my job at Kenza. Well most days I do, especially when Ruben stays out of the way, but recently every time I turn around he's there, glaring at me. He probably wishes he had an excuse to fire me, but as of yet, I've managed to keep my temper in check and have done what he asks. Honestly, I'm not sure how much longer I can work for him. Every horrid comment from him causes a sharp pain in my chest and recently I've even arrived home with tears in my eyes. As soon as the doors close behind me, I give in to them and collapse into a sobbing heap.

Why does he affect me this much? Well, you see, over the past nine months I've slowly fallen in love with him and it hurts so damn much because it's clear that he can't stand me. Over time, he's made that very clear.

He's handsome in a rough kind of way with his dark hair falling over his chocolate colored eyes all the time. He ended up with a crooked nose because of his love of boxing and then you have his muscular body. All solid.

I've seen him once without his shirt when he'd been working out back at the club, and I'd drooled. Oh, yes he reminded me of those tattooed male models all over Facebook with one hell of a 'V' leading into his jeans. My eyes had followed that 'V,' along with the dark tattoo inked there, down until both disappeared into his jeans. My mouth salivated at the thought of licking his tattoo. He'd caught me drooling, of course, and had spent the remainder of the evening being an ass.

"Ugh." Turning to head back before I'm missed, I freeze. The object of my bad mood is standing behind me blocking the exit. How long he's been standing there is anyone's guess.

"What do you want?"

His eyes narrow at the challenge in my tone. "I'm your boss, Rosie. Or have you forgotten?"

"How could I forget with the constant stream of orders that come out of your mouth?" I feel like stamping my foot, which I refrain from, but I stand with my hands on my hips.

"Any more sass from you and you can find a new job because I've had enough," he growls at me, moving closer.

My heart thumps in my chest. *Does he want to get rid of me? Does he really hate me?*

I swallow the lump in my throat, but I'm afraid of opening my mouth because my tears are so close to the surface. Not only is the man I've fallen for being hateful, but also there are things going on at his club that I don't think he knows anything about, which all goes back to Simon. The stress of it all is finally getting to me.

Taking a deep breath for courage, I answer, "I've never been fired before," I swallow a few times, "so I...I quit."

Before he can reply, I turn and take a few steps toward where the cars are parked, but I don't get very far before he grabs hold of my arm and spins me to face him.

"You. Are. Not. Quitting."

A tear slips from my eye, which his gaze follows as it slides down my cheek to my mouth.

"Rosie," he groans.

His lips meet mine seconds before his tongue pushes for access to my mouth, which I give in on a sigh. He tastes of coffee and mints. I break his hold on my arms and slide my hands into his hair, holding him to me as I start to take a more active role in this unexpected kiss, which has my toes curling and my pussy wet and throbbing.

Ruben takes hold of my hips, pulling me in flush against him. I can feel his erection grinding in to me. Then it suddenly hits me what I'm doing. Making out with the boss!

I push him away, breaking free of his embrace. Wiping his kiss from my lips, I stammer, "No. We can't." Turning, I flee to the car lot with tears running down my face, not having a clue what I'm going to do now. Can I really stay at Kenza? *Shit!* I just told him I quit.

1

Ruben

THE WOMAN TIED TO THE BED IS PRACTICALLY BEGGING me to fuck her. I've given her countless orgasms, and her pussy is so wet that I should be desperate to get inside her and ease the ache in my balls. So why am I waiting?

I'm not going there.

I grab a condom from the side table, roll it down my length, and climb between her spread thighs.

I don't know her name. I didn't ask. All I saw was her dark hair falling down her lithe back and the curve of her narrow waist and long legs. That was all it took to have me buy her a drink and arrange this evening of sex.

Looking at her now, I'm not sure why I came back to her place. She isn't the one I want. But getting laid is the only way to curb my lust for another brunette who shouldn't be on my mind when I'm with someone else.

Shaking my head to forget about Rosie, I slide my hands up the woman's quivering thighs and start stroking her pussy. She moans, encouraging me.

The only sounds in the room are hers. We haven't spoken. After we both stripped, she lay on the bed naked and waited for me to tie her up, which I was more than happy to do.

Her pussy is bare as I watch my fingers slide back and forth along her lips. It coats my fingers in her arousal. I insert a couple of digits inside her, making sure she's ready for me.

I just want this to be over with now. I've stayed longer than usual. It's not because I like her more than anyone else. It's because she's making me feel damn good with all the orgasms I'm wringing out of her. Despite my lack of enthusiasm, this woman has definitely stroked my ego—something I needed.

I take hold of my cock and pump my fist back and forth a few times as we both watch the cum leak out into the condom. I'm ready, but first, I lean back and untie her ankles from the bedposts. Sliding my hands under her ass, I lift her up and toward me. My dick slides easily into her entrance, and her walls spasm against me at the same time her pussy sucks me deeper.

I groan, place her ass back on the bed, and follow her down. I lap at her nipples while thrusting in and out of her. This is going to be quick. I've gone without sex for so long that I won't be able to hold back.

She arches her back, moans, and thrashes around under me, squeezing the life out of my dick with her climax and sending me shooting to the stars in an explosive release.

Slowly moving back and forth to prolong our pleasure, I drop my face into the crook of her neck. Biting down on her shoulder, I mumble, "Rosie..." and freeze. Fuck!

I close my eyes, trying to block out the name I just whispered to another woman.

This is a one-time deal with someone I don't even know, but that doesn't mean I can be a bastard. I felt her stiffen slightly when I said it, and I'm positive it hurt her. What the hell am I doing breathing Rosie's name while buried deep inside someone else?

Fuck! Fuck! Fuck!

I untie her wrists, jump off the bed, and walk to

the bathroom to dispose of the condom. I wash my hands, splash water on my face, and dry off. Seeing the huge shower in here makes me want to jump in. However, second thoughts have me walking back into the bedroom and reaching for my clothes.

I need to get out of here.

Tonight was supposed to make me feel better. It was supposed to be a release from the damn stress. Instead, I feel like shit, and it didn't relieve the itch I needed to scratch.

I finally slip my feet back into my boots and look at the woman I've just spent a couple of hours with. She's sitting back against the pillows now, a robe hiding her nakedness. Her ankles are crossed, and her head is tilted to the side as she watches me.

I've never felt awkward before, but I do now.

"My name's Miranda. If you were wondering," she tells me, reaching for her phone, which has just lit up.

"I wasn't." Fuck. Just leave. "Look, we both know this was a one-time thing, so let's just forget it. I need to leave."

I turn my back to the woman and quickly check my pockets for my wallet, keys, and cell phone. Then, I stride out of the bedroom.

As I make my way across the apartment, I reach the door. I yank it open and hear her walking up behind me. She says, "See you around, Ruben McKenzie."

I freeze. She knows who I am? How?

"The man at the bar told me who you are," she answers my unspoken question.

I don't quite trust her because something tells me she's lying. I turn back to her. She shrugs.

God, I need to get out of here.

As I walk through the back door of my club, I know something is wrong. I can usually come and go this way without anyone noticing, but tonight, everyone has stopped to stare.

Simon, the club manager, walked out of the corridor leading to my office. He was about to walk toward the front of the club when he spotted me. He pauses, then changes direction and comes toward me with intent.

"Ruben."

I nod. "What's going on?" I ask, walking in his direction.

"A couple of guys decided to fight in the club, and Rosie got caught in the middle."

My blood runs cold, and I stop in my tracks. "What the fuck does that mean?"

"One of the guys punched her. She's in your office on the sofa with a cold compress on her face. I just gave her two painkillers, so hopefully they'll kick in soon."

"And the guy?" I seethe.

"Tony and a customer, whom I set up with free drinks at the bar, wrestled the guy outside and handed him over to the cops. Tony's back at the door, and everything has calmed down—for now."

I nod. With Tony handling it, there isn't much I can do. He's damn good at being a security guard and always manages to keep the peace. I just wish he had gotten to Rosie before she got hit.

Simon turns away and heads back out onto the floor, leaving me undecided as to whether I should go check on Rosie or break the neck of the bastard who dared to touch her.

Rosie wins. Rosie always wins.

Before barging into my office, I try to curb my anger about what happened to her. The last thing I want is to scare Rosie, which will happen if I unleash the anger buried deep inside me.

I let my mask slip into place before she sees the concern I feel for her and stare at my office door.

Feeling anything for her is wrong. She's my employee. Michael went after Lily even though she was his employee first, but he knew as soon as he met her that she was the one.

I'm not looking for that. I like my life as it is. Hooking up with Rosie isn't going to happen, no matter how much I want her. I wasn't meant for what came after the hookup. I'm not into relationships, and if I hooked up with Rosie, I'd have to let her go afterwards. Not only that, but Rosie is innocent. I like being in control when I have sex. There isn't any way Rosie has experience with the kind of control I like. I'd probably scare the life out of her.

Shaking loose of my thoughts, I push into my office and feel my composure slip. Rosie is curled up on my sofa, facing away from me. Seeing her like this crushes me.

I gently close the door behind me so as not to disturb her and walk to where she is. I drop to my knees beside the sofa, my hands hovering over her. I'm not sure what to do. Should I touch her and do what I want to do? Or should I back away so she won't know I've been here?

Oh, fuck it!

"Rosie..." I gently place my hands on her hips and help her turn over. When she does, I want to kill someone. Her beautiful face... The left side is bruised, and her eye is swollen shut. Her face is dry, and I can tell she's close to crying but hasn't yet. She still looks heartbreakingly beautiful.

I need to remember that I'm the boss in this situation. How would I have reacted if it had been any of the other servers? I would have been angry and concerned, but I wouldn't have been kneeling on the floor, wanting nothing more than to take her in my arms and keep her safe.

Step back, Ruben.

Just as I'm trying to work up the courage, she bursts into tears. I'm done for.

"Dammit, Rosie. Come here, babe," I say, already standing and lifting her into my arms.

She drops the ice pack on the floor and wraps her arms around my neck, holding on tight.

I turn with her and drop onto the sofa, holding her against me.

Rosie gets more comfortable in my arms, and I'm sure that if she could, she would have climbed inside me. She buries her face in my neck, soaking my skin and the collar of my shirt with her tears.

All I can do is hold her until she calms down, praying she doesn't realize the hardness in her ass is my cock—which is so inappropriate right now. I have

no chance, though. Having her this close to me makes my heart turn over.

Rosie

My face hurts so badly that all I can do is cry all over Ruben, the sexiest man I've ever seen. He's the only man who has ever made my heart flutter with excitement and my legs quiver when I hear his voice. Even now, despite everything that has happened, my pulse dances with excitement at the feel of his strong arms around me and his distinctive musky scent.

I take another shuddering breath and push the images from earlier out of my mind. Tonight was frightening and not something that usually happens at Kenza. It was just my luck to get in the way of a flying fist as the jerk was hitting the guy who was being a coward by ducking behind me.

I'm surprised my teeth didn't fly out from the force of his punch. Thankfully, the shock of being hit froze everyone in place, allowing Tony and Hunter, a customer I'd been talking to, to haul the culprit outside to wait for the cops. Simon quickly lifted me into his arms and carried me back to Ruben's office.

I'm now being held in Ruben's arms, which feels amazing. I really don't want to move because when I do, he'll go back to avoiding me. His avoidance hurts. It hurts, especially when I know he spends some nights with other women, away from the club.

Simon has caught me watching Ruben on a few occasions. To make matters worse, Simon makes sure I know every time Ruben leaves with someone. This has me spending the rest of the night locked away in my apartment. My heart aches for him, but I try not to think about him being with someone else.

I'm stupid. What would he see in me? He has money, as does his family. I hardly have any. I have a small savings account for emergencies, but it's nothing special. Yet, I've fallen for him in a big way. Every time he does something nice for one of the staff—or even me—I fall deeper.

Ruben also frightens me a little. He has so much experience with women that if we ever had the opportunity to be together, he'd probably be disappointed. I've only been with three men—well, boys, I suppose—in my twenty-three years. How many women has he been with? Too many to count, I bet.

"Rosie, darlin'." He starts to caress my back. "Is the pain getting any easier?"

The painkillers are starting to kick in, and my other senses are waking up. I feel him. He's rock hard against me—and I don't just mean what's going on in his pants. I can definitely feel something hard down there. Ruben's hard all over and smells damn good, too. He has a dark, sensual scent that makes me want to lean in closer to lick the pulse throbbing in his neck.

"Mmm," I moan, moving closer to him. What did he ask me? Something about pain?

He has his fingers buried in my hair, holding me against him with one hand while the other continues to caress my back. I'm not sure if he realizes what he's doing.

"The pain is more of a throb now," I whisper, "instead of a fire."

My hands start to slide through the hair at the nape of his neck.

He shudders and presses me against him.

I wiggle my butt, trying to get closer, positive that I'm losing my mind, unable to help myself now that I'm in his arms.

He growls, "Rosie," when I rub against his hard penis.

Not having much experience with male anatomy, I have trouble calling it anything but a penis. Anne, a girl I'm friends with who lives next door, loves using the word "cock." I cringe every time she says it. "Dick" isn't that bad, but "cock". I just can't get my head around it. When I think of a penis, I think of Ruben and try to imagine what his looks like. From the way things feel, I'm right in thinking that he's long and wide. Is the head of his penis red or plum colored? Does he leak cum when he's aroused? I shudder at the images racing through my mind.

I really need to stop thinking about it because my panties are about to combust. Not to mention, the man beneath me is gripping my hips as if he's about to explode. His breathing is uneven. I put my mouth to the pulse in his neck and suck.

"Jesus! Fuck!" Ruben shouts, jumping up. Before I can think straight, I find myself sprawled out on his office floor with him looming over me, breathing deeply. The bulge behind his zipper twitches as he chokes out, "Rosie."

I'll never tire of hearing him say my name in that husky growl. He's only used it on me once before, at his niece and nephew's baptism. He used that same tone after kissing me, but then he kept his distance.

At least he didn't hold me to my resignation. That was something I supposed.

He runs his fingers through his hair, clears his throat, and rests his hands on his hips. His eyes sparkle as he glares at me. "What the fuck am I going to do with you?" He holds his hand up, silencing my response. "Don't say anything until you're back on your feet." He holds out his hand, and I take it, letting him haul me up from the floor. "Because I'm only human. Seeing you lying on my office floor, flashing your pink, lacy panties, has me seconds from joining you."

Blushing, I look around his office to avoid meeting his gaze. Ruben won't let me ignore him. Taking a gentle hold of my jaw, he turns my face back to his, so I can no longer pretend he isn't standing in front of me. Our gazes meet and hold before he starts to caress my face. He moves his thumb close to my cheek, and I suck in my breath from the pain. He curses like a sailor when I do.

I haven't seen the damage because I don't want to, but judging by Ruben's reaction, it's bad.

"It's a good thing Simon dealt with the fucker." He picks up the ice pack from the floor and puts it back on my cheek. Then, he rests his hand on my shoulder.

"I'm okay. Really. The painkillers are working." I

shrug my shoulders. "I'd better get back out there," I say, trying to move away from him. He stops me with his hand on my forearm.

"You're not going back out there tonight. You're going to go home and rest." He covers my mouth with a finger, stifling my argument, but quickly moves his finger away. "Don't be difficult, Rosie. You're hurting. You need to get in bed. Take some more painkillers, and try to sleep through the pain. You haven't taken time off since you started working here, so take the week off."

Needing space from Ruben, I break off our conversation. I let the ice pack fall onto the sofa and start to shuffle toward the door, but he follows me. "I'm just going to grab my things and head out. But I really don't need the whole week off—maybe just a few days." I can't afford to take time off.

With my hand on the doorknob, Ruben crowds me against the door, his front against my back, and puts both his hands on the door. His breath caresses my neck, sending shivers through my body. I shouldn't be shivering because of my boss. My heart flutters, and my breath catches in my throat as he puts his mouth to my ear.

"You'll take the week off with full pay," he whispers. "When you're back, you'll stay away from the floor. I'm putting you behind the bar."

His words don't register properly because I can only concentrate on his body. I feel his burning gaze as his wandering hand slowly moves down toward my hip. He squeezes it before pushing himself away.

"I'll get Simon to drive you home," Ruben says as I hear him walk away.

I take a deep breath, turn to face Ruben, and tell him, "Thanks, but I can get myself home." I don't want to be in a car with Simon, who's starting to give off the wrong kind of vibes.

"Simon will drive you," Ruben says, his voice firm and his eyes challenging. He does not look happy with me right now. "I don't want anything else happening to you between here and where you live."

I close my eyes. I take a deep breath and let it out in exasperation. "I'm not ten years old, Ruben. Simon isn't taking me home. There are plenty of cabs outside."

I pull open the door and quickly exit Ruben's office, making my way to the staff room to get my things.

The first thing I reach for as soon as I open my locker is my jeans. I kick off the shoes I wear for work and quickly slide my legs into the soft denim, wiggling around to pull them up around my hips. After fastening them, I quickly remove my skirt and toss it into my purse. I follow with my long-sleeved shirt. With my feet nice and secure in my boots, I shove the strap of my purse over my shoulder, making sure my locker is secure. I just want to leave and go back to my apartment to cry my eyes out for the rest of the night. Thanks to Ruben, my emotions are all over the place, and my face feels like it's been hit with a brick instead of a fist. I need to be alone. I'm used to being alone.

Stepping into the hall, I freeze.

"You win," Ruben says, pushing off the wall he was leaning on. Clearly, he's waiting for me. "But I'm going to make sure you get inside a cab in one piece."

I sigh. I can't complain about that. Truthfully, I wasn't looking forward to walking out the front door alone with the line of people waiting to get in. Sometimes they can be obnoxious.

"Thank you," I say as he takes my elbow. I take in the profile of his set jaw and smile. A wave of mischievousness crashes over me as I add, "But don't make a habit of bossing me around."

His hand briefly tightens on my elbow before slackening again. He chuckles. "We'll see."

Outside, in the cool air, Ruben ignores everyone

shouting for his attention and opens the door of a cab for me. As I'm about to climb in, he stops me with a hand on my arm. I turn to look at him. I know his face well, and I can see the internal struggle playing across it. But what he's struggling with is beyond me.

"Let me see your phone."

Uncertain what he wants my phone for, I hesitate before handing it to him. He begins typing on it, and then I hear the phone in his pocket beep. He removes it and checks the screen.

"That's my private number. Use it if you need anything. I mean it, Rosie. Anything." He hands me my phone, which I clutch as he shoves me into the cab. He slams the door closed and bangs on the roof a couple of times.

The cab pulls out into traffic, and I can't help but turn to watch Ruben. I hold his stare until the cab turns out of view.

2

Ruben

As I pull up to the side of my parents' house for Sunday dinner, I grin when I spot Lily and Carla on the front porch, each with a baby on their lap. Sabrina is leaning over Carla, playing with one of the twins.

My mom is overjoyed to have grandchildren, thanks to my brother Michael and his wife, Lily. But she is driving the rest of us crazy with questions. When are we going to get married and give her more grandchildren? Ugh!

Ramon always manages to give her the slip. Despite that saving grace, though, something has been off with him lately. He's looked troubled for a while now, which I'm not used to seeing since he's always been the more carefree brother. I definitely need to find time to chat with my youngest brother. Maybe I can get to the bottom of it, although he's the hardest of my brothers to crack.

Lucien takes her questions in stride, but he's definitely upset about Lily's friend Sabrina. We all see this except him. Because of his accident, he feels like he isn't useful to anyone, and he certainly wouldn't want anyone to wake up beside him and have to look at his scars. I hope he finally hooks up with Sabrina because I have a feeling she'll be good for him.

As for me, there's only one woman who makes me crazy, only one woman I can't get out of my head. One woman who gives me the hardest fucking boner that can pound nails—Rosie. Sweet, innocent Rosie. She's too innocent for my tastes, but I'd be lying if I said the thought of teaching her what I like doesn't turn me on.

It's taken everything not to visit her this past week. She listened to me and took the week off, and I wanted to check on her every single day—hell, every single minute. On Wednesday, I gave in and texted her to ask if she was okay. She responded with a simple "Yes, I'm fine." I'm not sure what I was expecting, but "yes, I'm fine" pissed me off.

"What the fuck?"

Lucien brought me abruptly back to the present by opening the car door and scaring the shit out of me.

"What, you daydreaming like a girl now?" Lucien asked, grinning like an idiot.

I push the door into him, and he takes a step back as I jump from the car. "I'm not going to dignify that with an answer."

I slam the door shut and ignore him, walking past to head toward the house. Under his breath, he says, "No need to get your panties in a twist because I caught you daydreaming about Rosie."

Fuck! I glare at my brother. "Do I have a sign on my forehead that says, 'Ruben can't stop thinking about Rosie?'"

He starts laughing and says, "I never thought you'd admit it," before rubbing his hand across his face and meeting my gaze.

With my hands on my hips, I exhale and shake my head. "I walked right into that one." I chuckle, but it turns into a frown. "Nothing can happen between us. She's about eleven years younger than me, and she looks innocent. I'd scare her off." I look toward the house, sigh, and continue, "I'm also her boss. She's the best employee I have on that floor. After the past weekend, though, she's on bar duty for the foreseeable future."

"Come on, Mom keeps looking at us through the window." Lucien gets me moving again toward the house. "I'll leave Rosie and your love life alone for now, but not forever." He grinned, then became serious again. "Ramon told me what happened to her. Do you think the fight had anything to do with the trouble you've been having?"

"That thought has crossed my mind a few times." My gut is telling me it has everything to do with it. But how does a fight in the club have anything to do with the vandalism and break-in? It doesn't make sense."

I can feel the worry lines on my forehead. Something has been going on at my club for a while now. The frustrating thing is that no matter what I do to try to find out who is behind it all, I always end up with nothing.

"I'll come hang out at Kenza a couple times a week. I'll see if I catch anything going on. Ramon can come too and be social for a change. I don't know what's up with him. He's been distracted since Carla moved in with Sebastian." Lucien frowns as we walk up the steps to the front porch just in time to hear the twins wake up—noisily.

We watch Lily and Carla cuddle the babies, who are getting big for eight-month-olds.

Lucien moves forward, kisses Lily on the cheek, and takes Michael Jr. from her arms. He straightens and places our nephew on his shoulder, which shuts him up immediately. Not wanting to be outdone by my brother, I greet Carla by kissing the top of her head.

"Get your hands off my woman, brother."

I snicker and tell Sebastian, "She's damn sexy with a baby in her arms. I didn't have my hands on her. I had my mouth." I grin at Carla, who rolls her eyes at our teasing. I pinch Charlotte out of her arms and get her to quiet down with her little face tucked into my neck. I take a deep breath and smile at the little angel in my arms.

"Besides, this is my girl right here," I announce, rubbing Charlotte's back. I move her away from my neck slightly and kiss her little nose. Charlotte and Jr. have me wrapped around their little fingers. There's nothing I wouldn't do for them, and nothing I wouldn't give them. I lose my "man card" when I'm around these two bundles of joy, and no matter what my brothers say, they're just the same. The twins have everyone wrapped around their little fingers.

"How are you, Sabrina? Haven't seen you for a few

weeks." Sabrina usually comes to the house every Sunday for dinner because my mom adopted her after witnessing her interaction with her own mother. Sabrina's mom seemed more interested in her nails than in Sabrina's sprained wrist, which she got playing a vigorous game of tennis with Ramon.

"I'm good. Thanks, Ruben," she answered with a quick glance at Lucien before moving toward the house's door. "I'll see if Pippa needs any help." She disappears inside.

"You have to stop scaring her off," I tell Lucien. "Otherwise, she's going to stop coming by, which will upset Mom. Plus, I really like her." I grin, and my grin turns into a laugh when Sebastian clamps his arm around Lucien's shoulders.

He grins at Carla and tells Lucien, "If it wasn't for my woman over there, I'd be doing something about her." He gets an elbow in the ribs from Lucien.

"I don't know what you're talking about," Lucien says as he takes the seat next to Lily. She leans in to offer her finger for her son to grasp.

"Behave and leave your brother alone," Lily tells us before kissing Lucien on the cheek.

Anyone watching would think Lucien was the father of these babies the way they carry on. I'm actually not sure how Michael has accepted her close relationship with our brother.

We all trust Lucien—that's the brother code—but Lily and Lucien have always seemed too comfortable with each other. Since Michael accepted her friendship with Lucien, I've wondered once or twice whether Lucien has stronger feelings for Lily than he lets on. But it's none of my business.

"Give me back my daughter," Michael grinned, walking out onto the porch. "Then again, carry on. I'm going to borrow my wife." He pulls Lily up from the sofa, pats her on the butt, and pulls her toward the barn. This causes Sebastian to act like he's fifteen by whistling.

I feel sorry for Lily. Although she's laughing, a lovely blush covers her face. Michael's a jerk. I shake my head as I watch him shove her into the barn. I don't need to guess what they're going to do.

I take the seat Lily vacated next to Lucien and bring Charlotte down into my arms. She isn't happy with this position, though, and tries to pull herself up. So, with her sitting on my knee, I gently bounce her up and down, which is met with lots of baby giggles.

I hear a camera shutter and turn to grin at my mom. If she isn't holding one of her grandbabies, she's capturing them and us with the digital camera.

"Hmm," Mom sighs. "So, which of my babies is going to be next to fall?"

Sebastian roars with laughter, and I feel pressure in my chest when I think of Rosie. Trying to ignore Mom, I glance at Lucien, who is fidgeting in his seat like he used to when he wanted to avoid a conversation. Some things never change.

"Lucien will be next...then again, I bet Ruben cracks soon as well, so I guess it's going to be a pretty close race."

I'd love to knock the shit-eating grin off Sebastian's face with my fist.

"What about Ramon? Why didn't you mention him?" I counter.

"What about me?" Ramon asked as he walked around the end of the porch.

I hadn't realized he was already here because his wheels aren't out front.

"Mom wants to know who's going to be next." I chuckle at the look on his face. "She wants more grandbabies."

"Oh, you hush up," Mom says, clipping me on the shoulder. "I'm hoping Sebastian will help me out with that."

"Hey now," Sebastian interrupts. "I want time alone with my woman before we have a baby." He pulls Carla up from her chair, sits down in her seat, and pulls her into his lap. She snuggles into him, and I realize that I want that too—my own woman, Rosie.

"Well, with all the practicing you've been doing, I'm sure you'll get it right when needed." Mom never ceases to amaze me with the things she says. At least Sebastian is keeping his mouth shut, probably because Carla is sitting with us, looking embarrassed.

"You can all laugh, but I want to see my other three sons having the love of a good woman. There's nothing more satisfying than seeing the love that Lily and Carla have for my sons. I want you three to have that." When Mom finishes, she dabs at her eyes. We groan, knowing that she's on a mission to get us all hooked up and off her hands.

Ramon cringes before turning and heading back around the porch, and I try to look anywhere but at Mom. The last thing she needs is for one of us to acknowledge her comments.

Lucien ignores her and plays with Jr., but unfortunately, I'm the one Mom has her eyes on. I hope it's because I'm bouncing Charlotte on my knee.

"Ruben, I'm worried about you." Her tone is quiet, but it makes me meet Mom's gaze. "You work too much," she says, giving me the "don't even think about opening your mouth" look. "Regardless of how much you and your brothers wish I was deaf, I'm not, and I know you've been having trouble at the club." Mom stops talking and starts to bite her lip. That's a sure sign she's worried.

How do moms always manage to find out what you don't want them to? "I didn't want you to worry." I lean over and kiss Charlotte on the head. Before I know it, Mom has taken her out of my arms and is making silly noises in front of her face.

"I always find out these things. You should know that by now. Please, just tell me you have it under control."

"He's going to be fine, Mom, and so is the club. I'm going to hang out there a few times a week, and we'll get Ramon down to the club to see if we can figure out what's going on," Lucien states.

"Hmm. Well, although I think it's a good idea for my two single sons to hang out at the club with another one of my single sons, I'm going to worry triple time now. But if you meet a nice young lady there, then I might not worry as much."

I choke back a laugh, knowing it won't be appreciated. I say what I know Lucien is thinking, "Nice young ladies don't hang out at Kenza. If they do, they're usually with their significant other."

"These babies are going to have no fingers left if

we don't feed them soon. And don't think you guys are off the hook," Mom says, ignoring my protests. I laugh as I watch Charlotte and Jr. shove their fingers in their mouths and suck on them. "And you, Lucien, can take Sabrina to the club. She doesn't really have any friends here except for Lily, Carla, and Sylvia. I'd like to see those two young ladies find true love," Mom adds, clutching her chest and looking sappy.

"I think it would be much better if you concentrated on fixing Sylvia and Sabrina up instead of us."

I stand and follow Mom into the house, holding the door for Lucien and Jr., with Charlotte in her arms.

"Now, it would be perfect if those ladies were to end up with one of my sons." Mom turns and grins at us both before disappearing into the kitchen with Charlotte. Luckily, she misses Lucien cursing under his breath.

We'd all love for Lucien to get together with Sabrina, but he's stubborn and fighting his feelings for her. Everyone can see this except my idiot brother. If he doesn't get with it soon, he's going to lose her to someone else. She's an attractive woman, and once she opens herself up to dating, he's going to be left behind.

The woman in question stands in the kitchen

doorway, staring at Lucien as he holds a one-sided conversation with Jr. The look on her face makes me think that perhaps she'll be the one to act and shake his world, not the other way around.

Sabrina glances toward me and blushes when she realizes I've been watching her. Instead of retreating, as she usually does when caught watching Lucien, she makes her presence known. Standing in front of him, she says, "Jr.'s dinner is ready. I'll take him."

Lucien pauses before holding Jr. out to her. She takes him into her arms, gives him a kiss and a cuddle, then retreats back into the kitchen. Lucien watches her retreat.

I grin and stare at him.

"What the fuck is wrong with you?" he grouches.

"Nothing's wrong with me." I laugh, then become serious again. "Why don't you ask her out? I don't think she'd refuse."

He looks surprised. Does he really think she'd refuse him after the way she always watches him?

"She doesn't want to go out with me. I don't have anything to offer anyone, and she's too close to home for anything else."

With a huge effort, I keep my mouth shut. He's been alone and shut off from the world for over five years. I know he was badly hurt in the car accident, but I've wondered for a while now whether his girl-friend at the time said something to him about his injuries. Since they broke up, I haven't seen him with a woman. He always goes out of his way to be stand-offish. It pisses me off.

"You don't do 'anything else.' When you start dating someone, it's going to be more than 'anything else.' We both know that. You've never done the casual fuck…"

"Ruben Elias McKenzie." I cringe when I hear my full name shouted out from the kitchen. "Stop using the 'f' word, and go find Ramon."

I could feel the heat creeping into my face, knowing that Mom had overheard part of my conver-sation with Lucien. He was lounging back on one of the sofas with a shit-eating grin on his face.

Busted!

Rosie

After stepping out of the shower, I quickly dried myself with my favorite pink, fluffy towel. I thought back to last night, my first night back at Kenza. I had been looking forward to going back to work so that I could see Ruben, but, much to my disappointment, he wasn't around. Simon, the bastard, had snickered when he caught me snooping around. He made sure I knew that Ruben was out on a booty call. Hearing those words, of course, made me lose my objective— to find out what was going on at Kenza. I went back to work, but toward the end of the evening, I chatted with Hunter, who helped break up the fight the night I got hurt.

If Ruben hadn't already captured my heart, I might have been tempted to flirt with Hunter. He has the most mesmerizing green eyes I've ever seen. When he looks at me, it feels like he's looking into my soul—intense and hot. It took a lot to drag my gaze away from his. He seemed to know this, considering the smirk he gave me. Arrogant ass!

I suppose he has a reason to be arrogant, looking the way he does with his chiseled cheekbones, square jaw covered in five-o'clock shadow, and unruly hair falling to his shoulders. I'm sure the ladies drop their panties for him. Although, I have to say, I don't remember him ever leaving with anyone the few times I've seen him at the club.

He has a sexy butt, which I may have noticed once or twice. There's nothing wrong with looking, even if

I've fallen for someone who doesn't know I exist. Perhaps I need to move on.

Sighing, I fasten my jeans before pulling on my red long-sleeved shirt. It matches the red Converse I grab from the floor of my closet perfectly.

My apartment is small, with three rooms—a bedroom, a bathroom, and an open living area with a small kitchen off to one side—but it's mine, and in the two years that I've lived here, I've made it homey. It's nothing like the home I grew up in but it's the home I always imagined having. Something cozy and my own space. I have pictures on the walls and colorful throws over the sofa and chair. Next to the kitchen is a fold-up, two-person table with two wooden stools. I'm rather proud of my small apartment and the things I've bought at bargain prices from the thrift store near me. Home sweet home!

I grab my keys and cell phone from the small coffee table and take one last look around before heading out the door and making my way downstairs. Have I mentioned that I live above a diner that makes the best coffee in Lexington? It isn't a chain like Starbucks or Costa. Liz makes the best coffee, but she refuses to tell me her secret or what kind of beans she uses.

I take a seat along the counter at Mama E's and

pick up the menu. I do this every time I come in here. I'm not sure why, since I know the menu by heart—it's just habit, I guess.

"Pancakes and coffee, sleepyhead?" Liz asks, knowing what I have for breakfast on Sunday mornings.

I grin. "Please."

Liz holds a large cup under my nose and fills it with hot coffee.

I smile, and warmth fills me. This place is just an extension of my home. Liz has been a constant presence in my life ever since she took pity on me and let me rent the apartment upstairs for next to nothing until I found a job.

She always wears a starched pink dress, matching shoes, a small hat, and a white apron tied around her slim waist. Liz reminds me of Frenchy from the movie Grease—she likes to experiment with the color of her hair. Today, though, it's back to its usual light brown color, pulled up into a neat bun on top of her head. She looks amazing for fifty-seven. I hope I look as good when I reach her age.

"Earth to Rosie."

I blink and realize that Ed, Liz's husband, has taken the seat beside me.

"How are you doing, Ed?" I ask, swiveling my

chair around to face him and resting my arm on the counter beside me.

"I'm doing good. Thanks, Rosie." He looks me over. "You can hardly see the bruising now. How's the pain?" he asks, concerned.

"The pain's gone now. So all is well." I smile to reassure him. "I went back to work last night, which went well. Even though I caught up on all the new books on my Kindle while I had the week off, I'm not used to being so idle, you know?"

"I know. I can't keep up with you half the time when you get a bee in your bonnet." He takes a drink of his coffee, which he no doubt helped himself to before sitting down.

"Here you go. Now eat it all up. You've lost weight this past week," Liz says in a motherly tone.

She places a stack of two pancakes in front of me, along with a small dish of warmed maple syrup. I smile. She usually gives me one pancake, but I guess this is her way of saying she's worried about me.

I haven't lost much weight this week, although I have lost some. I wouldn't have thought I'd lost enough for it to be noticeable, though.

"Well, come on. Eat up," Ed says, nudging me and starting to wolf down his sausage and eggs.

"This looks good as always. Your wife makes damn

good food, not to mention coffee." I pour syrup over my pancakes and start devouring them. I'm not sure I'll be able to finish the plate because one pancake usually leaves me feeling full and makes me undo the button on my jeans.

"Mmm, no matter how much you beg or butter her up, she'll never tell you her coffee secret," Ed smirks, munching on some egg.

I narrow my eyes. "Do you know the secret?"

He pauses, obviously not expecting me to start on him. He won't meet my eyes. I chuckle.

"I don't think so," he replies, his mouth full of food.

"I'll let you off the hook for now," I say, spearing a piece of pancake with my fork. "But I have a very good memory," I whisper.

He laughs. "Has anyone ever told you that you're dangerous?"

"Not recently."

We both concentrate on our breakfast. As I'd expected, two pancakes are too much, and I'm struggling to finish the second one. They're delicious but filling.

"Hmm, I thought you'd struggle, but I thought you'd at least manage half of the second one."

"Sorry, Liz."

She removes my plate and leans on the counter in front of me. "So, how is your young man?" she asks.

Liz and Ed are the only ones I've told about Ruben, and not willingly. They've been encouraging me to go after what I want ever since. They don't realize it isn't easy, especially since he doesn't seem to know I exist.

He certainly reacted to me last week when I was hurt. There was no way I could have mistaken the hardness against my hip or the bulge twitching behind his zipper when I ended up flashing him. I blush every time I remember him standing over me and commenting on my pink panties.

"Oh, this is going to be good." Liz leans even closer and says, "You don't blush for a handshake. What aren't you telling me?"

"You're impossible, you know that, right?"

"Ed tells me that all the time."

The man in question starts laughing, stands up, and takes his empty dishes to the kitchen.

"Okay, quick, before he comes back. What happened between you and Ruben?"

"I wish I could say something has, but it hasn't. I already told you about him holding me after I was hit last week. He texted me once to see how I was doing.

He wasn't there last night. Simon said he went out on a booty call." I shrug, feeling sad.

"Hmm. Do you believe Simon? Or do you think he's telling you that to get under your skin?"

That hadn't even entered my head. "I don't know. But I do know that Ruben prefers women who can give him more than I ever could." I swallow down the knot of sadness threatening to overwhelm me. Even if Ruben were interested in me, I could never give him what he needs.

"You won't know unless you try." Liz pats me on the arm.

"He's my boss. If I make a total idiot of myself, I'll have to leave, and I really like my job. It also pays an above-average wage." I let out a loud sigh. "Ugh! I don't know what to do, but I'm sure it'll all work out." I hope. For now, though, I need to go across the street and buy some groceries. I'm out of a few things." I slid off the seat, stepped on the foot rail in front of the counter, leaned over, and hugged Liz. "Thank you for being here," I whisper into her ear.

She smiles. "Take care of yourself, Rosie."

I grin. "I will. Always."

I wave back to Liz and Ed, push my way outside, and dash across the road to the corner grocery store, which always seems to be open.

I grab a basket as I walk inside and pick up a pack of apples, but I pause when I feel someone close behind me—too close.

"Hello, Rosie."

I quickly turn, recognizing the voice. *Simon.* "I didn't know you lived around here." I'm sure he doesn't.

"I'm on my way to a friend's house. When I saw you dash in here, I thought I'd stop by for a few minutes."

"Oh." I fidget with the bag of apples in my hand, but then I realize what I'm doing, so I drop them into my basket. Moving further around the fruit display, I pick up a bag of grapes and add them to the apples.

The hair on the nape of my neck prickles as I shuffle under Simon's stare. My skin feels like it's crawling, but I force myself not to turn and run. Why is he here? He's never shown any interest in me before, so why now?

"Have coffee with me," he suddenly asks, running his fingers over his head. "Shit, I can't right now. But another time."

"Um, okay." Why did I agree? *Because he frightens you.*

"That's great. I'll catch you later."

He left me standing there as he headed out

through the doors. He doesn't turn back, and I can't help but wonder what he's up to. I've suspected for a while now that he's involved in the problems at the club, but I have no real evidence. Simon started off as a friend when I first started working at Kenza. But he's been odd lately.

I really wish Ruben and his brothers would get to the bottom of all the trouble that's been happening. I sure don't want to admit to Ruben that I suspect someone is selling drugs at the club. Knowing my luck lately, he'd probably blame me.

3

Ruben

WITH MY HEAD BURIED IN THE PAPERWORK ON MY DESK, I try to avoid thinking about Rosie—but no such luck. She has been driving me crazy, especially since she started back at work and started avoiding me. I don't really blame her, considering the mixed signals I gave her the night she was hit. I've also done my best to avoid running into her because I have no idea what I'm supposed to say.

I'm thirty-five years old, yet I'm still clueless around Rosie. She turns me upside down, and no matter how many times I tell myself to stay away from her, I'm always pulled toward her.

She looks so innocent, and the thought of

teaching her what I like makes my dick hard as fuck and my balls ache. But it's not going to happen. I'd probably scare the shit out of her by introducing her to butt plugs and restraints.

I like my women tied up and helpless. It's their trust in me that turns me on, but only after I've made sure they're well taken care of. My brothers joke about whips and chains, but I've never used either. Silk scarves are gentler on a woman's wrists and ankles. Rosie would look beautiful spread out on my bed, her wrists and ankles secured to the posts, her gorgeous hair spilling over my pillow.

Slipping my hand beneath my desk, I rub my throbbing dick at the image in my head. I'd climb between her spread legs, using my mouth on her pussy to get her good and wet. Then, I'd work my finger into her tight, puckered hole before inserting a small butt plug.

My cock jerks with excitement.

"Ruben."

Fuck!

I grabbed my balls and squeezed. I sure as hell don't want to come while she's standing there in the doorway. "Yeah..." I croak, then clear my throat and try again. "Yeah, what's wrong, Rosie?"

"Simon wanted me to tell you the delivery you're waiting for just arrived out front."

"Okay," I say to the empty doorway.

Breathing deeply, trying to get rid of my hard-as-fuck problem, I count backwards so that I won't be a walking embarrassment when I go to sort out the delivery or confront Rosie.

We both need to stop avoiding each other, and she sure as hell needs to stop running off the minute she's said what she needs to.

Once I have my composure, I head out of my office toward the front of the club to check on the delivery. It should have been here four days ago, but someone claiming to have my authority supposedly canceled the order. It pisses me off that someone is messing with my business.

Just as I'm about to punch through the door leading out front, Simon comes barreling inside.

"Everything okay?" I ask.

"Yeah, I had them pull the truck around back now that the car blocking the alley has moved. They have the full delivery, so I'm going to check it as they unload to make sure there aren't any more screw-ups." Simon looks at the clipboard in his hand before glancing back at me. "Would you like to check it?"

"I was going to, but it seems like you have it under control, so I'll leave you to it. Grilling the driver about the cancellation won't help us find out who was responsible for that phone call." I run my hands through my hair in agitation. "Just make sure everything we ordered is delivered. I'm going to finish up some paperwork."

Simon dashes off to the back of the club.

On my way back to my office, I see Rosie dart into the staff room. I decide to put an end to this avoidance. No matter how much I want her, she's still one of my employees, and I certainly don't want her to think that she has to avoid me.

As she comes out of the staff room, she turns in my direction, but freezes when she sees me heading toward her. Rosie meets my gaze, which I hold with an intensity I haven't felt before. My heart feels like it's about to burst out of my chest, and when she sticks her tongue out to moisten her lips, my dick lengthens and throbs in anticipation.

"Ruben," she whispers when I stop in front of her.

I gulp, knowing I need to take a step back from her. However, my body is telling me something completely different from my head.

Just one taste. What harm can one taste do?

"I...I need to get back to work." Rosie bites her lip but doesn't move to walk away.

"Work can wait," I say, taking her by the arm. I quickly punch in my security code for the door leading up to my apartment. "But this can't."

As soon as I pull Rosie inside, our lips meet. The door slams shut behind me, but I barely notice as I press her up against the wall. I hold her head in place with one hand while devouring her mouth. My other hand clutches her bottom, bringing her in tight against my erection.

This woman drives me crazy, and her taste is hot and sweet—innocent yet sinful. I can't get enough of her.

She moans into my mouth as she wraps her arms around my neck. Her legs wrap around my waist, pressing her pussy against my straining cock.

Using my hips to hold her in place, I slowly move my hand up her ribcage, leaving it to rest under her breast, and continue assaulting her senses with my mouth. My tongue tangles with hers as I mimic what I want to do with another part of my body.

Rosie starts grinding against me, causing even more blood to rush south and giving me an erection to end all erections. I've wanted her for so long. Mix that need with her innocence, and I'm not sure I'll be able to last. She makes me feel like an uncontrollable teenager.

I kiss her jaw and neck, moving down to her collarbone. I cup her breast with my hand, rubbing her hardened nipple with my thumb. She arches against the wall, pushing her chest toward me.

Not one to miss an opportunity, I shove her shirt up, nearly coming in my jeans when I see her bounty covered by a pink, lacy bra. With a quick flick of the clasp in the front, I peel open the cups and watch her dusty nipples appear from beneath the fabric.

She's exquisite.

Bending down, I capture one cherry-colored nipple between my lips and suckle it. She lets out a loud moan, tightening her hand against the nape of my neck as I grind against her.

"Oh God, Ruben...please don't stop."

Fuck! I didn't intend for this to happen. I'm not complaining because she's in my arms, but at this rate, neither one of us is going to make it upstairs before climaxing.

Unable to pull away, I grab her hips and help her rub herself on me. I feel her hands slide into my hair, holding me against her breast. I switch to her other breast, covering it with my hand and twisting and pinching her nipple.

The minute I suck her nipple into my mouth, she groans and shudders against me. I pull my mouth away, clamping my lips shut to try to breathe, because I'm seconds from exploding.

I drop my head into the crook of her neck and pray that she doesn't move against my cock because I'm holding on by a thread.

"Rosie, I'm sorry," I mumble against her neck. "I only meant to talk to you, not attack you."

"You didn't attack me, but I don't think this should have happened. I'm not sorry, though." She pushes me away and lets her legs drop to the floor. She fastens her bra and pulls her shirt back into place.

"I'm not made for the things you like," she starts, looking nervous. "I don't do one-night stands, and I'm not into what I've heard you're into. I like my job, so it would be best if this doesn't happen again." She glances at the bulge in my pants before looking me in the eye and quickly looking away. "I better go."

With those words, she slides out the door, and she's gone. I'm left frustrated, knowing that I'm going to have to finish what she started with my hand. I'm also stunned that she could act so calmly when I feel as though I've been hit by a truck.

Pressing the heel of my hand against my dick, I hiss and quickly make my way upstairs to take care of business. It should have subsided by now that she isn't with me, but no such luck.

I shove my way into my apartment, lock the door so my brothers can't walk in on me, and head straight for the bathroom.

I don't have time for a shower, so I release my cock with a sigh, stroking from tip to base and letting my jeans hover around my thighs. I'll be lucky if this lasts more than a minute.

I quickly rub lube into my hands, take a firm hold of my shaft, and start bringing myself to orgasm with pictures of Rosie running through my head. Her breasts, which nearly overflowed my hands. Her nipples, large and ripe for my mouth.

Growling, I throw my head back and roar through my release. It squirts all over the shower floor and the opposite wall. Fuck me! I back up and drop onto the toilet—jeans around my ankles. Holy fuck! If that's how my body reacts to thoughts of Rosie, how will I ever survive being with her?

What the hell have I done?

Since when does talking involve bringing her to orgasm and jerking off in my bathroom?

Why the hell did she look scared when she talked about finding out what I like? For once, I wish the staff would mind their own fucking business. It also makes me wonder who's been filling her head with nonsense. But it's not all bad, is it?

I take a deep breath, clean myself up, and turn the shower head on to wash my cum off the wall. Then, I head back downstairs to deal with whatever arises tonight. I also need to give Rosie space so she doesn't have to avoid me. I hate it when she does that.

Rosie

"What's gotten you so riled up? Or should I ask who?" Hunter asks me, nursing his longneck.

I frown and ignore him.

Since my tryst with Ruben, I've felt out of sorts. Can you blame me? I finally end up in the arms of the man who's gradually crept into my heart over the past fourteen months. Well, maybe not from day one. And what do I do? I tell him I don't like kink, and that he won't have me in his arms again. I didn't say "kink," but there's no way he missed what I meant.

"Must be a heated thought to put that color on your face," Hunter observes, obviously not wanting to leave me alone.

I'd forgotten he was sitting in front of me, lost in his own thoughts.

"Sorry. I'm a bit distracted."

After finishing wiping down the bar between us, I lean back and try not to blush as I watch him look me over. He's a sexy badass, but he isn't Ruben.

"I'd say so. I can't remember the last time I checked out a girl only to have her frown when I finished. I've lost my touch."

I chuckle. "Sorry to burst your bubble, but I'm not interested. You have rough and sexy down pat, and I have a feeling you have a trail of burned panties behind you."

Hunter chokes on his beer before slamming the bottle back on the bar.

I quickly pass him some napkins to mop up with and smirk. I rarely get the last word, so it's nice to have it with someone who's probably used to having it himself.

"Rough and sexy, huh?" He grins.

I roll my eyes and place another longneck in front of him. But before I can pull my hand away, I find it engulfed in his.

"You look sweet and innocent, but underneath it all, you're a little spitfire," he tells me.

"Take your hands off her."

I yank my hand free and jump back at the sound

of Ruben's voice. I glance his way and watch as he glares at Hunter, who doesn't give a damn.

Eventually, Hunter shakes his head and holds up his hands in surrender. "Sorry, man. I didn't know she was yours." He turns back toward the bar and continues drinking.

For a guy like Hunter, turning his back on a threat probably goes against everything he believes in. I'm guessing Ruben realizes this, because he looks at me before striding off toward the back of the club.

"I'm not his. I don't belong to anyone," I tell Hunter before heading to the other end of the bar, angry with Ruben.

It's still early, so the few customers who have drinks are spread out on the other side of the club, where the tables and sofas are. This is my favorite time to be at Kenza, before it starts filling up and everyone starts shouting orders at us from all directions.

It's twice as bad when there's a live band, which happens every two weeks on Friday and Saturday nights. Since I started working here, Kenza has become one of the hottest nightclubs in Lexington, and I love it.

Initially, I'd dreaded taking the job because the last

thing I wanted to do was serve drinks, but I needed the money. Even though I've had my ups and downs during my time here, I still love it. I love the look of the place. I love that Ruben is against drugs. I love that I have full medical benefits here—no other club or bar around here offers that. I guess I'm also kind of in love with the boss, which isn't the smartest thing I've ever done.

"Hey, Rosie. How are you doing?"

Glancing up from wiping glasses, I see Lucien leaning halfway over the bar.

I'm surprised to see him here. He comes in from time to time, but not as often as his brothers.

"Hi, Lucien. I'm good, thanks. It's nice to see you here."

And it is nice. I like Lucien, and the way he hides really pulls at my heartstrings. Even with his scars, he's a handsome man. Because of his choice to be alone, I'm guessing a woman hurt him because of the damage done to his body. If I'm right, then that woman needs a fist to the face, although I could be wrong. I just always find it strange that he refuses company and insists that he has nothing to offer anyone. He's so wrong.

"How has my brother been treating you?" he asks as I set his usual glass of whiskey in front of him. I'm not even sure how to answer because it sounds like

I'm with his brother, which couldn't be further from the truth.

I go for neutral. "He's a good boss. I'm fine."

He watches me work, as though expecting me to say more. Luckily, he's distracted by Sebastian's arrival.

"Hey, gorgeous. Anyone snapped you up yet?"

I roll my eyes and pass Sebastian the same drink as his brother. "Nope. I'm still young, free, and single." Feeling like teasing, I add, "Unless you're offering," and bat my eyelashes.

Sebastian laughs. "Are you flirting with me, Rosie?"

I ignore his question and counter with, "Where's Carla?"

I know Sebastian is only teasing because there is no way anyone else is going to turn his head the way Carla does. He has eyes for only one woman.

"She's at home reading. I'm planning on joining her real soon."

"Then stop flirting with Rosie before Ruben catches you," Lucien says. "But, as I don't have a woman and love nothing more than to wind my brother up, I'll continue flirting."

"Rosie knows I'm only teasing, but I'm all for you flirting with her. You need the practice."

Lucien frowns at Sebastian's comment. Before the moment becomes awkward, I ask, "How's Sabrina doing?" That gets Lucien's attention, although I'm not sure he likes being asked about her.

"What's wrong with Sabrina?" he asks as Sebastian wanders away from the bar with his drink in hand.

"I bumped into her and her mom the other week. She looked upset, and her mom looked like she was gloating about something." I start wiping the new glasses that Derek just dumped on the counter without saying a word. "I don't think she gets along with her mom all that well. I could be wrong. I've been wrong before. It was just a feeling I had when I stopped to talk to them."

"Hmm." Lucien sighed, finishing his drink.

"Another?"

"Please."

After pouring another whiskey, I start to move back down to where I can see Hunter watching me. I hesitate, then gather my courage and ask Lucien, "Why don't you ask her out?"

He pauses mid-drink. "She needs someone strong. Someone who isn't an embarrassment to her. That isn't me anymore."

This man is so full of hurt that he's going to make me cry. I cover his scarred hand with both of mine and tell him, "Lucien, you are one of the strongest men I know. Any woman would be proud to be with you." I quickly release him and move toward Hunter, but not before noticing Ruben standing behind Lucien, frowning.

Hell! The McKenzie men are everywhere tonight, tugging at my heartstrings.

"You're popular tonight."

I push Lucien from my mind and smile at Hunter. "They're the boss's brothers. Would you like another?"

"No, thanks. I need to head out." He stands up from the stool he's been sitting on. Throwing some money onto the bar, he starts to move away. He stops, looks over his shoulder, and seems to come to a decision. With quick strides, he makes his way back to me, indicating with his finger that I should come closer. I do, meeting him halfway over the bar.

"There are dangerous things going on in this place," he whispers, his eyes narrowing. My eyes widen in surprise, but he continues, "I don't think your boss knows either. In fact, I'm ninety-nine percent sure he doesn't. If you see something that seems out of place, ignore it. I don't want you getting in the middle of anything."

Hunter straightens up, but I grab his arm. "Who are you?"

He smirks. "A rough, sexy good guy."

I follow him with my eyes across the club until I lose him in the dim lighting.

He hasn't told me anything I didn't already know, but he has confirmed that my suspicions are correct. As for staying away from it all, I can't do that. I need proof before I go to Ruben. I know he's aware of something going on here at Kenza, but I'm positive he doesn't know what it is. I have a feeling it has something to do with Simon. Ruben won't believe his trusted manager is up to no good unless I have proof.

I can't wait for my shift to end tonight so I can go home, think about everything that's happened, and figure out how to get the proof I need. I only hope that being in Ruben's arms won't be on my mind, but I have a feeling it will be at the forefront.

4

———————

Ruben

I CAME AWAKE ABRUPTLY AND LAY IN BED, TRYING TO decide what had actually woken me up. I waited. Thump, thump!

Someone is banging on the door, and my phone is buzzing. I put it on silent when I went to bed last night—or rather, in the early hours of the morning.

Rolling out of bed, I stroke my morning wood, which feels damn good. Grabbing my phone, I realize I've missed calls and texts from Ramon, telling me to open the "fucking" door. At least I know who's trying to break down the door.

I yank on last night's jeans and zip them as I make my way to the door. I open it and turn my back,

63

saying, "Give me a minute. I need to use the bathroom."

"Whatever," Lucien mumbles.

I hope they've brought breakfast and coffee. Lucien has a thing about Starbucks, so hopefully they stopped on their way over. I can hope.

I shove into the bathroom, praying my dick behaves now that it's started going down, and close the door behind me.

My brothers have a habit of dropping in unannounced, but not usually this early. It fills me with dread. What have they discovered?

No matter how many times my brothers tell me not to take the vandalism and break-in personally, I find it difficult not to. It's my place. Why wouldn't I take it personally? By causing shit to happen here, the person responsible is basically hitting me where it hurts. I'm angry about everything, and last night was the first night I'd slept properly in a long time.

I grin because that had more to do with Rosie than anything else. She's been under my skin for a while. Her soft skin calls for my fingers to touch her—her innocence, her sass. God, does she have sass! She's a hot little package that has managed to do what no one else ever has and caught my undivided attention.

Frowning at the thought, I put on a sweater and

grab some clean socks, thinking about my next move with sweet Rosie. I should leave her alone, but I can't. I've never wanted anyone the way I want Rosie.

"Ruben, what the fuck are you doing in there?"

"I'm coming," I reply to Lucien.

"Did we really need to know that?" Ramon comments, laughing when he sees me walking toward him.

"Fuck you!" I say, but there's no fight in my words.

I chuckle and help myself to a coffee and a chocolate chip muffin that they've brought with them before turning to face them. "Why the early morning visit?"

"Early morning? Have you looked at a clock since we obviously woke you up? It's eleven-thirty."

"Shit." I had no idea it was so late. I'm usually up by eight. I guess that's what happens when all the sleepless nights catch up to you.

Glancing at Lucien, who looks distracted, I turn to Ramon, who says one word, "Drugs."

I choke on my coffee and slam the cup down on the table.

"What the hell do you mean, 'drugs'? Is that what's going on at Kenza?"

Ramon nods in response.

"Who?"

"We don't know," Lucien says, joining the conversation. "Last night, I overheard a couple of guys talking about buying some heroin. One of them seemed to know all about it and said his supplier was here at the club. When they finished talking, I heard the door slam, so I went to follow them to see who it was. But there was no one there. I figured they'd gone back into the club, which was packed last night."

I sit and stew, not saying anything, wondering who the hell would bring drugs into my club. "It can't be the staff. They know what happens if I find drugs on them in my club, don't they?" I go through my list of staff, and doubt rears its ugly head. There isn't anyone who has been acting out of sorts. I pay my staff well so they won't be tempted to take advantage of the club.

"You need to get an undercover cop in here. I have a couple of contacts we can use, but you need someone who knows about this stuff to be in the club. Nothing is going to happen while you or us are around. It was pure luck that Lucien heard what he did last night."

I lean back on the sofa with my feet on the coffee table and my head on the backrest. I close my eyes and rub my temples. I'm furious that drugs are being sold right under my nose. God help the bastard responsible when I find him.

"Set it up," I tell Ramon. "It can't hurt to have someone here. I want to know if they put someone in the club."

"I'll tell him." Ramon slouches into the chair, looking exhausted.

He hasn't been himself for a while. It bugs me that my brother seems to have the world on his shoulders, yet he won't talk to me or anyone else.

Lucien watches him, too.

"I'll ask Simon to keep his ear to the ground as well."

"Do you trust him?" Lucien asks.

His question plays over and over in my mind. He's my manager and the one person in the best position to betray me, but I trust him. I gave him a job—a chance. I can't imagine him being responsible. "I won't mention the undercover cop you're trying to get here, but I'll tell him that I've heard we might have a drug problem, and I'll tell him to keep his eyes open."

"Okay." Lucien nods and starts eating his muffin.

I turn to Ramon and demand, "Talk to us. Don't give me that shit about there being nothing wrong.

You've changed. I'd even go so far as to say you look sad."

Ramon meets my gaze, then looks away. I know he's about to lie to me.

"Don't say anything if you're not willing to tell me the truth, because that will piss me off." I lean forward, resting my arms on my knees, and wait for Ramon to decide whether to speak or remain silent.

A while back, Lucien thought Ramon was gay. Then, Carla appeared as his so-called girlfriend. This made my oldest brother a telltale, but when we discovered he'd been pretending with Carla, it made me stop and think.

The thought of another guy touching my junk does nothing for me. If that's how my brother is, though, I'll support him no matter what. He's my brother, and I'd be damn proud to call him that either way.

Then there's Sylvia from the office, who works as Sebastian's and Michael's assistant. I've seen the way he looks at her on the few occasions she's been to a gathering at someone's house.

It's difficult to figure out what's going on in his life.

"Carla's brother is still missing." He rubs his hands through his hair. "No one seems to know where he's gone. It's as though he's disappeared from the face of the earth. The detective I hired was following his trail, but it's gone cold. I have no idea how I'm going to tell Carla." He laughs. "I've even thought about getting Sebastian to tell her, but Noah and Carla are my friends, so I can't really do that. I need to be the one to tell her. I just wish I knew if he was okay."

I sit back again and think about what he just said. I can't help but go back to the gay thing. "Are you gay?"

Lucien starts coughing. "Wrong way," he whispers, still coughing.

"Idiot." I shoot Lucien a glare before turning back to Ramon. "You didn't answer the question," I remind Ramon, who looks very uncomfortable.

He sighs and meets my gaze. "Not exactly."

"But 'not exactly' doesn't answer the question. Either you are or you aren't."

"Fuck."

"Look, I'm not trying to put you on the spot, but I guess I've done that. It doesn't matter to me either way. I'm just trying to figure you out. You've been troubled for a while now. I'm sick of hearing you say everything is okay when it clearly isn't."

We sit in silence for a few minutes before Lucien speaks.

"I'm with Ruben on this. You're our brother, no

matter who you love. We've always stuck together, and that isn't about to change, so spit it out."

"I'm bi. Fuck!" He leans forward, puts his coffee cup on the table, and rests his arms on his thighs. "I was with Noah in Canada. He lived with me until he disappeared. I like women. I just prefer men." He looks between Lucien and me. "Is this weird?"

I shake my head and answer, "No, we've suspected for a while now, although you threw us off when Carla was pretending to be your girlfriend. I've also seen you watching Sylvia." I grin. "Are you going to do anything about her?"

"I'm not in a position to do anything about her."

Well, my morning turned out to be a lot more informative than I expected. But I could use something more substantial than a muffin in my stomach. I decide to let my brother off the hook... for now.

A large plate of food at the diner is calling my name. I get to my feet and say, "If you ladies have finished, I'm going out to get something to eat."

"Ladies my ass," Lucien grumbles. "I'll come with you."

"I could eat. You both won't tell the others, will you? I'll tell them when I'm ready for them to know."

"I'll stay quiet, but the sooner you tell them, the better. They'll react the same way we did. Well, maybe Sebastian will act like he's five, but Michael and the others will be fine."

"I suspect Sebastian may know." Ramon shrugs. "Carla does, so she may have told him. But I don't know for sure."

Lucien laughs. "If he knew, you can bet he'd have let you know."

Ramon nods as Lucien and I follow him out of my apartment and downstairs to the club. I see Simon entering his office. I need to talk to him and hope that I can trust him with what I'm about to tell him.

I pat my brothers on the back and tell them, "I'll meet you at the diner. I'm going to talk to Simon about what we discussed."

"See you there." Lucien walks out the rear door.

Ramon looks relieved as he turns to follow Lucien out the door.

I walk toward Simon's office to tell him what I've discovered about the club, sighing with relief. The doubt from earlier creeps up, and I realize that I should try to gauge his reaction. This is awful—suspecting people I trust to run Kenza. But this shit is going to stop soon.

Rosie

"Hey, Rosie. How are you?" Hunter asked me as he took a seat at the bar I always seem to be wiping down whenever he arrives.

"I'm good." I put a beer in front of him and lean on the bar. "What's going on, Hunter? Do you know who's causing the trouble here?"

Taking a long swallow, he holds my gaze. Holding his drink in one hand, he leans closer to me, and I fight the urge to move away. He's invading my personal space, but I refuse to back up. "You're cute, and Ruben's a dick for letting you go."

I wasn't expecting that and respond, "Ruben has never had me to let go of. Now, you were saying?"

He laughs. "I wasn't saying anything."

"You were about to tell me what's going on with Kenza. I was about to listen." I offer him my best smile, which I've been told can turn heads.

He narrows his eyes and leans closer to me. "If you get any closer, you're going to face-plant in my lap—not that I'd complain, but I think your boyfriend might have something to say about it."

"Hmm. You're an ass, and you're trying to distract me so I forget my original question, which I haven't, in case you're wondering."

Hunter's eyes stay on me the whole time I'm serving a couple of other customers. He doesn't bother me because I know he isn't really interested. He's into the whole flirting from a distance thing, which is perfectly fine with me, considering my hang-up with my boss.

As I move to the front of the bar to collect a couple of empties that have been left lying around, I spot Ruben across the room, glaring daggers at me. What the hell has pissed him off, and why is he looking at me like that?

He's the one who likes all that stuff I'm not into. Plus, he's been ignoring me since our embrace—or whatever you want to call it—at the bottom of the stairs.

"Hmm. He might not have you, but he wants you, and he's jealous as hell that you're over here flirting with me."

"I'm not flirting with you, Hunter. If I were really flirting with you, you'd certainly know." I place my hand on his shoulder, slowly caressing down his back to the waist of his low-cut jeans, then back up to his other shoulder. He shudders.

Seeing the heat in his eyes, I retreat behind the bar. Maybe I've gone too far. I meant to tease and have a laugh, but maybe it backfired.

Clearing his throat, Hunter says, "Not that I mind you flirting with me, but you'd better keep your hands to yourself because that felt too damn good."

"Rosie!" Ruben practically roars from the end of the bar. "My office...now." He turns and heads toward the back of the club.

Shit! This isn't good. He looks really angry.

I start to follow Ruben, but Hunter grabs my wrist. "Are you afraid of him?"

"What?" I shook my head. "No."

Hunter lets go of me as Craig arrives to take over.

"I'll be fine. He won't hurt me."

I know this in my heart, or at least I know he won't hurt me physically. Whether he'll hurt me emotionally remains to be seen.

I offer Hunter a smile and turn to head to Ruben's office to face the grizzly bear.

While teasing Hunter, I temporarily forgot that Ruben was watching me from the back of the room.

Taking a deep breath, I knock on his door and enter to find him pacing back and forth in front of his desk. His agitation is clear in his step and the tightness of his shoulders. Then, he turns his wild eyes toward me, and I fight the urge to run back to the bar.

"Come in and shut the door."

I do as I'm told, but I feel perspiration on my

palms. Worry creases my brow at his agitation. I've never seen him like this before.

"Ruben—"

I don't finish because he's on me, pinning me against the door, nose-to-nose.

"You touched him. You caressed his back. Did your touch make him hard?"

Wow. He's really worked up over my teasing of Hunter. There isn't an inch between our bodies, and, being this close, I can feel Ruben throbbing against my belly.

"Stay away from him, Rosie. He isn't for you."

Screw this. "You don't have any say in who I'm with. I like Hunter, and he knows what he wants. I'm not confused about what he wants from me." He doesn't need to know that I don't believe Hunter wants to have sex with me.

I try to push him away, but he's unmovable. "Ruben, stop being an ass and let me go."

"Stay away from him," he says, glaring at my mouth.

"And what if I don't want to stay away from him?"

He blinks as though he can't believe I wouldn't do what he wants. "You are the most pigheaded woman I've ever met, and you drive me fucking crazy. I don't know anything about him, so I just want you to be safe."

I've had enough of this. He's an idiot if he thinks I could want anyone else when the only man I want is pinning me against the wall with his hard body.

"Make love to me, Ruben," I say. The words are out before I even realize I've said them. They shock us both, and we freeze, feeling the tension crackle between us. I groan inwardly. That was supposed to be a silent thought.

"Fuck, Rosie." His breathing increases, and his penis twitches against me.

"I've wanted you forever, but you're too innocent. But I can't let anyone else touch you."

What the hell does he mean? It's okay for him to sleep with whomever he wants, but not for me?

"Let me get this straight." My nostrils flare in anger, and I can feel the heat in my cheeks. "It's okay for you to go about your life, sleeping with whoever you want, but you're saying it isn't all right for me to do the same? Does that about cover it? Because I'm telling you right now, I'll sleep with whomever I want, and it won't have anything to do with you."

He rubs against my belly. "That's for you," he says, jaw clenched tight. "You need to be careful what you say to me because make no mistake—I want you. I want you so damn bad that no one else does it for me anymore. When I jerk off, it's because of you. I picture you lying on my bed with your legs spread open for me and me alone. I imagine you on your knees, sucking me off. This belongs to me. Are we clear that my cock only wants to get wet between your thighs?"

My heart feels like it's going to burst from his closeness and words. He's the sexiest man I've ever seen, and my head is telling me that, no matter what he said, it's now or never.

Sliding my hands into the back of his hair, I respond, "Crystal clear. Now shut up and kiss me."

I pull his head toward me. Before our lips meet, I catch his smirk, and then his mouth is on mine. Our teeth clash, and our tongues tangle.

I'll never get enough of Ruben. He sets my body on fire. His arms wrap around me, pulling me tight against him. I wrap my arms around his neck as we continue to kiss deeply.

"Let me love you, Rosie." He kisses down my neck to my collarbone, and I throw my head back and moan. My whole body feels like jelly, and I feel tingles running through my bloodstream straight to my pussy, which throbs with an ache that only Ruben can ease. I want this man so much that I don't have the strength to refuse him. Even though I asked first, he asked me to let him love me. He didn't say anything vulgar or sugary to seduce me, but he said, "Let me love you."

I wrap my leg around his hip, bringing myself up close and personal with the rock-hard bulge in his jeans. He rears back and hisses as I rub against him. "Don't stop, Ruben. Please don't stop. I want you inside me," I tell him, wondering where those words came from. I don't normally ask for what I want when it comes to sex.

"I'll love you, babe. But the first time I take you, it won't be a quick fuck in my office." He breathes heavily into my neck. "My apartment—now."

I let him push me away without question and watch him adjust himself in his jeans. Then, he drags me out of his office and through the door that leads to his apartment. He locks the door behind us. "I don't want us to be disturbed."

When he turns to look at me standing on the stairs, I can't think straight. His eyes are hot, and he has an aroused flush on his cheekbones.

"Rosie, stop looking at me like that, or I won't make it until we're in my apartment." He clenches his fists at his sides.

Knowing this man wants me so much is a

powerful aphrodisiac. That he's close to losing it right here, right now.

I turn and start walking upstairs with an added sway to my hips. Halfway up, I nearly stumble when I feel his hands on my hips. Then, I stumble again, ending up on my hands and knees on the stairs when he bites me on the bottom.

I can't think with his hands everywhere—on my breasts, belly, hips, and legs—before he moves under my skirt and rubs me between my thighs. Moaning, I drop forward, and Ruben follows me.

"You're *very* wet. Do you have any idea how hot it is knowing that I make you this wet? I need to taste you."

He wraps his arms around my waist and hauls me up a few more stairs to the landing. He turns me in his arms and lays me down, staying kneeling on the stairs between my spread legs.

My skirt is around my hips when Ruben slides his hands up my thighs to my panties and rips them off. He holds them to his nose, closes his eyes, and inhales before shoving them into his pocket.

He strokes my pussy lips, coating his fingers in my wetness and driving me crazy. Losing all inhibitions, I yank my shirt and bra over my head.

"Fuck, Rosie," Ruben hisses, staring at my breasts.

Wanting to tease him, I bring my hands up to play with my nipples. I hear Ruben cuss before he inserts a finger inside me. I arch up from the floor in pleasure, not wanting him to stop.

I drop my hands from my breasts when I feel Ruben's talented mouth on me, his tongue lapping me up before darting in and out of my channel.

I thread my fingers into his hair and hold my quivering thighs open while he goes to town on me. I've never come this way before, but I feel the ball of fire gathering in my belly and the tightening of my nipples.

"Ahhh... Oh God... Ruben!" I shout as my orgasm rips through me, making my toes curl and my head feel like it's going to explode. It feels too good. He's still lapping me up. I can't take much more. "Ruben, I want you inside me. Oh God, please." I'm begging. I'm lost.

Ruben lifts his head from between my thighs, crawls over my body, and seals his lips with mine. My taste is on his lips. I wrap my legs around his hips and push him down onto me with the heels of my feet.

I shove a hand between our bodies and try to undo his belt, but it's too difficult, so I give up and rub him through his jeans, scraping my fingernails along his rigid length. I need to feel him—see him.

"Help me," I beg, moving back to his belt.

Ruben knocks my hand away, lifts up from me, and sorts out his belt while I unzip him. I shove my hand into the opening and wrap my fingers around his width. I hear him gasp when I bring him out from where he's been hidden.

He's gorgeous and pulsing in my hand. I rub my thumb over the leaking head of his shaft. My nail presses into the slit, causing more pre-cum to leak out. He knocks my hand away, rears back into a kneeling position, and pinches the head of his long, thick penis with one hand while squeezing his balls with the other.

5

Ruben

"Fuck, fuck, fuck!" I almost came from her touch alone.

Kneeling between her thighs, I held my cock and balls in an attempt to stave off my orgasm. I tried to control my breathing and lust for this woman.

I've wanted her for so long that now that I have her under me, I'm too excited to go slow. But I need to.

"We need to get inside. I want you on my bed. I've dreamed about you lying naked on my bed in my arms."

She scrambles away from me and quickly picks up

her clothes. I slowly get to my feet, holding on to my jeans to keep them from falling to my ankles.

God, she's beautiful.

She's standing in my apartment, breathing as unevenly as I am. I walk up to her and slide my hands under her skirt, bringing it up to her waist. This allows me to caress the golden globes of her smooth ass.

I let my cock rest between her buttocks, wrap my arms around her, and let her lean against my chest. Then, I dip my head and kiss the curve of her neck. She shivers against me.

"Ruben," she whispers.

"Mmm."

Removing her skirt, she stands naked before me. My cock jumps, trying to get to her. I quickly remove the rest of my clothes and walk toward her, unable to wait any longer. I pick her up in a fireman's lift, striding into my bedroom and depositing her on my bed.

"Gorgeous."

I crawl onto the bed and spread her legs so I can get closer to her, not knowing what to taste or touch first. Whatever I choose, chances are I'm going to climax. She has me so worked up, and my passion for her hasn't dimmed at all since we moved from the landing to my bed. I want her with a desperation unlike anything I've ever felt before. Keeping myself in check so I don't frighten her is killing me.

I settle over her, using my forearms on either side of her chest to support my weight, and I teasingly caress her breasts. I know where she wants my hands, but I want my mouth on them. Dipping down, I capture one nipple between my lips and suck. Rosie reacts as though she's been struck by lightning.

Having her rub her pussy against my aching dick is driving me insane. My balls are tight against my body, and I'm leaking all over her from excitement. I need to be inside her.

I quickly shove a finger inside her to make sure she's ready—and boy, is she ready!—and take my cock in hand. I push the head of my dick inside her. I clamp my teeth together and try to breathe through the pleasure I feel as I enter her body. Moving deeper and deeper inside her, I pray I won't come too soon. Fuck! I've never lost control of my body's responses before, but I'm damn close to doing just that. Then, I'm balls deep inside her. She's so good—so wet, hot, and tight. I bite down on the orgasm threatening to overcome me. She's just so good.

She arches under me, and—fuck! "Oh God, no! Don't move. Please, don't move. I don't have a condom." I've never been inside anyone without a condom before. Not once. I'm in way over my head with this woman.

I slide out of her and grab a condom from the bedside table. I quickly put it on before slamming back inside her, seconds from exploding.

Holding her gaze, I slowly slide out to the tip and back in just as slowly.

She pulls me on top of her, reaching up to search for my mouth, which I give her. Her legs wrap around mine, and we're skin-to-skin. I'm closer to her than I've ever been to anyone before.

I lick a path from her mouth to her breasts, taking one engorged nipple into my mouth as I slide back and forth inside her, my balls slapping against her.

"Ruben," she says, kissing me on the forehead. "You make me feel...feel...never before...not like this."

Her words make my head swell—and I don't just mean the one inside her that's about to explode.

"Rosie, I need to come. I can't hold off. I'll make it up to you." I kneel up between her legs, my cock half-buried inside her. Grabbing her hips, I pull her bottom to my lap, and she wraps her legs around my waist.

Having her spread out and open to me is so fucking hot. I start moving, feeling the prickling sensation start in the base of my spine as she arches up against me, clinging to the quilt beneath her.

I reach between us, find her clit, and roll it between my fingers. I watch as she flies apart, taking me with her, as the fire in my balls explodes through the tip of my cock.

My release goes on and on as I fill the condom, with Rosie still squeezing more cum out of me. Her aftershocks flutter up and down my dick, keeping me hard as fuck even after my orgasm.

I collapse forward and wrap her tightly in my arms, bringing her against my chest. I roll onto my back, still connected to her in the most intimate way a man and woman can be. I never want to give this up.

WHILE GETTING DRESSED AFTER OUR SHOWER, I FOUND that I was too distracted by the image in my head of Rosie on her knees in the shower, sucking me off. It was unlike anything I had experienced before. Her innocence and enthusiasm had me spilling my seed within minutes of her hot little mouth wrapping around me.

I shove my feet back into my boots, stand, and leave my shirt hanging loose to hide the fact that I want the woman across the bed from me, who doesn't seem to know what to do about her missing panties. She won't get back the ones I ripped from her. They're mine.

I walk to my dresser and grab a pair of black boxers. I root around for a pin or something to hold them up on her slim hips. The thought of her walking around Kenza in my underwear is fucking hot.

"Here, you can wear these." I hand them to her, throbbing when she hits her skirt up and slides the boxers up her legs. "Let me."

My hands shake as I pull the top band together and fasten it with the pin. I pull her skirt back down over her legs and crouch down, unable to resist sliding my hands up and down her mouth-watering legs.

"Ruben... Mmm... Simon's waiting for you."

"He can wait," I breathe against her leg. I'm so close to rutting against her like a dog in heat.

"Nope, come on." She steps back and takes my hand, pulling me up to my full height.

I kiss her quickly on the lips, then slide my fingers between hers, holding her hand tightly. "Stay with me when Kenza closes."

Being with her terrifies me because I sense that nothing will ever be the same again. At the same time, though, I want more with her. I don't want her to be just another notch on my bedpost. I want her for much longer.

"Ruben," she says softly under her breath. "I want to be with you, but I'm afraid I won't satisfy you. I'm not into toys." She bites her lip.

"I like playing with toys, but if it means getting to spend my nights with you, then I can do without. Hasn't our time in my apartment shown you just how much I'm satisfied with you? Good God, you almost made me come on the landing, and I wasn't even inside you." I give her an embarrassed chuckle. Because, hell, nearly coming like a randy teenager is damn embarrassing at thirty-five.

"Then I'll stay." She offers me a slight smile.

I open my apartment door and let go of her hand, catching the frown that crosses her features. How do I tell her to keep this between us without sounding like a jerk?

Wanting to get it off my chest, I say, "Rosie, we need to keep this between us. I don't want the rest of the staff to know you're sleeping with the boss."

She gasps, and I realize I could have worded it differently so that it didn't sound sleazy.

Rosie backs toward the stairs. I reach out to her, but she ignores my hand.

"You know what? I don't think sleeping with the boss is such a good idea. Especially when he's too embarrassed to tell the rest of the staff that he's sleeping with the hired help. Maybe you don't want them getting excited and wondering who's next." With that, she flees down the stairs.

"Rosie!" I shout. "Rosie, fuck! Stop! I didn't mean —" I trail off as the door at the bottom of the stairs slams shut behind her. "I've never fucked an employee," I whisper, "but I just made love to one..."

Rosie

A week later, the idea of "sleeping with the boss" still resonates with me. During my late-afternoon tryst with Ruben, I fell more in love with him. He made me feel like I was on top of the world—more so after he asked me to spend the night with him. But then he opened his mouth and ruined everything.

Sighing, I moved toward Hunter when I saw Ruben enter the main floor. His eyes always follow me. I've sensed his urge to talk to me since I left his place last week, but he's stayed away. I wanted him to come after me so badly that night, but he didn't. He let me go, and it hurt badly.

"Hey, gorgeous." Hunter brings me out of my distressing thoughts. "Who put that look on your pretty face? Do I need to knock some sense into him?"

Without thinking, I step into him and wrap my arms around his waist. I just need someone to hold me. I need comfort from anyone, just a warm body to hold me and make me feel like everything is okay.

He pauses before I feel his arms wrap around me. "Hey, babe. You have me worried."

I shake my head, look at him, and say, "I'm okay. I've missed you."

"Well, if that's what it takes to get you in my arms, what will it take to get you under me?"

I pinch him on the ass. "Don't be a dick. I need a friend."

He chuckles. "Well, pinching me on the ass isn't going to earn my friendship. I love being pinched on the ass by a hot little spitfire—it turns me on."

He pauses when he sees the glare I shoot him.

Clearing his throat, he continues, "I've never had a female friend before, but I guess there's a first time for everything." He grins and, keeping his arm around me, leads me to the bar. "Did I do good that time? Maybe I deserve a drink for controlling my urges."

I walk around the bar, grab a longneck, open it, and pass it to him. "You're a big flirt and would probably run a mile if this little spitfire accepted what you keep offering."

I wink at him, turn, and leave him with his mouth hanging open as I make my way down the bar to serve Ramon. The grin on my face says it all—I love having the last word. It doesn't happen often, but that felt good.

I place a whiskey in front of Ramon and look back up the bar at Hunter, laughing out loud. He's grinning at me and toasting me with his beer.

"Rosie, stop flirting with the customers," Ruben tells me. Anger flashes in his eyes as he walks toward the floor.

I stick my tongue out at his back, and Ramon laughs. "I take it you and my brother aren't getting along."

I snort—very ladylike—but he's starting to piss me off. His anger is even worse now that I'm not crying every time he looks at me with disgust. "You could say that," I respond to Ramon's observation. "He might be your brother, but he's a dick."

"Hmm," he says, nursing his whiskey. "What's he done now?"

I ignore his question.

But he persists. "Rosie, if you're calling my brother a dick, don't you think I have the right to know why?"

Slowing my movements as I wipe the bar top, I meet his gaze and try to hold back my tears, but it's obvious that I'm upset. I tell him the truth, "After...after...well, I think you know what I mean. Afterward, he told me not to 'let the staff know I'm sleeping with the boss.' I don't want to be with someone who isn't proud to acknowledge our relationship. He was more than a quick fuck, and I thought it meant more to him as well. But I was wrong. I've been there before, and I'm not going there again. So now you know why I think your brother is a dick."

I uncapped a bottle of still water and took some strong gulps. I nearly spluttered when Ramon opened his mouth.

"I think I'd have to agree with you. He is a dick for that. But, in his defense, Ruben does have a habit of saying one thing and meaning something completely different. Whatever you have going on with Hunter will make him admit his mistake sooner rather than later."

"I don't have anything going on with Hunter. He's

a friend. He doesn't want me either. It's nice to have a male friend who doesn't want anything else from me. It's refreshing."

Leaning on the bar, I take a closer look at Ramon. He's cute, the baby of the McKenzie family. Although he looks nothing like a baby, with his overgrown long hair, blue-green eyes, and five-o'clock shadow.

"Rosie, you're staring."

"Yes, I am. You're cute," I blurt out. I watch as Ramon blushes. Grinning, I take the hand he just ran through his unruly hair. Sobering up, I say, "We're both in love with someone who has no idea." I meet his sad eyes. "I'm here if you ever need to talk. And I don't just mean because I'm in love with your idiot of a brother. Sometimes it's easier talking to someone you're not close to. Anyway, the offer stands."

Ramon slides his fingers between mine and holds on. That's how Ruben catches us.

"What the fuck is going on? Isn't Hunter enough for you that you have to move on to my brother?" Ruben snarls.

I try to pull my hand free, but Ramon refuses to let go. He winks at me before turning his head toward his brother. "You screwed up. What's it to you who she chooses to be with? And before you get your shorts in a wad, it isn't me." Ramon looks back at me. "I'm comforting a friend and offering her suggestions about how to get a guy like me to take her home for more than just sleeping in the same bed."

"Screw this! Rosie, I'll pick you up tomorrow at eleven." Ruben heads back the way he came but stops and walks back to us. "Keep your hands off my woman," he growls at Ramon, making sure to include Hunter in his statement.

Ramon releases my hand and grins like an idiot. "Well, well, well. It looks like my 'dick' of a brother wants more than to scratch an itch," he says after Ruben disappears into the back of the club.

"He sure does," Hunter comments, sitting beside Ramon. "Are you sure you didn't misunderstand what he said to you?"

I shake my head. "How could I misunderstand 'I don't want the rest of the staff to know you're sleeping with the boss'?"

Ramon slams his whiskey down. "You have a point. It's entertaining watching my brother eat crow." He looks at Hunter, then turns back to me. "You want some advice, Rosie? Actually, I'm going to give you some regardless. Don't let him get between your legs until you've made him sweat. Keep 'em shut tomorrow. Let him beg. I like the idea of you making my brother beg." He grinned, and I couldn't help but laugh at the glee on his face.

"Don't you love your brother?"

"Yeah, I do. But he's being a dick with you, which tells me you mean something to him. More than he's ever felt before. Go knock him dead, Rosie."

"Hmm, we'll see. He really hurt me last week, but I'd rather change the subject to you. You're much more interesting."

"Rosie, I'm not interesting at all."

I stare at Ramon and Hunter for a moment, until I finally get the hint—they want to be left alone. Hmm. I think I've figured out Ramon's sexual preference, but what about Hunter?

6

Ruben

"I'M SUCH A GIRL!" IS THE FIRST THOUGHT THAT RUNS through my head when I look at my bed, having finally decided on my favorite pair of soft, pale blue jeans and a long-sleeved T-shirt in a darker shade of blue. They were the first items I took from my now half-empty closet.

I shake my head at how stupid I'm being, all because I have a date with Rosie. That doesn't stop me from spraying on some of my favorite cologne or looking in the mirror to make sure my hair isn't sticking up everywhere.

She has me tied in knots. The other week, when she caressed Hunter's back, I felt like killing him. I came close to ripping my brother's hand off last night. I'm not the jealous type—at least, I never thought I was until Rosie came along.

With nerves in my stomach, I grab my phone and dial Sebastian. This call isn't going to go well. In fact, I bet Sebastian will kill himself laughing at my expense. Hopefully, Carla will be the one to answer.

"Hello."

Yes!

"Carla, I need your help. I'm taking Rosie out today, but I'm not sure where to take her. I'd have been okay in the evening, but I told her I'd pick her up at eleven. Help!"

She chuckles. "Ruben, calm down. Rosie isn't high maintenance. It's a beautiful day, so why don't you take her to the mountains and have a picnic? She loves nature, so she'll love it."

"Okay, I can handle that." I continued to pace, wondering where I could get a picnic at such short notice. "Where—"

Carla interrupted me. "One minute, Ruben. Your brother is being his nosy self."

I listen as Carla tells Sebastian to do something else while she finishes talking to me. He's probably more interested in the fact that I'm going on a date than anything else.

"Carla, it's cool. I'm good. Thanks for the help."

"Stay calm, Ruben. It'll all work out fine. Just go and have fun with your girl."

After hanging up with Carla, I grabbed my keys and wallet, slipped my cell phone into my back pocket, and headed out. I planned to stop at the deli.

I climb into my SUV and drive the three blocks to see the woman who is going to save my date, wondering how I don't know anything about picnics at my age.

Probably because I haven't been on a picnic since I was a kid. That one was with my parents and brothers down by the river on my family's property. We had fun jumping into the river while Mom shouted at us not to drown each other.

Grinning at the memory, I push into the store and sigh in relief when I spot Lorraine at the counter.

"Ruben, what a nice surprise! What can I get you?" Lorraine asks, coming around the counter to hug me.

She has worked here as long as I can remember and has always had a smile for my brothers and me.

I release her from my arms and grin as I admit, "I'm taking someone on a picnic, but I have no idea what to bring. I'm ashamed to say I've never done this before, at least not one that I've arranged myself."

Lorraine chuckles. "That must mean she's

someone special." There's a gleam in her eye as she waits for me to agree, but I stay silent. "Ruben McKenzie, I do believe love is in the air."

My face heats up as I look anywhere but at Lorraine. "Maybe," I mumble.

Rolling her eyes, Lorraine asks, "Well, let's get this picnic sorted out. I'm presuming it's going to be just the two of you?"

I nod.

"Okay. Take a seat over there while I make you a coffee. Then, I'll get your picnic together."

"Thanks, Lorraine. You're a lifesaver."

I take a seat and drink the coffee that Lorraine sent over with one of the other staff. With her "sunny disposition," she looks as though she wishes to be elsewhere. It's a good thing Lorraine hasn't seen her serve me with attitude. Lorraine wouldn't stand for that and the girl would be gone.

Shaking my head, I turned to stare out the window, wondering if Rosie would be happy to see me. I caught her off guard last night when I told her I would pick her up at eleven today. There was no way I could sit back and watch her with my brother and Hunter without staking my claim. I figured a date would be much better and cleaner than pissing on her leg. I chuckle at the thought.

"Daydreaming?" Lorraine asked.

I turned to look at her, my eyes widening in shock when I saw the huge basket sitting on the table beside me. "Did you leave anything in the store?"

She swats me on the shoulder. "Don't be silly. You need to show your girl how special she is...and Ruben." She waits until I meet her eyes before continuing. "Don't screw it up."

"That's the last thing I want."

"I know, honey. Now go get your girl."

I push away from the table and say, "Thank you," as I hand her some money. I end up shoving it into her pocket when I hug her again because she refuses to take it. "I'll be offended if you give it back to me." I quickly kiss her on the forehead before heading out the door to my SUV and going to get Rosie.

After storing the basket in the back, I'm behind the wheel and on my way to Rosie's apartment building. As her employer, I didn't need to ask for her address. I have it on the secure staff program on my laptop. I've known the address for a while and have driven past the building on more than one occasion, but I hadn't been able to work up the courage to drop in on Rosie. I might keep that bit of information to myself, though. I don't want her to think I've been stalking her. I haven't been stalking her, have I?

Whatever. I know I'm not a sick idiot. She's been mine since she stepped foot in Kenza for her interview with Simon.

I asked him to conduct the interviews so that I could be elsewhere, but the minute our eyes met, I was lost. I buried those feelings for so long, trying to get rid of them with other women. But my heart always beats frantically in my chest when I'm around her. After having her under me and knowing what it's like to be inside her, I want more—a lot more.

My feelings for her are complicated as well because part of me knows she's sweet and innocent. However, she didn't act very sweet or innocent when she was wrapped around me. Would she be willing to play?

It's too late to start thinking about this now, though, because I have an erection bursting to get free, and I've pulled up outside the diner where she lives.

I look it over, trying to take my mind off my arousal.

The diner reminds me of the diners that sprang up all over the States in the '50s and '60s. It looks well cared for. The chrome exterior and interior are spotless and shine brightly in the sunlight. The pale pink and blue colors blend well.

"Ruben?"

Shit! I'm losing it. Lost in thought again.

Rosie climbs in with a frown on her face. "If you don't want to do this, just say so. I'd hate to force my company on anyone."

Great, this is off to a good start.

I turn in my seat to look at her. "I want to take you on a picnic, okay? I was just admiring the diner's chrome and colors and how they blend together."

She starts to laugh. "Do you want to go inside and meet everyone? I can introduce you if you'd rather eat here."

What is she talking about? "No way. I'm not sharing you. Besides, I have a basket full of food in the back."

"You do?"

"Yeah, I do. Fasten your seatbelt, and we'll go up into the mountains to one of my favorite spots. There's a stream, and we'll be able to eat there with an amazing view of the valley below."

"Mmm, that sounds wonderful."

I quickly glance at Rosie, who is snuggled into the seat, before moving my eyes back to the road.

Rosie

As we drive by the beautiful landscape of Lexington, I have time to think. Ruben and I have both been avoiding each other since I slept with him. He makes my body react in ways it never has before, and it frightens me. It also makes me think that I'm heading for heartbreak with him. He's not the settling-down kind of guy. Even if Simon hadn't pointed that out a few more times than necessary, I would have known. For some reason, though, Ruben has taken a liking to me. He gets jealous whenever someone else shows interest in me, which tells me that this thing between us means more to him.

The silence of the engine finally registers, and I turn toward Ruben, who is grinning at me. "Stay," he says before jumping out of the SUV.

He opens my door and holds out his hand. I place my hand in his, and he pulls me out of the car. Without letting go, he kisses me on the knuckles.

"Let me grab the picnic basket and blanket." He walks to the back of the SUV and pulls out a large basket. The thought of the food inside makes my stomach grumble. I was so nervous this morning about seeing Ruben today that I couldn't eat breakfast. All I managed was my morning coffee—I needed that to wake up. I'd be "a bitch" all day, otherwise. Liz's words, not mine. My words would be "sweet as an angel."

Coming out of my thoughts about bitches and angels, I watch Ruben struggle to hold on to everything. I stepped forward and grabbed the blanket. "Here, let me help."

"Thanks." He releases the blanket and locks his SUV before taking my hand again. He leads me through trees that have grown into a tunnel-like shelter. We walk straight through it. On the other side, I gasp. It's the kind of thing you'd expect to see in a movie, but not in real life. The view is breathtaking.

There is a small stream practically at our feet that, from this position, looks like a snake winding down the mountain to the right. The view is just as Ruben described—you can see for miles. I could easily sit here forever and never move.

Ruben squeezes my hand, gives it a slight tug, and gets me moving again toward a shaded spot. He puts the picnic basket down, releases my hand, and holds out his hand. "Give me one end of the blanket, babe. Let's get this picnic started."

I do as he asks, enjoying the sound of his voice. When he's aroused, it's dark and husky, like melted chocolate.

"Sit."

I sit down and watch Ruben fish around in the basket, smiling. He's happy—happy to be here with me.

I nibble my lip and ask, "Are you planning on sharing?"

He stops and looks sheepish. "Sorry. Do you know Lorraine at the deli?" He asks this while starting to unload the basket, revealing tub after tub of food.

Just how many people is he planning on feeding?

"I know Lorraine. She makes the most amazing cinnamon buns." I kneel forward and remove some lids, my stomach grumbling. My eyes have trouble deciding what to look at because it's a tough choice. It's either the food on the picnic blanket or Ruben, whose thigh muscles flex with his movement. Then he looks at me and grins.

My heart thumps in my chest at the uncensored look he gives me. Without thinking, I lean over the food, grab his T-shirt, pull him toward me, and kiss him—not passionately, but tenderly.

I am so filled with love for this man. Will my feelings ever be returned?

Sighing, I pull away from a shocked Ruben and pretend to ignore him while continuing to remove lids. But I can't hold back a squeal, which makes Ruben jump, when I spot the cinnamon buns.

"I take it you want dessert first?"

"Mmm," I mumble, licking my lips as I take a cinnamon bun. Taking my first bite, I close my eyes and sigh in pleasure, savoring the spicy sweetness.

"Fuck," Ruben mutters under his breath.

My eyes pop open to meet his lust-filled gaze. When I start to lick the sugar from my lips, he inhales and closes his eyes. "Rosie, you're really trying my patience." His eyes pop open, and my heart starts beating frantically. "I want you, but doing things like that," he waves his arms around, "sends all my good intentions out the window. We need to talk, and I want to spend today with you to get to know you better, so please behave."

I nod and take another bite of the sticky bun. Then, I grin at Ruben, who shoves a chicken leg into his mouth and ravishes it. The grease from the food coats his lips as I stare at him longingly. Before he can comment, though, I turn my gaze to the valley below and try to ignore him while finishing my bun.

He's hard to ignore, and his scent makes me tingle from top to toe. If I knew what he wanted with me, then this whole thing about us going out on a picnic or "date" wouldn't make me feel out of my depth. I'd know where I stand.

Over the past week, while Hunter has been at the club, I've wished I'd reacted this way with him. However, he's probably just like Ruben, with his love-'em-and-leave-'em philosophy.

I'm also having trouble getting past the words Ruben said to me after he rocked my world. They hurt—a lot.

I've calmed down a bit, and I've been wondering ever since what he would have said if I had stopped when he called to me. At the time, I was so close to tears that I didn't want him to see how much his words affected me. He's a guy, though, so I suppose I should have made allowances. But after the amazing sex, I didn't think he deserved any.

"Talk to me, Rosie," Ruben says, interrupting my thoughts. "You've been scowling at the sticky bun for about five minutes."

"Have I? Hmm." I have no idea what he wants me to say, and I'm pretty sure not sharing my actual thoughts isn't such a good idea. "What do you want to talk about?" I ask, realizing that the playfulness from ten minutes ago has disappeared as I got lost in my thoughts.

Ruben sighs, dragging my gaze back to him. "I never apologize," he smirks, "but I owe you one."

He scoots over to me, kneels against my hip, takes my hands, and brings them up to his lips. Ruben pinches the last piece of bun with his teeth, his eyes alight with humor, and starts to lick my fingers clean of the sugary confection.

The heat from his mouth lands straight between my legs, and it takes everything in me to stay still and not squirm around to ease the ache he knows he's creating.

7

Ruben

LICKING ROSIE'S FINGERS WAS A BAD IDEA. I'M NOT
sure what I was planning to accomplish, but I gave
myself an erection. It's going to be noticeable if Rosie
glances at my lap. But I can't help but smile when I
see the look on her face. She wants me just as much,
and I bet she's forcing herself to stay put.

I don't think she realizes that when she's aroused,
the color of her eyes darkens, and a delightful flush
covers her cheekbones. She's beautiful.

I don't apologize often, but I need to apologize to
her. I'm not sure what else I should do.

Releasing one of her hands, I run my fingers
through my hair and go for it. "I'm sorry." It wasn't as

difficult as I thought it would be, and I have her attention. "Look, I've never slept with, dated, or wanted an employee until you. When you left and I mentioned keeping quiet, I could have phrased it differently or explained myself, but you kind of took off." I smile. "I'm new to this...whatever it is between us, and I handled it wrong. I was trying to protect you when I mentioned the staff. I didn't want them to treat you differently because of me."

Our hands entwine, and when I feel a gentle pressure against mine, I feel as though all might be right between us. This woman drives me insane, and no matter what I do, she won't leave my thoughts.

She places a kiss on my knuckles and meets my gaze. "I thought you were ashamed to be seen with me. A waitress."

Is she crazy? I release her hands, rise up, take her face in my hands, and tell her, "Rosie, I could never be ashamed of you." I kiss her lips. "Oh God, babe. Don't ever think that. I was just trying to protect you in your work space."

I kiss her again. Just small, feather-light kisses around her lips and nose. "I'm sorry you thought that. I'm sorry I upset you after the most amazing connection I've ever had with a woman."

I'm not ready to talk about the love I think is

behind my obsession with Rosie. I can't call it sex, though. It was so much more than sex.

"Will you forgive me for being an ass and blurting it out the way I did?" I try to give her the saddest puppy-dog look I can muster, but it doesn't work too well when she bursts out laughing.

"I'll forgive you. Just don't keep looking at me like that, because you look so funny, and I could eat more food now."

"I promise."

Grinning, I handed Rosie a plate. Sitting back, I watched her fill it with all of Lorraine's delicious food. Now that everything is cleared up, I feel as though the huge lump of anxiety in my stomach has finally lifted.

Rosie sits back with her plate in her lap, ready to start eating, but then she notices my lack of movement and asks, "Is everything okay?"

"Um, yeah. Actually, it's great. I was enjoying watching you eat, but now that you're all set, it's my turn."

I feel giddy around Rosie, like a child. She's so fresh and young and gorgeous.

I settle beside her and eat some seasoned rice with chicken as we both gaze down the valley.

This has been one of my favorite hangouts since I

was old enough to drive. Even as a young man, I used to come here for peace and to think. Until now, I've never brought anyone else out here. I used to bring my Golden Retriever, Rex, when he was alive. Not even my brothers know about this spot. If they do, they've never mentioned it.

"What were you like as a boy?"

Rosie's out-of-the-blue question surprises me, especially because I was lost in the past.

"There's almost two years between each of my brothers, and as you know, I'm the middle one. When I was young, I hated being in the middle, even though my mom used to tell me that middle children are special." I laugh. "My brothers hated that and would try to beat me up. That only happened once until Lucien taught me how to fight back. Good days."

I chuckle, remembering, and ask, "What about you? Any siblings?" As I ask Rosie this question, I realize that I hardly know anything about her.

She looks out toward the distance before going back to her plate of food. "I was an only child. Both my parents are dead—thank God. So there really is only me. Although, I think Liz and Ed, the owners of Mama E's diner, treat me like a daughter." Rosie meets my eyes. "Sad, huh? I don't have a big family like you."

She's alone. I can't stop thinking about it, and I'm tempted to ask her to be part of my family, but I can't—at least not yet. She'd probably run a mile.

I keep the questions about what happened to her parents to myself because I sense it would ruin the picnic.

"I'm sorry you don't have a close family, Rosie, but at least you have Liz and Ed, right?"

She smiles. "Yeah, I do."

"And I've seen you with Lily and Carla. They're becoming your friends, right? I guess we better not forget that you're also a favorite with my brothers and that guy."

She starts to laugh, which is music to my ears after she looked so sad talking about her family.

"That guy?"

"Hunter," I say grudgingly.

She rolls her eyes and nudges me with her leg. "He's a nice guy, but lonely. Cute, too," she teases. "If you gave him a chance instead of giving him the 'stay clear' look, then you might have a new friend—or even an employee."

Hearing her say "employee" has me sitting up and taking notice. "Employee?" Why would she suggest hiring Hunter?

"He helped out at the club the other week. I admit

that I don't know anything about him, but he always makes time to chat with me and your brothers. I just feel safe with him around." She shrugs.

I'm an idiot. It's been a few weeks since she was hit in the face on the dance floor at Kenza, but the fact that she doesn't feel safe bothers me. I don't want her to be afraid to come to work. However, there isn't much I can do about staff getting caught in the cross-fire. How can I make it safer?

I set my plate down beside me, remove hers from her hands, and place it alongside mine. "Rosie," I say, tilting her chin up with my hand so that our gazes meet. "I never want you to feel unsafe at Kenza. If you want, I'll ask Hunter if he wants a job. I want you to be safe and feel safe."

On the night of the fight, two security guards were out sick, or so they said. But I'm going to do my best to keep her safe.

"I don't want you to do anything just because I'm nervous after being hit. I mean, it isn't the first time I've been hit, but it still hurt." She gives a nervous laugh. "I don't want to talk about this anymore. It's ruining our time together."

It isn't the first time she's been hit! What the hell is wrong with that? I'm willing to leave it for now, but I'll want answers eventually.

With a slight push, she falls backward, laughing. I lie down with her but rest on my elbow, looming over her. A lock of hair has become loose from her braid. I wrap it around my finger, feeling its silky texture.

"You are beautiful," I say, leaning in to kiss the tip of her nose. I grin. "And you are such a huge distraction that I'm sure I'm behind on the paperwork. All I think about is you. I think about how you tasted, spread out before me. I think about how you looked in my bed, with your hair on my pillow."

My breath catches when she reaches up and places her palm against my chest. The heat from her hand burns through my shirt as she caresses my side. My body hardens with her hands on me.

"Ruben, will you kiss me?"

"I'm yours, Rosie. You never need to ask, but I'm going to kiss you slowly." With that said, I roll on top of her, push her legs open, and settle between them. Supporting my weight with my elbows on either side of her, I look at her, starting from her slim torso and moving up along the curve of her breasts toward her neck, finally meeting her gaze.

As I continue to hold her gaze, my hand has a mind of its own, lightly rubbing her aroused nipples.

Her mouth opens slightly in pleasure as I do it again. There's no way she can't feel my growing arousal with me pressed up close and personal like this.

She watches me through her half-closed eyes as I lower my face to hers. When our lips are a breath apart, I say, "Don't let me take this too far. Promise me, Rosie. Today is a date that won't end with us getting naked."

I press a soft kiss to the corner of her mouth, then use my tongue to slide across her lips to the other corner, which I also kiss. I love teasing her as I move back to the middle and dip my tongue inside to gain entry. Our tongues meet, and all I can think about is her taste, which explodes on my tongue—cinnamon and my woman.

Deepening the kiss, I take her wrists in one hand and bring them above her head. She arches up against me, rubbing against my hard dick. I use my other hand to caress her side and hip. I grip her flesh, trying to stop myself from ravishing her completely.

"God," I breathe into her neck. "I wish I had some-thing to tie your wrists together, so my other hand would be free to touch you."

She freezes against me as if she's suddenly turned into a statue.

"Let me go. Get off me." She pushes at my chest.

I release her wrists, but it takes a moment for my

lust-fueled body and brain to comprehend what's going on before I start to move. She's panicking about something.

"Ruben, please get off me. Let me up," she gasps.

I quickly roll away from her and get to my knees to help her, but she's already up and walking around, holding her stomach protectively.

I jump to my feet and go to her, but she stops me by holding out a shaking hand in front of her.

"I can't be what you want, Ruben. I'm sorry."

"What..."

She walks away and starts resealing the tubs, tossing them back into the picnic basket.

I guess our picnic is over. I just wish she would talk to me. What the hell did I do? Then it hits me. I mentioned tying her up, and then she said she couldn't be what I want. She's running scared.

"Rosie, please stop. Let me speak."

She shakes her head. "Ruben, please don't. It's okay." She continues placing everything neatly away. "Well, it's not that I don't want to be with you, but you like things that I don't like or want. I can't be the person who trusts you to tie them up without abusing them. I can't do it. Please don't ask me to do that."

I take the containers from her hands and try to

hold on to her. "Rosie, damn it. I'm sorry I frightened you. Wait..." I see red. "Who abused you? I'll kill him."

She stops with her back to me as she makes her way to the SUV. "My father used to tie me up and leave me sitting in the middle of my room all day when he thought I'd been naughty. The first time was after I left an apple in my lunch bag. The second time was because I missed the school bus. I missed the bus because he couldn't find the keys to unlock the door, and I refused to climb out the window with all the other kids at the bus stop watching. I'll never relinquish control of my body to anyone. Please don't ask me to talk about it again. I'd rather leave it where it belongs—in the past."

However, I'm not sure that leaving it buried in the past is healthy for her. She needs to deal with it to fully move on. She can't just let it fester. But now she sounds exhausted. "Please just take me home. I can't do this. It isn't fair to either of us."

Having never been in this situation before, I'm at a loss as to what to say, but I don't want to take her home—at least not until I've said something. It would be great if my brain started working again first, though.

"Rosie," I say, standing behind her and clenching my fists, itching to comfort her. "I'm sorry I frightened you. That's the last thing I wanted. I want—no, I need—to see you again. I know the rumors about my appetites—for want of a better word—but I can do without them. I don't need it. Yes, I like all that, and I like playing with toys for pleasure, but I don't need it. God, I need you more."

I'm begging like a pussy. I've never begged for anything in my life, but I'll beg for Rosie.

"I hear you. Please just take me home, and I promise to think about what you've said."

"Okay, I'm not going to let you go so easily. You realize that, right? You're under my skin, Rosie." I leaned forward and kissed her on the back of her head.

"Let me grab everything, and then we'll head back. I'll give you some time to think about it, and then we can go to the movies or something. I really do want to date you properly."

Rosie

After my afternoon out with Ruben, I was torn about whether to show up at work tonight. He didn't do anything wrong. It was my fear. Because of how he reacted, I was able to tell him about my fear, which surprised me. It's something I've never told anyone, but he didn't flip out, and I found myself speaking. I feel relieved that he knows because now he won't pressure me into anything like that.

My heart fluttered when he said he wanted to date me properly. I'd like that as well. More than he could possibly know. Today had been wonderful until my fear hit.

Sighing, I dabbed at my face with a napkin in the restroom, trying to hide from Simon and the guy sitting with him. I've seen them together about five or six times now, and every time, the guy stares at me in a totally creepy way. I suspect Simon is behind what's happening, and I've wondered the past couple of times if the guy with him is involved. But I can't hide in here all night. I'm supposed to be working the bar with Craig.

"Okay, here goes nothing." I pull the door open, pop my head out, and check if the coast is clear. Then, I laugh at myself. I'm glad there isn't anyone around to see me. Idiot. Too much late-night television.

I slip through the door and head toward the bar, managing to make it behind without incident until Craig steps in my way.

"Where've you been?" He frowns.

"Restroom."

"You can't keep running to the restroom every time Simon and that guy come in."

"What the hell!"

"Don't give me that wide-eyed stare. I'm not stupid, regardless of what you might think." Craig continues wiping glasses while watching me out of the corner of his eye.

I had no idea I was so obvious. I shrug and say, "He's weird and freaks me out. I can't help that."

He grins. "Sorry. I was teasing. He freaks me out too, but the guy he arrived with is really freaky. He's built like the Hulk."

I give him a quizzical look. "I haven't seen anyone else."

"That's because he always stays outside. I saw him once when I went outside for a smoke. I never go outside when Simon's friend is here anymore." He shudders. "Speaking of friends, Hunter is here." He nods toward the end of the bar, where Hunter is sitting and staring in our direction.

"Okay, thanks. Let me know when he's gone."

"Will do."

I grab an apron and fasten it as I walk toward Hunter, who is frowning at me. "What's up?"

"You okay?" he asks, ignoring me and glancing at Craig.

"Yeah, I'm fine."

I wave the bottle of whiskey in front of him, causing a grin to spread across his face.

I pour him three fingers of the hard liquor and place the bottle down in front of him. I notice he still looks distracted, but I don't think it has anything to do with me this time.

"What's wrong?" I lean on the bar toward him. "And don't tell me nothing. You're still frowning."

His eyes meet mine, but the worried look remains. I'm starting to worry now. It can't be a good sign if Hunter has that look.

"Stay away from the guy with Simon. I'm not telling you anything else. Just stay clear, and don't go outside while he's here. If you can do that, then I'll be happy."

"That's easy to do. He freaks me out, and Craig already warned me not to go outside because Hulk is apparently out there." I offer a wry smile, but I should have known he'd see straight through me.

"Rosie," he said, taking my hands in his. "As long as he's here, I'll be close to you, okay? Don't worry about that."

He does make me feel safe. However, I don't want

to ruin his evening by having him babysit me, which is basically what it comes down to. I'm also wondering if Ruben has spoken to him about the security job he mentioned. I wouldn't put it past him.

"Hey, babe."

Hunter releases my hands.

Speaking of the devil.

Ruben wraps his arm around my waist, kisses me on the side of my head, and turns to face Hunter while keeping his arm around me. He's marking me. Regardless of what happened this afternoon, I think I like being marked by him.

"Is this okay?" he whispers into my ear, squeezing my waist to indicate what he's referring to.

His cologne makes my knees weak, and he feels so good pressed against me that I'm going to turn to mush at his feet soon.

"Yeah, it's fine."

Hunter coughs, drawing my gaze back to him. He's laughing behind his hand.

I'm lost for words, glaring at him while enjoying Ruben's presence next to me.

"Hunter doesn't want to work for me," Ruben says. "He has other things to do. But he promised to make sure nothing happens to you and to hang out when he can."

"Okay, I'm not mad at you for thinking I need a babysitter after what I said earlier. But I think it's just nerves after what happened, you know? I'll settle down eventually."

Looking back at Hunter, I say, "But it's good knowing you're going to be around." I smile.

Hopefully, everyone will think twice about causing trouble when he's around. Right now, he looks approachable and friendly. But the night I got caught in the middle of a fight and got punched in the face, he looked anything but friendly.

"I've got work to do on the computer." Ruben kisses me again before taking his arm away. "Stay safe, babe." With those words, he disappears as quickly as he arrived.

"Hmm, that was cozy," Hunter observes.

I ignore him and spend the next hour serving drinks and drying glasses. Boring, I know. But I'd rather do this with the bar between me and everyone else. Safer.

I'm also unsure about Ruben. Why is he showing affection after saying he'd give me space? I'm totally confused about the guy, and it's giving me a headache. I know it probably has something to do with me talking to Hunter, but still.

Never mind. Liz says everything usually works itself out. I hope she's right this time.

As I finish putting the glasses away on the shelf, I turn and come face to face with Simon. Thank God his friend isn't around. "What's going on, Rosie?"

"Um, I'm busy. Why? What's wrong?" I mumble, my stomach full of butterflies.

"I saw you flirting with Ruben. I've told you before that you need to stay away from him. You're too young and innocent to hang out with him."

As if I didn't already know that. But it pisses me off that he thinks I'm an idiot who can't figure that out on my own.

"I'm well aware of that. Did you want anything else?" I just want him to leave because I've had enough of his warnings about Ruben.

His eyes narrow before he grins. "Yes, bring two Americanos to my office, please." Simon smirks and heads toward his office, and my stomach drops.

I presume that's where he disappeared to with his friend, which makes me want to hurl. There is no way I'm going into that office alone with them in there. I don't trust Simon to protect me, and his friend looks at me as though he wants to hurt me. And I don't mean in a nice way.

I place my hand over my stomach, inhale, and try

to calm my nerves. I can do this. I can do this. I can't send Craig in with the drinks once they're made. He'd trip on his way in from nerves.

"I'll take them," Hunter says, dragging me out of my panic. "Make the drinks, Rosie, and I'll take them in there. Make some excuse for why you can't go in."

I want to jump at him and say yes, please, but I can't. This is my job, and Hunter won't always be around to protect me. "I'll manage, but thanks."

"Rosie," he says, waiting until I meet his eyes before continuing. "This is non-negotiable."

I shake my head and place my hand on his arm as he leans across the bar toward me. "I'll let you open the doors for me. You can wait for me to exit the office, but I need to take them in. I don't want Simon thinking he can scare me off."

I quickly make the coffees, place them on a clean tray, and add a small plate of handmade chocolates, delivered directly from Marcella's Sweet Treats twice a week. I shift the coffee cup slightly on the tray and take a deep breath, unable to delay any longer. I lift the tray and walk toward the end of the bar. Hunter lifts the hatch for me, clearing a path through to the back of the club and the offices.

He's been here often enough that he doesn't need directions. With a quick look over his shoulder, he opens Simon's door and whispers, "I'll keep the door open," as I walk past him into the room.

I place the tray on the corner of Simon's desk, in the spot where he's cleared off his mess. Without making eye contact with either man in the room, I turn and start walking toward the door, seeing my escape within sight.

"Hold up, Rosie," Simon says.

My heart starts to thud in my chest. What does he want now?

"You can go," Simon says, dismissing Hunter.

"I'll wait. Ruben asked me to escort her to his office."

Has he?

"Hmm, really?"

"Yes, really," Hunter replies, holding his hand out to me. "Rosie, come on."

I don't need to be told twice. I dash out of the office, hearing the door close as Hunter grabs my arm and pulls me around the back corner, out of sight.

"Breathe, Rosie."

He's standing in front of me, trying to calm me down, but he's making me more worked up. I was already nervous about the guy before Hunter said anything, but he's made me even more aware of him. That, combined with my imagination, has me terrified. After taking a few deep breaths, I gradually start to calm down. I feel heat fill my cheeks as I realize that maybe I was a little stupid for reacting the way I did to Simon and that guy.

Simon has been here since I started, so I'm being ridiculous. No matter what, Simon would never let anything happen to me.

"Are you okay now?"

"I'm fine." I push away from the wall. "I'm going to pop in and talk to Ruben."

"Okay, I'll be out front."

I watch Hunter make his way to the front of the club before walking to Ruben's office. With the door ajar, I'm about to push through when I hear a woman's voice.

"I have a hotel room booked close by. You'll come play, won't you, Ruben?"

I can't believe what I'm hearing.

At least, that's what it sounded like when Ruben sighed. Then he said, "Yeah, I'll come to your hotel."

What the hell?

He can't mean to take her up on her offer to play, can he? Surely he can't. Not after the way he's been with me. What was the picnic all about if he planned on continuing to "play"?

"I've missed you, Ruben. Now come on, I want to play."

"Veronica,"

"Your paperwork will still be there tomorrow, but I won't be. I'm flying to LA at ten in the morning."

After a moment of silence, Ruben says, "What the hell." I hear a chair scrape against the tiled floor.

Suddenly realizing that I'm going to get caught, I quickly move away from the door. This will give me a view of the back door of the club as they exit. At least, I presume they're going to exit by the back door.

"Ruben, you are so funny," Veronica says, using a fake laugh.

If I weren't so angry and upset, I'd laugh at her artificiality, but right now, I feel like jumping back around the corner and poking her eyes out and kicking Ruben in the groin. Would that make me feel any better? Probably for all of five minutes.

"Just be quiet. I'll follow you back to your hotel. I don't like being without my wheels."

Then, the door banged shut, leaving me stunned with tears silently running down my face.

8

Ruben

IT'S STUPID TO SIT IN MY SUV OUTSIDE VERONICA'S hotel. Other times when she's stayed here, I've always been inside before she could even get undressed in her room. Now, I'm sitting here, trying to work up the courage to go upstairs with her.

I've never dated anyone until Rosie came along. Veronica and I have an agreement, though. Whenever she's in town, we get together.

Things have changed for me, though. That change is Rosie. I can't go upstairs and have sex with Veronica or anyone else because I won't be able to face Rosie again if I do. It's not just the thought of Rosie finding out that's stopping me from getting naked. I can't bring myself to be with anyone but Rosie.

This afternoon, something clicked when I was thinking back over my time with Rosie and her reaction at the picnic. I realized that I don't need as much control as I usually like to have. I'll still need to be in control, but with Rosie, I can make love to her without using restraints and toys. I proved this the other week when I made love to her. I never thought about anything other than the woman beneath me.

My brothers like to joke that I'm into kinky stuff, but what I'm really into is much milder than they'll ever know. It's certainly not a topic I'm going to discuss with them.

I can't sit out here all night. I need to go inside and explain to Veronica that whatever we have is over and that she needs to move on because I'm no longer interested.

Ruben, stop fucking around and get inside!

"Shit."

I quickly make my way into the hotel, avoiding the reception desks and heading straight for the elevators. I find an empty one ready and waiting.

I press the button for the fifth floor and lean back against the mirrored walls, trying to breathe through my nervousness.

I'm not usually this nervous, so I'm not sure what the hell is wrong with me. I know I'm worried that Rosie will find out where I've been tonight, and all it will take is for Simon to open his mouth, and she'll get the wrong idea. Rather, she'll get the correct impression from a month ago, but now that information would be so wrong.

The elevator comes to a stop, and I slowly exit and drag myself three rooms down to Veronica's. She could afford the penthouse, but that would leave a trail she didn't want.

I tap on the door and hear her shout, "Come in!" in her grating, husky voice. Why am I only now noticing how annoying her "squeak" is?

I push open the door and make my way inside her dimly lit room, closing the door behind me.

"Ruben."

"Yeah."

"You're taking your time tonight."

Oh boy!

I step into the main room and have a hard time looking anywhere but at Veronica, who is lounging on the bed in all her naked glory, legs spread, as she inserts a vibrator between them. I stare. I'm a guy!

The twitching in my jeans tells me my cock likes what I'm seeing. But this is not happening. She's familiar, which is why I'm reacting to her as well as to her nakedness.

"Fuck," I curse, turning around to give her my back. "Stop, Veronica. Veronica, you have to stop. I'm not here to play tonight."

I hear rustling behind me and freeze, wondering what she's up to now, as she's been too quiet—which is usually not a good sign. Feeling vulnerable with my back to her, I turn around and come face-to-face with her.

She reaches out and caresses my arms as she takes a step closer, bringing her breasts up against my chest.

I try to step away, but she follows.

"Ruben, tsk... tsk. I know you want me." She grabbed my dick through my jeans and started to rub it.

I'd be lying if I said she wasn't arousing me, because she is. I've been with her so many times that my dick knows what she can give me. But my brain is telling me no.

I knock her hand away and step back out of her grasp. "Not this time... or any time."

"You're serious."

I nod.

She backs up, grabs her robe from the chair beside the bed, and wraps it around herself.

"There's someone I'm interested in. She's not into all this, but I am, and I don't want to jeopardize that."

God, it feels good to finally get that out. It's like standing up at an AA meeting for the first time—not that I'd know, but I went with a friend for support a long time ago.

"Well. I can honestly say that I never expected to hear that from you." She sits on the end of the bed, crosses her legs, and hums. "I know you're not immune to me. I felt the evidence. But I can see you mean what you say, so I'm not going to try to change your mind."

I'm surprised, and I can't hide it, which sets her off laughing.

"Oh God, Ruben. I'm not a heartless bitch. The woman who has you acting like this must be someone special."

"She is." I run my hands through my hair and sit down on the edge of the desk opposite the bed. "I can't believe you're being so good about this. I thought you'd be disappointed. Honestly, it's a relief you're so accepting."

"I'm disappointed. I was looking forward to our little get-together, but we both know that my tastes lean more toward the dark side than you're comfortable with."

She's right about that. I'm not into whips and floggers. She's hinted on more than one occasion that she wouldn't mind if I used them. I ignored her.

As I'm about to leave, I hold my hand out to her. "So, no hard feelings."

"Is that all I get after months of sex?" She stands and offers me a hug, which I hesitantly accept. "That's better."

I kiss her on the side of her face, then untangle myself and make a quick getaway. But once I have the door open, I turn back to look at her. "Look after yourself, Veronica."

She nods, smiling.

BACK AT THE CLUB, I START LOOKING AROUND FOR Rosie when Hunter stops me. My heart sinks, thinking that something might have happened to her.

"You need to stop playing games with her. She's too sweet for you to treat her this way," he says, his jaw tight with anger. He doesn't look happy. In fact, he looks ready to hit me.

"What the hell are you talking about? Where's Rosie? Is she okay?" I try to look around, but I can't see anything with the dim lighting and him blocking my view of the club floor.

"She hasn't been attacked again, if that's what you mean. I took her home earlier after she saw you leave with a woman you'd arranged to meet at her hotel."

My heart sinks, and I feel the blood start to pound in my ears. Fuck! Fuck! Fuck! I didn't see her around. How the hell... "I need to talk to her and explain." I pace back and forth. "Yes, I used to fuck Veronica, but that's all it was. I followed her back to her hotel to talk to her. I needed to explain that I couldn't carry on with her anymore because of Rosie. Shit. I didn't do anything with her. After I explained, we hugged. I kissed her on the cheek and left. That's it."

I run my fingers through my hair and look at Hunter. "What am I going to do? There's no way she's going to believe that nothing happened. Was she really upset?"

"If by upset, you mean trying to hold her tears in while silent ones ran down her face, then I guess you could say she was upset."

"Fuck." I sag against the wall beside my office door.

"The only advice I can offer is to give her a day or

two. She was upset, but she was also pissed as hell. If you want her to listen to you with an open mind, then you need to give her time to calm down. You might make things worse, otherwise." He groans. "And please don't tell anyone that I gave you advice like a pussy. You'll ruin me."

I shake my head. "You're safe." As he turns to head back into the club, I shout, "Hunter!" He looks toward me over his shoulder. "Thanks for making sure she got home safely."

He nods and leaves me alone with my sorrow.

I should have trusted my instinct to break up with Veronica in my office instead of going to her hotel. I'd chosen the hotel because I didn't want Rosie to witness a scene, but it all backfired anyway.

Nice going Ruben.

Rosie

It's been three days since the picnic with Ruben and the disastrous evening. I'm supposed to be back at work at eight, but I'm having trouble finding the will to go. I really want to see Ruben. Something tells me there's more to the story than what I overheard. But I'm afraid it's wishful thinking. I want to believe that he wants to be with me as much as I want to be with him. However, after a lifetime of craving someone who wants me for who I am, I'm having trouble believing that he does.

"Rosie."

I nearly jump out of my skin when someone touches my shoulder and says my name at the same time.

"It's Sabrina." She gives me a quizzical look.

"Sorry, you startled me." I laugh. "Have you settled back into Lexington life?"

She threads her arm through mine and says, "Have coffee with me, and I'll tell you about it," not giving me a choice in the matter. I grin. This is just what I need to take my mind off Ruben.

"Let's sit here since it's a nice day. Is this okay?"

I nod and watch her dash inside. I presume she's ordering coffee because she never asked me how I like mine.

"Here you go. I remembered you like vanilla latte, so I hope you still do because I forgot to ask you before I shot off inside." Sabrina places the drinks on the table from the tray along with a third coffee and a plate of amaretto biscuits—my favorite.

"Carla's joining us," Sabrina comments, noticing my raised eyebrow. She takes the seat opposite me. She's the woman who has Lucien tied in so many knots, he doesn't know whether he's coming or going. She looks different than she did the last time I saw her. Her hair is shiny and a vibrant shade of red that falls to her shoulders. It suits her, especially with her green eyes and freckles over her nose and underneath her eyes. She looks young and fresh.

"You asked me if I'm settled, and I am. But it's kind of lonely, you know? My mom is here, but she only points out my weaknesses and never sees anything positive. She blames me for everything that isn't going right in her life. It gets lonely."

"I know that feeling. I'm really alone, although I do have Liz and Ed, who own the apartment I live in above their diner. I like working at Kenza, but I'm not interested in the people who hang around there. They're not bad people, just not for me. Ruben's brothers come in for a drink every once in a while, especially lately, so I talk to them. It isn't the same, though. God, my life is so sad."

I take a sip of my latte, sit back, and savor the

flavor while enjoying the peace. This part of Lexington tends to get quiet in the late afternoon. If you look through the coffee shop's glass window, you can see the reflection of the snow-capped mountains.

"I think we should be friends. What do you say?" Sabrina asks, looking unsure. When I start to grin, she returns the smile.

"I'd love that. It would be great to have a female friend again, at least one close to my own age."

"Let's shake on it." Sabrina holds her hand out over the table, just avoiding the plate of biscuits with her chunky bracelet. "Shit, let me take this off. I only wear it to annoy my mother. She hates it."

I chuckle at her. "To friends," I say, shaking her hand.

"Friends."

Sabrina gives me a sly look. "So, if we're girl-friends, that means I can ask you anything, right?"

"Why do I get the feeling I'm not going to like this part?"

"Oh, come on. I only want to know what's happening with Ruben."

"Oh, that's something I wanted to ask," Carla says, sitting between us. "Especially after the picnic."

I choke on my drink, not expecting them to know

that there might be something between Ruben and me. They don't miss much.

"There's nothing happening with Ruben."

Carla pauses as she reaches into her purse, and Sabrina raises her eyebrow. I continue, "No, seriously. We went on the picnic, had a good time, and that's all it was." I shrug, not wanting to go into detail about what happened afterward. However, I have a feeling I'm not going to escape it.

"Rosie, I saw you both at the baptism. Plus, I've noticed Ruben's been distracted these past few months, and I bet you're the reason why." Carla rubs her hands together, and I feel a blush creeping up from my neck into my cheeks.

Carla practically vibrates in her chair. "This is going to be good."

"Grrr... I'll make you a deal. You—I point to Sabrina—tell me what's going on between you and Lucien, and I'll tell you what's going on with Ruben." I smile.

I've seen Sabrina, and I know damn well that she has it bad for Lucien—and he for her. I've tried to push him, but he won't budge because he thinks he isn't worthy. He makes me want to wrap my arms around him and hold him tight. Of course, I don't think he'd appreciate it if I did. I really hope my new

friend can get through the wall he's built around himself for protection since the accident that caused his burns.

"There isn't anything to tell about Lucien."

"Hmm."

"What does 'hmm' mean?" Sabrina rests her chin in her hands on the table and watches me.

"Rosie's 'hmm' probably means the same as my 'hmm' from yesterday. And don't think I didn't notice how quickly you left Lily's house the other day, right after she asked you about Lucien," Carla says, laying her hand on Sabrina's arm in quiet sympathy. It's obvious that Sabrina is hiding her true feelings, probably out of fear of rejection.

"You like him more than you would a friend, so while it's just us and not Pippa trying to marry off her sons, talk to us. Why won't you go after him? You'd make a lovely couple," Carla asks.

Sabrina sighs. "I don't think he likes me much. He spends far too much time with Lily." Now, she looks sad.

"You know there's never been anything between him and Lily, right? I really believe he thinks of her as a sister," Carla says, frowning.

There's no way he's still hung up on Lily. Is there? I've seen him with her a few times, and they always act like siblings. Plus, I've seen Lucien moping around Kenza. I've certainly gotten his attention a couple of times when I've mentioned Sabrina.

"Enough about my miserable life. What about Ruben?" she asks, trying to divert the conversation back to me.

I sigh loudly and look out at the snow-capped mountains, trying to collect my thoughts. Finally, I say, "I like him, and I thought he liked me too. But then I saw him leaving with another woman. I over-heard him say that he would follow her back to her hotel." I nervously start to wrap my hair around my finger. "So I don't think he can be all that into me, you know?" I can't keep the sadness out of my voice.

"Join the club. We should have a night out and meet two different guys to take our minds off the mess of our current love lives, or rather, lack thereof. What do you say? Do you want to go out with me sometime, get drunk, and have a night of meaningless sex? Carla can come along to make sure we don't end up with an axe murderer."

Carla chuckles. "That sounds good, but you can bet Sebastian will follow me. He always needs me close. I thought that would get old really fast, you know? But I miss him when he's away. I guess that's love for you."

"That's sweet," I say, wanting what Carla has with Sebastian with Ruben, but knowing it's not going to happen. I'm also not sure about one-night stands, and I really don't believe Sabrina is like that, but I'll agree for now. "Sounds good. I'm not free for the next couple of weeks, but then I have a few days off, which would be good."

"Then it's a date. I'm so glad we bumped into you," she says, gathering her packages. "But I better go. I have a hair appointment that I'm about to be late for."

"Okay, I'll be in touch. Oh wait, I don't have your number."

Sabrina grabs her phone, takes a picture of me, and waits for me to give her my number, which I do. "I'll message you so you have my number."

Damn, she's quick! No sooner had she said that than my phone started pinging with a message. Sabrina had already left. I feel like a tornado just hit me.

"You'll get used to her," Carla laughs, seeing my stunned expression. "She's not as reserved as she was when she first arrived, or even a few months ago. It's as though she's gone through a makeover. It's good, and it drives Lucien nuts when Sunday dinner is served and she's present. He tries to avoid looking at her, but his eyes always find her. A bit like you and Ruben, really." She grins.

I won't comment on that, but I smile, wondering what will happen between the two of them. I really hope Lucien comes to his senses, and perhaps Sabrina will help him.

Ruben

"YOU NEED TO STOP BEING SUCH A PUSSY AND GO AFTER her. Get on your knees and beg."

Sebastian's words cut through me as we walk down the street on our way to meet Carla. I glanced at him out of the corner of my eye, biting back the urge to knock the grin right off his face. He assumes my unenthusiastic response to his idea of playing a round of golf is because of a woman. He's right, which I hate. Sebastian being right isn't good because he'll never let you forget it.

"I'm right. You've messed up with cute Rosie." He laughs, but he's really going to meet my fist if he keeps it up. "Oh, come on. I seem to remember not too long ago you laughing at me when Carla had me tied in knots."

"Rosie doesn't have me tied in knots." I watch the cars as we cross the road, but my thoughts are with Rosie. I don't know how, but she definitely has me by the balls. "Fuck! This isn't funny. She thinks I'm messing around when I'm telling her that I want to date her."

Well, that shut him up.

"You told Rosie you wanted to date her?" He shook his head. "Seriously? You want to date?"

"Stop being a dick. Yes, I want to date her." There's no reason to lie to him. He may act like a three-year-old, but I know he'll keep it to himself. "I took her out, but then she saw me leave with Veronica, who was in town that night. I didn't want to break our agreement at Kenza, so I offered to follow her back to her hotel, where nothing happened. Afterwards, I returned to Kenza, only to have Hunter tell me that he'd taken her home because she was upset." I run my fingers through my hair in agitation.

"What did she say when you explained everything? I hope you didn't go into too much detail about Veronica."

"I haven't yet."

"What?"

Hunter suggested I let her calm down so she'd be more inclined to hear me out, and I agreed. But it's been a few days, and she's due back at the club tonight, so I can't decide whether to drive to her place and talk to her before she leaves for work or wait."

This is all new to me, and it isn't sitting well with me. I like things to be clear-cut, but I'm uneasy because I'm not in control of the outcome.

As I turn the corner to the terrace, I see that there are only a few people around, which suits me just fine. The fewer crowds, the better. I have to suffer through crowds in Kenza on the weekends, so the thought of dodging everyone in Lexington isn't appealing.

"Um, Ruben."

I hear the strain in my brother's voice and glance at him, then in the direction he's staring. "What the..." I pause mid-speech, not expecting to see Rosie sitting at the table with Carla.

"I had no idea Rosie would be here," Sebastian says in defense.

"Yeah, right. You really didn't know? That's why you called and asked me to meet Carla with you."

Sebastian shakes his head. "Seriously, bro. I would have told you once we arrived. But I really didn't know she was going to be here. At least it solves your problem of when to talk to her."

My feet have a mind of their own, and I'm drawn toward the girl who won't leave my mind. She doesn't know I'm approaching yet. I really hope that when she sees me, I won't see disappointment on her face. That would crush me.

Hell! Carla has spotted us, and she can't seem to smile widely enough when she looks at Sebastian. Sometimes my brothers make me want to hurl, and that's no exaggeration.

I watch Carla say something to Rosie, who sits up from her slouched position in the chair and turns toward us.

"Oh, you're in for it now, brother," Sebastian says, chuckling as he pulls Carla out of her chair and sits back down with her on his lap.

I can only hold Rosie's gaze, and I feel hope when her eyes look happy. Unfortunately, that look doesn't last. She obviously remembers the last time she saw me, when she'd misunderstood what was going on. It's something I need to clear up with her if we have any chance of moving on. I only hope she believes me.

Feeling like a teenager speaking to a girl for the first time, I take the seat next to her and say, "Rosie, how have you been?" I hope Sebastian takes Carla elsewhere so I can talk to Rosie privately.

"I've been okay, Ruben. You?"

"Ruben, would you like a coffee?" Sebastian asks.

Without taking my eyes off Rosie, I reply, "No, I need to talk to Rosie."

"We'll go," Carla says, standing up and pulling Sebastian to his feet. She passes him her shopping bags. "And give you two some privacy."

"Can't I stay and watch my brother beg?"

I turn to look at him. But his attention is on Carla as she gives him a sultry look. I almost chuckle, since just a wiggle of her eyebrows gets my brother going. "Would you rather stay here than come back to our place and enjoy what's in these bags?" she purrs.

"Put like that, I'll let him beg in private. Come on, woman, let's go." He wraps an arm around Carla before looking back at me. "Beg, brother. Women like a man who begs for forgiveness."

"Don't worry, Ruben. Your brother is going to find out just how much this woman likes to watch him beg for forgiveness if he doesn't shut up," Carla adds, running her fingers up the front of his button-down shirt.

Rosie starts to chuckle as she listens to the

exchange between Carla and my brother. He's immature, but he's my brother.

Not wanting to waste time, I turn to Rosie, taking her hands into mine. I'm delighted when she makes no move to remove them.

"Hunter told me what you overheard, and I need to explain."

She yanks her hands away, making me feel sick at the loss.

"Please listen, Rosie. You didn't hear everything." I run my fingers through my hair, agitated. "Before I was with you, Veronica and I would hook up whenever she was in town. It hasn't happened in months." Her eyes narrow, and I feel like I'm losing her. I hurry to say, "She happened to show up that night, and I'd honestly forgotten about her."

I hope she doesn't think I'm a jerk for forgetting about someone I hook up with. I didn't realize how bad it sounded until I'd said it.

"Look, no matter how I put this, it sounds bad, so please just hear me out." I take a deep breath and try to calm my racing heart because I know I'll only get one chance at this. "We had some kind of arrangement at the club that I didn't want to break. She didn't deserve that. Yes, I followed her to her hotel room, but I swear nothing happened between us. I told her it wouldn't be happening anymore, then I left. When I got back to the club, Hunter told me he'd taken you home because you were upset."

After a minute or so of silence, during which she looks into my eyes, she reaches out and takes my hands in hers, caressing my thumb. "Why didn't you tell me sooner?"

"I wanted to give you time to calm down, hoping that you'd be more willing to listen to me. Also, I promised to give you time, remember?" I meet her gaze and hold it.

She whispers, "I remember."

"That's the truth about Veronica. I don't know how to prove to you that nothing happened, but trust me. If something had happened, you'd know about it. I'm terrible at hiding things when I feel guilty. That's how I'd feel if I'd slept with her." I wince. "Please tell me you believe me."

"I believe you, but I can't keep doing this, so if there's anyone else you want to tell me about, please tell me now, because I'm new to all this..." She pauses and bites her lip. "I'm not going to be able to handle sharing. I don't share. Ever."

I grin. "I don't share either." I feel heat creeping into my face, and Rosie raises an eyebrow in question. "I'll rephrase, I guess. I don't share anymore."

She laughs. "Well, as long as that's agreed, then I guess we can move on. I still have doubts about what we talked about at the picnic. But, if you can take it slow and give me time to get comfortable with being around you, then maybe I can open up a bit. That's only a maybe, though."

I shake my head and tell her, "You don't need to give anything. The other day at my apartment, nothing entered my head. Rope, not ribbon, nothing. Eventually, I'd like to introduce you to a few toys that are made to heighten your pleasure, but nothing frightening." I quickly kiss her on the lips. "But don't think about that for now. There's plenty of time, and I'm going to make sure you get comfortable with me quickly." I kiss her again.

"Will you come up to my place tonight? Let me cook you a late supper. Just you and me. We'll have a proper date with candlelight and soft music. It'll be my first time wining and dining someone, but with you, I want to experience a lot of firsts." The more I talk, the more I like this idea. I'll have her to myself in my apartment for the evening. She can have the evening off, and we can watch a movie.

"Are you sure this is what you want?" she asks. I smile. Although she seems cool and collected, she reveals her vulnerability by chewing her bottom lip and trembling slightly while holding my hands.

Releasing her hands, I lean forward and cradle her face in mine. "I'm serious about you, Rosie. It's frightening and exciting at the same time, but I want what we have more than anything."

"If you're sure, then I'd love to have dinner with you later." She smiles, surprising me when she turns her face and kisses the palm of my hand. The sensation shoots straight to my wayward body part, making it sit up and take notice that Rosie is giving us a second chance. Hopefully, my hand will get a rest. I can hope.

"I have to be at work soon," Rosie reminds me. "What time do you want me at your apartment, or should I just go there after work?" She pulls away and starts collecting her things.

"I'm the boss, so let me call and get someone to cover for me. Then we can start the evening. I don't want to let you go now that I finally have you with me." I wrap my hand around hers, sliding my fingers between hers. "I've missed you."

"The other staff will be upset with me for getting time off so easily, but I've missed you, too, so I'm not going to worry about them. I'll deal with it. I'm just going to enjoy being with you."

This would normally fill me with dread, but instead, I don't want to let this girl out of my sight. I'm even willing to have her over for a sleepover involving sleep and cuddles—nothing else—to keep her close. Another first.

I bring her close to me again and tell her, "We'll deal with it. If anyone hassles you about being with the boss, I want you to tell me. We're in this together, okay? You don't have to keep things to yourself. Promise me."

"Hmm," she mumbles. "I can't make a promise when I'm not sure I'll be able to keep it. But if I need you to step in, I promise I'll tell you." She grinned and quickly kissed me on the lips, leaving me stunned as she started walking toward the market. "Are you coming with me?" she asks over her shoulder.

Recovering quickly, I jog to catch up with her, slide my arm around her shoulders, and pull her close.

I'm starting to crave being near this woman. She packs a lot into her small, curvy frame. She's had my eye for months, and the fact that I can finally touch her makes me want to shout it from the rooftops. "This is my woman—stay away." Not sure Rosie would appreciate that, though. Then again, maybe she would.

Smiling to myself, I guide her closer to the market so we can buy ingredients for the romantic dinner I'm planning. This time, I'm not going to let her leave until she knows that she's the only girl I'm interested in.

Rosie

I'm in love with Ruben, and the more time I spend with him, the deeper I fall. His cute dimples cause my heart to flutter. Most of all, I find him endearing when I see the uncertainty in his eyes, like when he forgets to put on his fun-loving mask. He wants everyone to think he's a fun-loving guy, and he is. But there's so much more to him than his devil-may-care attitude.

I'm thinking about him as I lie on his sofa, having just enjoyed the most amazing spaghetti and meatballs. It's a favorite of mine, and apparently, Ruben's as well. It was delicious, and Ruben made it all without any help from me. I've truly been looked after, and my guy is across the room from me, finishing cleaning up in the kitchen. He banned me from the kitchen when we arrived back here. I, of course, had no objection, being the least domestic person ever. Ruben, however, looks to have it all in hand. I lie here watching the muscles under his shirt play as he moves. When he bends over and stretches the denim over his ass, my mouth waters. Seeing him like this makes me want to do things to him that I've never done before. Now, the thought of having him in my mouth, at my mercy, makes me fidget on the sofa.

I let my eyes trail up from his firm ass to his broad shoulders. I meet his gaze when he turns his head to look at me over his shoulder. Silently groaning, I hold his gaze and pray my blush stays away.

Ruben throws the dishtowel on the counter and starts to walk slowly toward me. I'm unable to look away. My heart starts to pound, and the throbbing between my thighs intensifies with my desire for this man who looks like he's going to eat me alive.

I have no fear of being vulnerable to him right now because all I want is for my clothing to disappear so that I'm ready for him. I want him to know I'm his for the taking.

He kneels beside me. Taking my face in his hands, he asks, "Do you have any idea what you do to me?"

He drops his forehead against mine and rests his

arms on either side of me. I slip my hand down the front of his jeans and caress the bulge.

"Fuck," he curses, pushing into my hand.

I squeeze, and he throws his head back with a groan.

"Rosie... God." He breathes heavily. "I'm trying to do the right thing, but I'm slowly losing my mind over you. Who am I kidding? I lost all sense and reason the minute I first tasted you."

As he pulses in my hand, I realize he's telling the truth. That's the deciding factor in my next move.

Releasing his erection, I turn onto my side. Sitting up, I maneuver my legs to each side of his, bringing us chest to chest. I start a slow caress up his arms, shoulders, and neck. He shudders against me as I make the most of touching his amazing body, which I've admired all night, from his well-defined muscles to his strong jaw.

I feel his eyes on me, but I continue my journey of discovery, wanting to really feel this beautiful man on his knees in front of me. I know his family is of American and Spanish descent, a trait that shows up more in Ruben than in his brothers. His thick, dark hair feels like silk as I run my fingers through the slightly too-long strands at the nape of his neck, then move further up to trace the curve of his ears.

He shudders against me and places his hands on my hips, pulling me against his stomach. His hands flex when I smooth my thumbs over his high cheekbones.

He has me so transfixed that I can't think of doing anything other than what I'm already doing. I rub my thumb along his parted lips and drop my face into the crook of his neck. Inhaling his scent catches my breath in the back of my throat. He always smells delicious. My tongue slips out between my lips, and I lick up his neck, tasting him, and nibble on his earlobe as a growl slips between his lips.

"Rosie," he whispers, sealing his lips over mine in an open-mouth kiss that shows me what part of his anatomy wants to do next. The kiss goes all the way to my toes as he wraps me up in his arms and I wrap mine around his neck.

I return his passionate kiss with everything I have. I'm on fire in his arms as I grind against his swollen erection. He's long, thick, and heavy against my mound and stomach. I want to taste him, feel him inside me. I want him to remember me always.

Breaking away from his kiss, I place my hands on his chest to push him back. "I want to taste you."

I take a deep breath, inhaling slowly before exhaling. I try to work up the courage to ask for what I want for a change instead of always being told what to do. "I want you naked on this sofa." I've said it!

He looks momentarily stunned before shooting to his feet and stripping in record time. Before I know it, he's standing in front of me, naked as the day he was born, with a proud erection pointing toward me. There are beads of moisture on the tip, and more appear the longer I watch.

I move slightly away and quickly remove my clothes. My effort is rewarded when I see the fire in his eyes, alight with passion.

Admiring his body, I say, "You're beautiful," before I can censor myself. Ruben just throws his head back and laughs.

I know how to shut him up. Leaning forward, I lick up the moisture, swirling my tongue around the crown of his penis. As I thought, the room plunges into silence until I lick along the length of him to his balls. He groans and slides his fingers through my hair. I start to trace the tattoo around the base of his shaft with one finger. A Celtic knot.

"You're the one who is beautiful, Rosie." His breath catches when I take him further into my mouth. "You feel amazing. I've dreamed about having your mouth wrapped around me again. Having you play out my dream is going to make me come too damn soon." He caresses my face as I wrap my tongue around him and suck him deeper.

"Fuck...stop! Oh, Christ! I'm going to come. You have to stop," Ruben begs, managing to withdraw completely from my mouth.

"I need to sit down before I hit the floor." He chuckles as he drops onto the sofa—the perfect position.

I crawl between his legs, kissing up his thighs and licking his balls. I trace around his tattoo with my tongue, which I think is sexy as hell. The tip of his penis is wet with excitement. I spread it around with my finger, causing his breathing to hitch.

"You're really good at that."

"Hmm, am I now? What about this?" I don't give him time to think, sucking him straight into my wet mouth with strong suction. His hips arch up from the sofa and his fists clench on either side.

I'm so aroused that I'm not sure I'll be able to finish without climbing on top of him. My core aches to be filled with his length. I want him with a desperation that I've only ever felt with him. No one else has ever aroused me the way Ruben does.

His groans set my body alight. He's clearly enjoying my mouth on him—his breathing is heavy, and his thighs are quivering. I move my hand and start massaging his heavy sac while continuing to use my mouth and tongue on him.

"Babe," he pants. "I can't hold off."

Hearing that makes me feel on top of the world. The fact that my mouth can make him lose control is empowering.

I take him further down my throat, inhaling, and start to gently hum as I stroke him between his legs. There's nothing more powerful than having this guy at my mercy. He is at my mercy—he probably couldn't even tell me his name right now.

"Oh, fuck, Rosie. . . I'm coming. . . Ahhh. . . Oh, God!"

Swallowing everything that shoots out from the head of his penis makes me wetter. After bringing Ruben to orgasm with my mouth, I'm in desperate need of relief. It was hot.

I let him slip from between my lips after swirling my tongue around the head and along the slit of his penis.

"Enough," he pants. "You are so fucking sexy. Let me catch my breath, and then I'm carrying you to my bed. You're not leaving it any time soon."

Smiling, I rested my hands on either side of his hips and placed butterfly kisses up from his stomach to his nipples. With his semi-hard penis lying between my breasts, I quickly swipe my tongue across each of his nipples. So soon? If the growing evidence against me is any indication, he sure doesn't need long to recover.

I raise my head and meet his laughing eyes.

"Only with you, baby," he laughs. "Come sit up here. I want to hold you."

I don't need to be told twice and crawl further up his body, straddling his thighs. I let the wetness between my legs coat the root of his penis as I settle against him.

God, he feels good as I wiggle over him.

"Ahh... Rosie, you need to stop doing that. We're going to use the bed...right now."

He sits up, sliding his hands under my bottom. "Hold on, babe, because I'm about to take you for a ride."

I roll my eyes, press my throbbing nipples against his chest, wrap my arms around his neck, and groan. He feels so good.

10

Ruben

I STUMBLE SLIGHTLY WHEN HER BREASTS PRESS AGAINST my chest. They feel hard and ready for my mouth. As her legs wrap around my waist, my dick slips out from between us and rubs against her ass.

My bedroom is too fucking far away right now, because all I want to do is fuck her until neither of us can walk. Considering that I just came, my dick is hard as fuck. The more she grinds against my groin, which in turn rubs and coats my dick with her arousal, the more I leak and get closer to another release.

Without letting her go, I crawl onto my bed, laying her down in the middle with her head against the pillows and my cock between her thighs. She's just where I've dreamed she would be time and time again.

"I'm on the pill," she blurts out.

"What?"

I pull back slightly to look at her, watching as she blushes.

"I mean, if you want to." Well, You know. Without."

"Rosie, are you telling me that I don't need to use a condom?" I grin.

She tries to turn away, but I won't let this conversation end just yet. I've never had sex without a condom before, but I want to with Rosie.

Chuckling, I tell her, "I'm clean, and I can't wait to get inside you bareback. It'll be a first for me."

"Really?"

"Really." I kiss her on the nose.

"Now, I'm going to touch you the way you touched me," I tell her, praying for strength. Whenever I'm close to this woman, my senses take over and my brain shuts down. But right now, I want to arouse her the way she did me.

Her touch made me feel cared for. I'd even say it made me feel loved. These thoughts don't frighten me the way they would with anyone else. The thought that the feelings I'm picking up from her might be real causes my heart to thud wildly in my chest. Until now, I hadn't realized that's what I want with this amazing woman. I'm certainly not going to scare her away. I need her to know that my feelings for her are much deeper than casual. She left casual the minute my lips met hers at my niece's and nephew's baptism.

Now that I'm emotionally invested, I briefly kiss her lips before moving down the bed and kneeling between her legs.

I take in her beauty as she watches me, her eyes showing as much passion as I imagine mine do.

My dick is hard again in her presence. I grip my shaft and slide my hand up and down a few times. Her eyes drop to watch me touch myself. The pre-cum leaking from the tip causes her to lick her lips. Groaning, I move my hand to my aching balls, pushing down to try and slow my excitement.

I relax my grip on my balls and move in to start exploring her delicious body, beginning with a caress of both ankles.

Her feet are dainty, with slim ankles leading to the sexiest pair of legs—smooth, silky calves and thighs leading to her hidden treasure. I settle fully between her thighs, needing to taste her sweet nectar. I hiss when my lower body presses against the bed, making my dick throb with desperation to be wet where my mouth is about to be.

Slowly, I use my fingers to open her up for my view, feeling her gaze on me. Looking up, I hold her stare and kiss the small landing strip of hair on top of her pussy. I watch her eyes glaze over with need.

I inhale. "You smell really good." I slip my tongue between her wet folds. "You taste even better than I imagined." Sliding a finger through her pussy lips, I dip inside her core. My dick leaks more pre-cum. She's so wet for me that my balls ache. I place another kiss on her pussy and force myself to withdraw my fingers. I suck them into my mouth, hearing her gasp as she watches me.

"Will you try something for me?" I ask, dipping my finger back inside her wet heat. I hope I'm not frightening her. I didn't lie when I told her that I don't need toys when I'm with her. I just want to show her how her pleasure can be heightened by what I have in mind.

Coating my finger in her excitement will lubricate the area where I want to use a small toy. As I gently rim her anus, I hear her breath catch in her throat. She's enjoying this. I dip my head and lick her pussy, sucking her clit into my mouth and massaging it with my tongue, causing her to arch her back. My cock jerks and expands as my finger slips inside her to the knuckle.

She moans, "You're driving me crazy, Ruben."

"Good, because that's how you make me feel."

I quickly stand up, open the drawer beside the bed, and withdraw a small toy. I meet Rosie's eyes, dip down, and kiss her beautiful lips. I whisper, "Trust me, Rosie. I promise I'll stop the minute you tell me to, no matter what stage of this we're up to." I kiss her again.

"Okay," she whispers. "Just do that again." She blushes. "With your finger."

I position myself back between her legs and tease her with my finger, circling around her wet entrance before dipping inside to lubricate it. As I rim her again, I slide the butt plug inside her and tease her.

"Oh God, Ruben. That feels so good," she moans. "More."

My cock is leaking uncontrollably from excitement, and it won't take much more stimulation for either of us to orgasm.

I remove the slim plug from her sex, withdraw my finger, and gently insert the butt plug into her ass. When it's secure, I lick her pussy and feel her vibrate around me.

Kissing my way up from between her legs, I caress

the underside of her voluptuous breasts, teasing her. I take one of her nipples into my mouth and suck while pinching and rolling the other between my fingers.

She arches and grinds against my cock, which is now wedged between her pussy lips. Not wanting her to climax yet, I ease up and kiss between her breasts. Moving further up, I place small kisses along her collarbone, leading up to her earlobe, which I nibble.

Her arms go to my shoulders, sliding into the hair at the nape of my neck, holding me to her. I start placing small kisses all over her face, avoiding her lips.

Supporting my weight with my elbows on either side of her breasts, I slide my hands under her shoulders to hold her close as I look into her eyes.

She's beautiful on the inside and out. I lean in to steal a kiss from her lips and, reaching down, guide my dick into her tight sheath. I nearly blow my load when she surrounds me in her tight, wet heat—the butt plug makes her sheath tighter than usual.

Breaking from the kiss, we both gasp in pleasure as I sink all the way inside her. My balls slap her ass. I drop my head to her neck, trying to get a grip, praying the tingling in my balls doesn't spread. I'll come before I even move, otherwise.

"You have me so worked up. I'm not sure I'll be

able to last long," I whisper into her ear, feeling her clamp down hard on my cock.

My eyes roll back in my head, and I grit my teeth, chanting inside my head. *You will not come. You will not come.* Fucking hell, she has me by the balls—literally.

"Ruben," she moans. "Please move. I'm close."

I stay pressed against her and say, "I want to pound into you, but this is going to be slow. I've never done slow before." I slide all the way out, then slide all the way back inside. "But I want to do slow with you."

It takes everything I've got to keep the slide of my dick inside her slow, but I want this to be special. I need it to be special. I may not be ready to tell her how I feel, but I can show her.

I dip down and plunder her mouth with mine, tangling my tongue with hers. I suck her tongue into my mouth and start imitating with my tongue what my cock is doing inside her.

No sooner have I started than I feel tiny flutters up and down my dick as her orgasm builds and builds until...

"Ruben!" she screams, thrashing around under me. She tightens and releases around my cock. I grit my teeth and continue the slow back-and-forth motion of my hips. Then, I join her and start coming. I thrust deep inside her, over and over again, unable to stop the spasms of my cock as my creamy liquid fills her up.

There mustn't be anything left in me after that, because I collapse on top of her. I bury my face in the curve of her neck, and she holds me tight in her arms.

"I have no words," she whispers, stroking the back of my head. "That was...intense."

"It was. I can't move, baby. You've taken everything I have."

Wanting to stay inside her but not wanting to crush her, I start to withdraw as regret fills my heart. Not regret at what we've just done, but regret that I'm no longer as close to her as possible.

"Stay," she says, tightening her arms around me. "Please, Ruben. I want your weight on me."

How could I refuse her when I want that too? If it were up to me, she would always be in my arms and in my bed, because I couldn't bear it if she were ever with anyone else.

While I've been with her, I've never thought about tying her up because I love feeling her touch. I'd planned to keep the butt plug hidden, but after feeling how she reacted to my finger, I wanted to see how she'd react to it. I was blown away that she allowed me entry there.

"You're hard again! How can you be hard again after that?" she asked, looking surprised.

I'm surprised as well that I'm hard again, but after thinking about Rosie and toys, it's no wonder. "I'm always hard thinking about you, babe." Kneeling between her thighs, I take hold of the butt plug and gently slide it free before tossing it in the direction of the bathroom.

Before I can react, she says, "My turn to drive," and quickly turns the tables, having me flat on my back as she straddles me and takes my cock straight inside her.

I grab her hips, keeping her pressed down on me while grinding up into her.

She throws her head back, giving me a great view of her swaying breasts, and starts to ride me.

Rosie

Pretending to sleep while Ruben tries to wake me is incredibly arousing. It isn't easy, with his hands and mouth all over my back and breasts. His fingers keep slipping into my core, which is wide awake and wanting more attention from him. I was surprised by the attention he gave me last night because, right up until he started applying pressure where I'd never been touched before, I'd had no idea that I was okay with him playing there. I think I surprised him as much as I surprised myself.

Gasping with pleasure, I focus on what Ruben is doing as the head of his penis slips inside me from behind.

"About time you woke up."

"Hmmm," I hum in pleasure. Reaching behind me, I slide my fingers into the hair at the nape of his neck. He shudders against me as he buries himself deeper inside. "God, you feel so good." I push back against him.

Ruben wraps me tightly in his arms, cupping my breasts with his hands as he starts thrusting in and out of my wet heat. My body constantly craves having him inside.

His wide, long penis stretches me well as it slides back and forth inside me so fast that I quickly reach my peak.

I reach behind me and rest my hand on his hip. He pinches my nipples, sending me into orbit. I grip him tightly while convulsing around his thick shaft, causing him to twitch inside me. He groans and curses loudly in my ear.

Ruben slides slowly in and out of me while trying to prolong our pleasure. I take one of his hands from my breast, bring it up to my mouth, and kiss his palm. I hold his hand against my cheek. I love this man so much.

He slides out of me and turns me over. He gets comfortable between my thighs and wraps his arms around me, dropping his forehead against mine. Our gazes meet and hold.

After kissing my lips quickly, he says, "You're my girl, Rosie. I want to do this with you. I have no idea how to do this properly, so you may have to hit me upside the head every now and again. But please, don't walk away from me again."

I caress his face, trying to control my emotions. Ruben always has his emotions turned up high, and hearing him tell me he really wants "this" makes my heart feel lighter. As much as I want to shout from the rooftops, I hesitate before jumping on the ledge. I need to know what he means by "this." So I ask, "What is this, Ruben? I don't want to misunderstand."

"Oh, baby. You're my girl. My girlfriend. My lover. You're only mine. Exclusive." He swept in and kissed me passionately before lifting his head. "I'm serious, Rosie. I want to be your girlfriend. I want you to be with me at family events. Sunday dinner at my parents' house." He groans. "But you have to promise not to run a mile when my mom asks you about weddings and babies. Thanks to Michael and Sebastian, she won't stop."

"I won't run away." There's no way I'd run away from Ruben. He's my everything. Unable to let him off easy, I tease, "I'll just tell her the wedding's next month and to expect another grandbaby in nine months." I grin, but the grin slips when I see the frown on Ruben's face.

He doesn't want that. My heart sinks when I realize that this isn't going to lead to anything permanent and that it's just until he gets fed up with me.

I try to move from under him, but he won't budge, so I start to struggle. I really need to get away from him before my tears begin to fall. I can already feel them threatening to spill over.

"Dammit, Rosie! What's wrong?" He holds me tight, refusing to let go. "Talk to me."

"You're an ass," I shout. "Now get off me, please." My tears are still hovering, but now I'm angry at him for being a jerk and at myself for reading more into what he said than I should have.

"Not until you tell me what set you off."

Is he for real? How could he not know?

"I was teasing about what I'd say to your mom," I whisper. "But by your reaction, you didn't think so. I thought you really wanted this to work between us, but your reaction made it seem like you don't see us lasting. It made me feel like you're only in this until you've had enough of me. That isn't me. Now, please let me up."

"No."

"No," I repeat.

"You're messing with my head. God, woman! I knew you were teasing, but marriage and kids hadn't even crossed my mind! I was thinking—I sure as hell wasn't thinking that we wouldn't get to that point. It really hadn't occurred to me. I'm in this for as long as you'll have me." His gaze is serious, and I grow still under him as the fight goes out of me. "If I only wanted sex, I wouldn't want you with me at family events. In my thirty-five years, I've never taken a girl-friend to meet my parents and brothers. Never Rosie. So, does that answer your question about my motives?" He asks this with a frown, the lines across his brow still evident. He's worried about my answer.

I need to stop reading into things because that's how all the upsetting things happen between us. At the end of the day, it's about trusting him. I do trust him. It's just difficult when I'm confronted with his past, not to mention my misreading his reaction.

"I'm sorry." I pull his face toward mine, kissing each of his eyes and nose before settling on his lips. I suck his bottom lip into my mouth. "I'm sorry, Ruben."

He shakes his head. "No, I'm the one who's sorry. Let's forget about this morning. I want to remember waking up with you in my arms. I want to remember what it felt like to have you wrapped around my cock."

His cock has risen again, and as I look at him, I see the sincerity in his eyes.

I'm going to do this with him because it would hurt too much not to. I grin. I have a boyfriend.

"What are you grinning at?"

"I have a boyfriend," I tell him. I pinch his ass and soothe it with my hand, feeling his shaft twitch between us.

"Say it again?" He kisses me. "Say it again, Rosie."

I pull him forward, bite his earlobe, and whisper, "I have a boyfriend," feeling his penis surge against me.

He pulls back panting, kisses the tip of my nose,

and says, "As much as I'd like to spend the day in bed with you, we need to shower and get dressed. I want to take you to breakfast."

Is he for real? His penis is hard as hell, resting against my thigh.

"Breakfast," he says, and I'm not sure who he's trying to convince.

I rub his leaking tip, coating the head with his precum. His eyes are shut, and his breathing catches. "Please stop, Rosie," he begs.

Releasing him, I bring him down to my mouth. To my disappointment, he won't deepen the kiss.

"I can't. You have me on a razor's edge." He rolls onto his back and entwines his fingers with mine, giving my hand a squeeze. He jumps up from the bed and turns to me. All I can do is admire the man before me. He's all muscle, with a sinfully sexy "V" leading to his erect penis that makes my mouth water.

"Fuck. I'm going to shower. I'll be quick, then you can hop in. If I get in there with you, there isn't any way we're going anywhere soon."

I chuckle and snuggle back into bed as I watch him walk to the bathroom. This time, I admire his tight buttocks and well-defined back.

I'm not sure what I've done to deserve him, but

I'm done questioning it. He makes me happy, and he hasn't mentioned anything like what happened at the picnic. I know it will come up again, but for now, I'm going to enjoy my time with the handsome man who wants me as his girlfriend.

11

Ruben

AFTER SHOWERING AND GETTING DRESSED, I STAND AND look down at Rosie, who is curled up and asleep in my bed. It's the place I never want her to leave if I have my way.

While I showered, I thought about Rosie. Although my heart beat frantically at the thought of being in a relationship, I decided that I don't care. I want Rosie, and I've decided that I'm through letting anything come between us.

Sighing, I crouch down at the side of the bed and tell myself that I'm not going to climb back under the covers with the gorgeous nymph who is now stretching. A breast and nipple peek out above the covers. I reach out and gently rub it with the palm of my hand.

"Mmm, come back to bed, Ruben." She opens her eyes and smiles. "Breakfast is overrated." With a flick of her wrist, she throws the covers to the other side of the bed, displaying her naked body for me.

I gulp. My hand freezes on her breast. She leaves me breathless.

"Touch me, Ruben. I want to remember having your hands on me this morning for the rest of the day," she says, bringing her hand up to cover mine over her breast. She holds my hand and moves it down her stomach, finally stopping at the top of her pussy.

"You've already had my hands on you this morning, but who am I to refuse? I only have to look at you, and I'm hard. It's painful, and I'm not going to lie to you. I want to climb back onto the bed with you because you're making it difficult."

My cock throbs behind my zipper. I know the only way I'll get any relief is to unzip and let my swollen dick out to play. But not this time. This time, I'm going to pleasure my girl.

Swallowing the lust in my throat, I throw off my shirt and move to the edge of the bed. I slide my hands around her ankles, yanking her to the edge of the bed with her legs over my shoulders. My face is now inches from her wet pussy.

When I look up and meet her gaze, I know she can see the lust I can't hide. "Hold on. I'm going to treat you really well." As I speak, she clutches the covers.

I spread her open with my fingers to my hungry gaze and lick her up, tasting her. My Rosie is sweet and insatiable. Her hips thrust forward, wanting more of what only I can give her. And I'm going to oblige.

I circle her opening with two fingers, letting her wetness coat them to make them slicker for rubbing between her pussy lips. I can't go slow anymore. I slide my fingers inside her, hitting the right spot. She bolts on the bed as though she's been hit by lightning. I return my mouth to her pussy and start lapping her up. I press my tongue onto her hardened nub, causing her to pant.

Trying to push my discomfort aside, I continue to pleasure her, scissoring my fingers in and out while caressing her clit with my tongue.

Rosie starts to whimper, causing my dick to jerk. Shit. I'm going to be lucky if I don't explode in my jeans from the noises she's making pand the taste of her.

Curling my fingers inside her, I feel the first wave

of her release building. I quickly withdraw my fingers, move to her clit, and use my tongue to bring her to a full-blown orgasm. She moans and writhes against my mouth as her arousal floods my tongue. I slowly bring her down from her high.

Eventually, her thighs go slack on my shoulders, so I lower them back to the bed. I groan at the sweet scent of her orgasm as I inhale. I clench my fists, come up from the floor, lean over her, and give her a soft kiss. Then I ask, "Are you okay?"

She gives me a satisfied smile. "I'm more than okay. That's the first time I've ever come that way. But what about you?"

"I'll survive," I tell her, knowing I'll probably be semi-aroused until I can get her under me again. Then, I register what she said. "Never before?" I'm stunned. "No one has ever gone down on you before?"

She looks embarrassed, and I didn't want that. I rest on my elbows and caress her face, making her look at me. "Don't be embarrassed."

"I haven't been with that many people. On the rare occasion that someone tried to go down on me, I froze and couldn't relax. You're the only one ever to get a reaction out of me down there."

I grin and seal our lips together before pulling back and saying, "I'm glad, and you can bet that I'm the only one who's ever going to get a reaction out of you down there." I kiss her again, trying to ignore my leaking dick. "You need to get that sexy butt out of bed and shower so we can get breakfast." I kiss her cute little nose. "Do you want me to take you home to change? Then we can eat downstairs, and you can introduce me to Liz and Ed."

"You really want to meet them?" she asks, rubbing her hands up and down my sides.

"They're like your family, right?"

She nods.

"So, yes, I want to meet them." I smile, push her away, take her hand, and haul her to her feet. "Go shower," I say, patting her on the ass. "We can leave as soon as you're ready."

"Okay."

I watch the bathroom door close and fall back onto my bed, stroking my erection and wondering if I have time to finish myself off before she comes back out.

"Liz, I'd like you to meet Ruben," she says nervously to the older woman standing beside her.

I hold out my hand, and Liz looks between the two of us before sliding her hand into mine and shaking it.

"It's nice to meet you, Liz. Rosie's mentioned you and your husband a few times," I say, overwhelmed with nerves.

I'm a grown man, but I can't shake the feeling that I should be nervous about meeting Rosie's family. Being here with her means something to me, and I really don't want to mess things up.

"Ruben brought me here to meet you and Ed and to feed me before taking me somewhere for the day." Rosie grins and moves closer to me, slipping her hand into mine. Staking her claim.

I can't wipe the smile off my face as I let her lead me to a booth in the back of the diner. She pushes me down into it. When she sits beside me, I pull her to me for a hard, fast kiss. Keeping my arm around her, I grab a menu from between the ketchup and mustard tubs. "What would you recommend, babe?" I continue reading the menu but glance at Rosie when she doesn't answer. "What's wrong?"

I let the menu drop to the table and give her my

full attention. Her silence worries me. Is she regretting being with me? If so, I'm not going to let her go without a fight. It's taken me this long to realize that she's what I want and need in my life. She's the only woman I want to call mine. She's the only woman to ever get under my skin, and despite our age differences, I know our relationship can work.

"I can't believe I'm here with you. It's surreal that we're starting a relationship when I've wanted to be with you for so long. Do you know what I mean?"

I sit and listen to her, and it takes me a minute to realize that she doesn't regret anything about us. When this finally sinks in, I drop my forehead to hers and sigh in relief.

She gives me a quizzical look but slides her arm around my shoulders and runs her fingers through the hair at the nape of my neck. Shivers run down my spine.

"I thought you were having second thoughts about us. Regretting last night. Regretting bringing me here to meet Liz, and hopefully Ed..."

Sealing her mouth to mine, she effectively shuts me up. "Mmm, you taste good," she says, pulling back slightly. "I loved being with you last night. I loved waking up with you this morning. I love being here with you. Most of all, I love being with you, no matter where we are. Please relax, Ruben. I'm not going to run away. I would have at one time, but with you, I speak my mind." She grinned.

"Ready to order?" Liz asks, looking between us as Rosie practically sits in my lap. "Um, my choice is on the menu," she adds, making us both laugh.

Rosie sits back down beside me but keeps her side pressed up against mine, as though she doesn't want to be away from me. I can't take my eyes off her profile. I move some hair behind her ear so I can see more clearly. Only when I hear a throat being cleared do I look up at Liz and realize that Rosie had me completely enthralled.

"I'll have the pancake, sausage, and syrup, thanks, Liz," Rosie says before turning to me. "Ruben, have you decided yet?"

I prefer to stay lost in my thoughts, even though they're probably dangerous to have in public. I quickly reply, "I'll have the full breakfast, thanks." I smile at Liz, who removes the menus. With one last look in our direction, she walks off to place our order.

"She likes you," Rosie says, turning to me. "And I mean really likes you." Smiling, she leans into me and quickly kisses my cheek. "The two times I've been in here with a man, she's been rude. She didn't even bother asking them what they wanted to eat. But you got the better treatment."

I don't like the idea of her bringing other guys in here. I thought she said she lacked experience.

"Ruben, I can see the wheels turning in that hard head of yours. I can't decide whether to let you think they meant something to me or tell you they were just friends," she smirks. "Liz vets everyone I bring here, and you're the only guy I've brought here who I've slept with."

It's going to stay that way."

She rolls her eyes. I decide to change the subject.

"What do you want to do for the rest of the day? I have to show my face at the club, but other than that, I'm all yours." Little does she know that I really am all hers.

"I'd love to go back to your place, cuddle on the sofa, and watch movies all day. I just want to be close to you before real life gets in the way."

"That sounds good, and before I forget, I want you to come to Sunday dinner at my parents' house. My mom might go crazy, but just ignore her. It'll be fun."

At least, I think it will be.

"Hey, you don't look too happy about that." She went pale, and her smile slipped when I mentioned Sunday dinner. She gets along well with my family, so that can't be the problem.

"You've never taken anyone before, right? So, well, won't it look odd if you take me?"

"What the hell! Rosie, I'm taking you because you're my girlfriend," I grinned. "I'd like you to be with me when it's family time at my parents' house. You're part of that now. You get along with my brothers and their partners. You'll rock it. I promise."

"If you're sure."

I wrap her in my arms and kiss her forehead. "I've never been more sure about anything. You're my girlfriend and part of my family."

She moves her head back to meet my gaze, and her eyes are swimming with tears, but she's glowing.

"Thank you," she says, snuggling against me. We're the perfect fit, as evidenced by my grumbling stomach.

Rosie

Today is Sunday, and we're on our way to Ruben's parents' house for dinner with his family. Up until he lifted me into his SUV, I was nervous about today. But as soon as the door closed, I wondered what I was nervous about. I'm familiar with his family. In fact, I enjoy talking with his brothers when they come to Kenza. Twice this past week, I met Carla, Lily, and Sabrina for coffee. All my nerves about today, other than meeting Pippa again, have disappeared.

I also believe that spending this past week with Ruben has helped me relax. We've alternated between spending the night at his place and mine. Now that I've allowed him to steal my heart and work his way into my daily life, the thought of not being with him is frightening. I should ask for space, but that isn't what I want. I want to be with him, and I feel as though something is missing when I'm not.

Sighing, I watch the fields on the outskirts of Lexington rush by as Ruben skillfully drives the SUV. My eyes are drawn to his hands flexing around the steering wheel.

"Rosie," he growls. "We're going to be late to my parents' place if you keep looking at me like that."

I smirk. "Like what?"

As if he doesn't know. I want his hands on my body instead of on the steering wheel. I want to be back at his apartment, naked, with his hands all over me. I fidget in my seat, aroused.

"Fuck," Ruben curses, pulling over to the side of the road. He slams on the brakes, unclips my seatbelt, and hauls me into his lap.

I straddle his hips, and our lips meet. We cling to each other while he arches against me, rubbing his penis against my wet panties. Moaning, I slide my fingers through his hair and hold him against me. I don't care that I can't breathe. All I want is to feel. There are too many clothes between us.

Ruben pulls his mouth from mine, breathing hard. "I'm not fucking you at the side of the road," he says, brushing the hair that has fallen into my eyes back behind my ears with unsteady hands. "But I will make love to you later, when we have a bed under us and you're under me."

His words make me want to melt into a puddle at his feet, especially when he says "make love" as opposed to "fuck" because it tells me that I mean more to him than he realizes.

I climb from his lap, fasten my seatbelt, and glance at his groin, noticing the bulge of his arousal against his zipper. Reaching out, I run a finger along the hard ridge, feeling him tense at my touch before he removes my hand.

He gulps. "Keep your hands to yourself for now. I don't want to embarass myself." He glances at me, his tone almost a whine. "Please."

I roll my eyes. "Now that you've given me permission to touch you, I'm finding it hard to keep my hands to myself. You should know that by now." I pretend to pout, knowing it's getting to him.

He unleashed the sex-starved part of me, and now there's no going back. Up until I met Ruben, I'd only ever had plenty of practice with my mouth. That's all I did before I turned nineteen, but only if they wore a condom.

I smirk to myself when I glance at Ruben and see him adjust himself in his jeans. He's unaware that I'm watching him out of the corner of my eye. I love making him react so quickly, but I'll stay quiet for now. Regardless of what he's been telling me, he's nervous about bringing me to a family dinner. For the rest of the journey, I stay silent and watch the changing scenery through the window.

"WE'RE HERE," RUBEN COMMENTS, SOUNDING enthusiastic. I glance at him as he climbs out and runs around to my side of the vehicle.

"Come on, babe." He reaches in, takes my hand, and pulls me out of the SUV and into his arms. He presses me tightly against his body, and I can't help but feel safe in his arms. "You smell so good," he murmurs.

Sighing, I snuggle against him, burying my face in his neck. He smells good, too, and feels even better. His hard muscles press against my soft curves, and there's nothing more erotic than him holding me like this, every part of me touching every part of him. I should have worn jeans today instead of this sundress, so there would be more between us than a thin piece of fabric. But I wanted to look like the girl his mama probably expects him to bring home.

Ruben seems to like me in this dress, though. As I feel his hand come to rest on my bottom, I hear footsteps behind him. I raise my head and meet a grinning Sebastian.

"It's Sebastian," I whisper into Ruben's ear.

Ruben shudders against me as my breath tickles his ear. His penis twitches, pressed against my hip.

"Mom's about to come out, so I suggest you hurry up and get Rosie inside to meet her." Sebastian stands with his hands on his hips, enjoying his brother's discomfort. Apparently not giving a damn, Ruben turns to face him—erection and all.

"Mom has already met Rosie." He takes my hand and starts walking toward the house, passing Sebastian.

"You might want to wait until it goes down first," he sniggers, moving out of hitting range.

I try not to laugh, but with Sebastian, laughter is almost guaranteed, especially when he's trying to get a rise out of one of his brothers.

"Go back to your own woman instead of trying to embarrass me in front of mine."

"Well, it's about time you admit Rosie is your woman. We've all been waiting a while. As for Mom, she may have met Rosie before, but she's never met her as your girlfriend."

Now, the nerves are back in my stomach at the thought of having to meet Ruben's parents again. I've spoken to them numerous times in the past, but, as Sebastian said, never as Ruben's girlfriend.

Ruben stops, plants a quick kiss on my lips, and says, "Don't worry, Rosie. They're just the same as before, although Mom might get carried away now that you're with me. She gets excited when one of us brings home a woman because it doesn't happen often."

He gives my shoulders a quick squeeze before wrapping an arm around my waist. I take a deep breath as he urges me forward to greet his mom, who is waiting on the front porch. She looks excited, practically bouncing where she stands. Pippa is a petite woman, which makes me wonder how she gave birth to five strapping sons. The mind boggles.

"Rosie," Pippa greets me, rushing forward and taking me into her arms. She gives me a really tight hug. And I mean tight. Tight as in, "I can't breathe" tight.

"Mom, I kinda like my girlfriend breathing," Ruben says, untangling me from his mom's arms. He kisses my forehead and wraps his arm around me. It's as though he's afraid I'll disappear if he isn't touching me. I'm not complaining, though, because I love having his hands on me.

"Girlfriend," Pippa says, dabbing at her eyes. "I never thought I'd hear those words out of your mouth," she tells Ruben as Elias, Ruben's father, wraps his arm around her shoulders.

"Rosie, it's a pleasure to have you in our home. Let's go inside, and hopefully Pippa will dry up soon." Elias leads his wife inside.

Ruben nudges me, and we follow them inside.

I knew Pippa would be overjoyed that Ruben brought me here, but I wasn't expecting that kind of response. Tears!

"You okay?" Ruben whispers in my ear.

I turn more into him and whisper back, "I'm fine as long as you stay with me."

He chuckled. "Don't worry. Mom is the only one who's going to cry."

"Wait until you announce that Rosie's pregnant, and then you'll see some big, ugly tears," Sebastian says, patting Ruben on the back with a huge grin on his face. When he winks at me, I realize that the whole room has fallen silent and that Pippa's tears have disappeared.

Ruben starts laughing along with Sebastian, but I don't see what's so funny about that statement. I'm not pregnant, and joking about it with his mom is wrong. Eventually, Ruben notices that I'm not laughing along and abruptly stops laughing. "Um, sorry." He coughs into his hand and elbows Sebastian in the stomach.

"Ouch! What was that for?" Sebastian rubs his stomach, looking between his parents and me. "Oh, um, Rosie isn't really pregnant. Sorry."

"Sebastian, are you causing trouble again?" Carla

saunters over, carrying Jr. on her hip. Sebastian is speechless. Anyone can see the love in his eyes for the woman standing before him, and I'm guessing he likes the way Carla looks with a baby in her arms. Hmm.

"He's always causing trouble, Carla," Ruben responds, smirking as he adds, "You need to keep him at home so we're all safe."

"And who would help run McKenzie's? He'd drive poor Carla crazy if he's under her feet all day," Pippa adds.

"That wouldn't happen because she'd be under me all day," Sebastian says cheekily, earning a shove from Carla. She blushes right up to the roots of her hair as she passes Jr. to Ruben, then drags Sebastian out of the room.

Jr. looks just like his father, Michael, and seems to love his Uncle Ruben. As soon as Jr. is in Ruben's arms, he lays his head on his shoulder and puts his little arms around his neck. The picture they portray brings tears to my eyes. Ruben looks choked up as well.

"I think the little tyke's tired." He sits back on the sofa, rubs Jr.'s back with one hand, and holds the other out to me. He doesn't need to make it any clearer.

I sit beside them and watch Jr. drift off to sleep while Pippa and Elias sit across from us.

Glancing at Pippa, I see that she has a dreamy look on her face as she gazes at Ruben and her grandson. They make quite the picture. Lucien snaps a picture with his cell as he appears from the kitchen.

Ruben takes my hand, kisses my knuckles, and brings our joined hands to his lap, leaving them there. My heart flutters in my chest at the look he's giving me.

I hear a throat being cleared and turn to face his mom, who is tearing up again, and his dad, who has a large grin on his face. Lucien hides his smirk behind his hand but manages to swallow it back when he catches me glaring at him.

Hmm. "So, Lucien," I say, straightening up. "Is Sabrina around?" His eyes widen at my question before narrowing.

"I've no idea."

"Really?"

He sighs. "She's in the kitchen with Lily."

Pippa jumps up. "Why don't you come with me into the kitchen, Rosie?" We can leave the men in here. I'm sure Ramon and Michael will join them soon, as will Sebastian, wherever he disappeared to with Carla. Tsk. He can't leave the poor woman alone. I don't know how she can still walk."

Ruben releases my hand, chuckling at his mom's comment. "I'll be here, babe, if you need me. Go have fun with your friends."

"Okay."

I let Pippa drag me into the kitchen, where Lily, Sabrina, and Sylvia are sitting and drinking coffee. They soon make room for me to join them.

12

Ruben

HOLDING JR. ON MY CHEST OVERWHELMS ME WITH emotion, so I breathe a sigh of relief when Mom ushers Rosie into the kitchen. I know Rosie saw the longing in my eyes. I want what Michael has, but hopefully, it will stay unspoken between us for now. It's taken me all this time to accept that I can be in a relationship without freaking out. My dad set a good example with his love, and I guess that's why it's always frightened me. Having someone rely on me for their happiness? Even forty-five years later, he still seems to be in love with Mom.

Jr. lets out a small cry against me, abruptly bringing me out of my thoughts about love and commitment. He settles back down, snuggling into my neck. There's nothing like cuddling a baby to make all your walls crumble. Who would have thought that Michael would be the first to have the much-wanted grandbabies?

"Wearing a baby suits you," Michael comments as he sits beside me. "Even if the baby belongs to me."

Hmm, brotherly love. "You have two. Go find Charlotte." I kick back with my feet on the coffee table. Snuggling a sleeping baby is making me want to nod off with him. Though I think that has more to do with Rosie keeping me up half the night. I grin.

"I'm not sure why you're grinning like that, but please behave around my son."

Michael is so easy to wind up. "I was thinking about what you have to do to get one of these."

"I'm getting plenty of practice," Sebastian interrupts as he joins us. "I can't get enough of my woman."

"As though we haven't noticed, son. But I'm not sure you need to keep mentioning it out loud. You'll embarrass Carla."

Judging by the look on Sebastian's face, he'd forgotten that Dad was sitting with us in the living room.

"Ruben, take your feet off the coffee table before

your mother catches you. You know what she's like when we have company."

Mom always has to have the perfect house—all the time. It keeps her busy, which she likes, and I love that no matter how long I've been away, I only have to walk through the front door to feel like I'm home again. The apartment above Kenza's is my home now, but I don't think I'll ever be able to call this ranch house anything other than home.

"Is anyone going to tell me what's really going on at Kenza?" Dad asked, pulling me away from my thoughts. "I know you boys don't like to tell me when there's trouble, but I need to know you're all okay. I worry."

I hadn't realized that, by keeping my dad out of the loop, he would worry as much as he just admitted. In fact, I hadn't realized that he knew I was having problems at the club.

"Dad, I'm sorry." I sat forward and passed Michael his sleeping son. "I didn't want to worry you or Mom. I'm okay, and the club will be too. Ramon and Lucien overheard talk of drugs."

My dad's eyes widen in shock because he knows how much I hate drugs. "Oh my."

I chuckled. "Well, that's an understatement." I rest my elbows on my knees and run my hands through my hair. "We'll get them, Dad, and we'll be okay. There's a guy at the club, Hunter, who is helping out. He's a customer and a friend of Rosie's. I know he'll take care of her, and I'm sure he won't overlook anything. I'm not sure who he is or where he's from, but he's been good to Rosie, so I trust him for now." I'm trying to put my jealousy aside, even though I saw the way he looked at Rosie at first. Now, he seems more like a friend to both of us.

"He's cool. I don't think you have anything to worry about," Ramon adds, having come through the front door.

"If you need any help, you know you can still come to me, right? I might not be as young as I once was, but I still have plenty of life left in me."

"Thanks, Dad. I'll let you know. I'm actually hoping this will all be over soon."

"I hope so, then you can focus more on Rosie and less on messing up. She's a nice girl, and the women seem to love her."

For some reason, my brothers find Dad's comment funny. I don't—really. Okay, maybe slightly. "No matter what you idiots think." I scowl at my brothers, then look at my dad, who also has a grin plastered across his face. "I'm capable of having a rela-tionship with Rosie without messing it up. She's the only woman I want, so I'm not going to risk messing things up."

"Who's being a dick?" Mom asks, walking back into the living room with a large tray of drinks and snacks. She places it on the coffee table and frowns in my direction. "You know you're not allowed to put your feet on the coffee table."

How the fuck does she do that? "Yes, ma'am."

"Hmmm, I notice you didn't deny it." She grins. "I don't think you've ever sat there without putting your feet up on the table, so I guessed right."

Dad starts to laugh. "She's got you there."

I ignore everyone and focus on Mom, wanting to know if Rosie is okay. Before I can open my mouth to ask her, she says, "Rosie is fine. She's teasing Sabrina with Carla and Lily." Mom glances at Lucien before bringing her attention back to me. "All joking aside, Ruben, I'm glad you're dating Rosie. She's a lovely girl, and although I was doubtful at first because of the age difference, she's the one for you. I've never seen you smile so much, even when you're not egging on your brothers. I'm really happy for you." She kisses the top of my head, then goes back into the kitchen, leaving me speechless. Mom loves teasing us and going on about us finding our one and only, but she's never been so open about one of our relationships. She's also damn observant.

Shaking my head, I try to think of an excuse to leave my dad and brothers so I can join the women.

"RUBEN, WHEN YOU SAID, 'LET'S TAKE A WALK,' I WASN'T expecting to sneak off to the hayloft," Rosie giggles, and my cock stands at attention.

I haven't felt this out of control since puberty. Now, all I want is to be naked and buried balls deep inside Rosie. I take the two steps needed to bring me chest-to-chest with her, whose breathing is as erratic as mine.

"I can't get enough of you," I say against her cheek, starting to place small kisses all over her face. "I have a permanent erection whenever you're close. Hell, who am I kidding? I've had a permanent erection ever since I've known you." My hands slide down her back, land on her bottom, and pull her in tight against me so she can feel for herself what she does to my body. She rubs against me, dragging a groan from my lips. Catching my breath, I tell her, "It's worse than ever now because it's been buried in your heat, your wetness, and it doesn't want to be anywhere but between your legs."

I slowly lift the skirt of her dress to her waist, so I can get to her panties and the heat beneath. She gasps as I rip off her panties and toss them behind us. I caress each cheek of her bottom before slipping a finger between her buttocks and moving down toward her entrance. She's wet, and she begins to moan, throwing her head back, as I start to rub her clit and dip my fingers inside her. She shudders around me.

Without moving her lust-filled gaze from mine, she quickly unzips and unbuckles my jeans and shoves them past my hips. She looks down at my huge, hard-as-a-rock cock. With her eyes on me, I twitch uncontrollably with excitement, leaking and coating the head of my dick with precum.

Meeting my gaze again, she steps back, pulls her dress off over her head, and quickly removes her bra. God, she takes my breath away. She's so beautiful. I love how she's slim but has breasts that overflow my hands when I cup them.

I feel my control slipping away as I nearly come all over us when she drops to her knees. I'd love to have her mouth on me, but I'm not sure I'll be able to control myself.

"Please, Ruben. Please, let me taste you again. You've tasted me so many times. I need this." I reach out and stroke her jaw. I cup her face and try to hold off my need as I bend to kiss her.

"As long as you promise to stop when you need to. I don't need this to be with you. Don't ever think I do."

In response, she burrows her face into my hands. She kisses my palm and starts to yank my jeans down my legs, but they get caught on my boots.

I toss my shirt off over my head, then get shocked when my bare ass touches a bed of hay.

"God, you look hot," Rosie tells me as she crawls between my legs. "I've wanted to do this since last time."

Without another word, she licks me from balls to the leaking crown of my cock. She swirls her tongue around me and laps up all the precum before licking back down and massaging my aching balls.

I try to open my legs wider, but my jeans restrict me. Rosie realizes my predicament but, instead of helping me, gives me a mischievous grin and sucks my cock into her mouth.

I stop breathing. My heart feels like it's about to jump out of my chest, and my balls pull tight to my body. Just as I feel my orgasm rushing forward, she releases me from her lips. She gives the tip a kiss and turns, presenting her ass to me. I quickly close my eyes, grab the base of my cock, and squeeze hard. I'm not going to come until I'm deep inside her, even though I'm tempted to ejaculate all over her ass.

Rosie has removed my boots, jeans, and undershorts, so I'm now free. I get to my knees and place my hands on Rosie's hips. "Stay." I swallow, trying to control the urge to shove myself deep inside her. "Rest on your arms, keeping your bottom up in the air." She does as I ask, and I can't describe how sexy she looks. I move backwards slightly, crouch down, and spread her legs. I place a kiss slap bang on her pussy. She wiggles against my face.

As I get drunk on her scent and taste, my hands reach under her and start to massage her breasts, pinching and squeezing her nipples. They're plump and swollen with need in my hands. I imagine her nipples are the color of a ripe cherry, my favorite fruit.

The more I lap at her pussy, the more aroused she becomes. My dick is desperate, and I'm not sure how much more I can take before I come. I managed to prevent my orgasm once. I'm not sure if I'm strong enough to do so again.

"Ruben. Oh God. Get inside me."

Thank you, God!

I reared up and took my cock in hand, pumping a few times and watching more precum leak out. I'm beyond excited now.

I position my twitching dick at her entrance and slip inside, immediately feeling her heat envelop me. She sucks me deeper and deeper until I'm buried balls deep in heaven. I need to move, but I know that if I do, I'll come in twenty seconds flat. I grip her hips to keep her still.

"Rosie." I drop my head against her back, my hands shaking with the need I'm holding back.

"It's okay, Ruben. Ruben, it's okay. I'm here, but please move. I need you to move."

I kiss her back along her spine, pulling out to the tip before slamming home. I lose control. My hips start pistoning in and out of her. My hands reach around to the front and hold her against me, her breasts spilling into my palms. I pinch and roll her nipples, getting rewarded when I feel her little cunt flutter with small tremors as her orgasm makes its way through her.

"Oh, oh, Ruben! Help me! I'm coming…" A gargled wail escaped her mouth as her cunt pulsated along my length, signaling my balls to erupt. A pleasure unlike anything I'd ever known spread along my shaft and out through the slit.

"Ahhh... Sweet Jesus..." I pant, coming and coming. Each little flutter of her vagina against me makes me come even more, leaving me breathless.

Rosie collapses face first into the hay beneath her. This causes me to groan as my cock slides out of her wet heat. A strand of cum holds us together, stretching from her wet pussy to the tip of my sensitive dick. Seeing my cum on her is so fucking hot that I start to get hard again.

Breaking the connection, I collapse beside her, pull her against my chest. She snuggles into me, her knee coming to rest on my erection.

She chuckles. "Really?" she asks, raising her head from my chest.

"You're hot, and I like seeing my cum on you."

Rolling her eyes, she drops her head back to my chest and mumbles, "Men!"

Rosie

I never expected to find myself lying in a hayloft on Ruben's parents' ranch one afternoon, or anywhere, for that matter. What has he done to me?

I stretch and rub against his swollen penis, smiling. He certainly doesn't have any trouble getting hard again. I'd always thought it took guys a while to get hard again, but not Ruben.

"Keep rubbing against me like that, and we'll be up here much longer than you're comfortable with. Before long, Mom will send one of my brothers to see what we're doing. She'll know, of course. That's why she'll send one of my brothers. So you won't be embarrassed in front of her."

Ruben kissed me on the head before rolling me onto my back and looming over me. "You make me happy, Rosie. Thank you." He kisses me on the lips, untangles himself from me, and starts hunting for clothes.

Hearing him tell me that I make him happy has me fighting back tears. He's a gorgeous man, and he's mine. I believe that with every breath I take. He's mine.

I smile as he bends over to pick up my dress,

pulling bits of hay from the material as he straightens up.

"You have a nice bottom."

He pauses and smirks at my comment. "Bottom?" He raises an eyebrow. "I'd prefer 'ass,' or 'butt,' but 'bottom'—thats for girls."

"Whatever you want to call it, yours is 'nice.' It makes me want to bite it." His eyes darken. "And while I'm biting your 'butt,' I'd use my hands to explore between your legs and tease your penis."

I'm lying on my stomach, chin resting on my hands, watching his penis harden under my stare and the image I've put in his head. I feel so comfortable being naked with him that teasing him to arousal doesn't bother me in the least. The only problem is that my teasing arouses me as well, to the point that I'm having trouble staying still.

As he grabs his shaft, I lick my lips, watching him caress his length from tip to base. "So, when you have me in your hands, what will you do to me?" he asks, continuing to massage his shaft.

I really want my hands to be the ones stroking him. He's beautiful, and well—not that I've seen that many—but he's above average in size.

"I can't think when I'm watching you do that." I can't take my eyes off of what he's doing.

"Lie on your back for me." He stays standing above me.

As I turn onto my back, he moves to stand beside me. As he looks down at me, his penis leaks. He uses the precum and spreads it over his lengthening erection.

"Are you wet, Rosie? I don't mean wet from my cum. Are you wet from arousal? Touch yourself and tell me."

Can I really do that? With Ruben, you can do anything. Trust him.

I open my legs and use one hand to spread my lips open to his gaze. I dip my finger inside. My whole body shivers with need.

"Rosie," he pants. "Don't stop touching yourself."

Are we really doing this?

If he's up for it, then so am I.

I insert my finger further inside my channel and start sliding it back and forth. I use my other hand to pinch my nipples. It feels so good, causing arousal to run through me.

I keep my eyes on Ruben's hand as he works himself faster and harder. His penis lengthens, and he leans back against the wall behind him. I see his legs quiver.

"I want you to come with me."

"I'm close. Oh God, Rosie," he whispers.

I put my feet together and spread my knees to the side, giving him a better view of my pussy and my fingers slipping in and out of me. He curses.

The sensation starts in my stomach and spreads outward. With one rub against my clit, I shut my eyes in ecstasy. I come apart against my fingers.

"Fuck, fuck, fuck."

I open my eyes and watch as Ruben ejaculates into the hay, narrowly missing me. He drops to his knees.

"Ruben, are you up there?"

Our eyes meet.

"We'll be down in ten," he says, inhaling.

"Make it five, otherwise Mom will be out here," Sebastian says, laughing. I can tell from his tone that he's not sorry at all.

God, I can't believe we just did that. It was hot and arousing, but damn. I feel the blush that I've been trying to hold at bay since we started rise into my face. There's no way Ruben won't notice how embarrassed I am. Even more so now that we nearly got caught.

"Rosie." Ruben crawls over to me and kisses me on the lips. It's just a quick kiss, without tongue, but it's still possessive. He starts helping me dress. The only problem is that when I stand, I feel his cum sliding out of me and down my thighs.

"Um, Ruben? Do you have anything to clean me up? You're kinda running down my legs," I say, getting a grin in return. "Today, please."

"I told you before, babe. I love being all over you." He finishes putting himself back together while I'm left floundering. I feel like hitting him over the head with whatever I can find.

"Rosie." He cups my face in his hands. "I'm sorry for being a careless jerk. Now, I'm going to take care of you."

I roll my eyes. "Isn't that what got me into this predicament in the first place?"

I place my hands on my hips and refuse to smile at him while he looks so smug. Before I can register what he's doing, he's kneeling at my feet, hands on my thighs, head beneath my skirt. "Ruben?"

"Hold still. I'm cleaning you up." And he does. I'm not sure what he's using, but he's being especially careful while wiping my thighs and the area between them. It's frustratingly slow.

"Oh God! What am I going to wear now that you've ruined my panties? I can't go out without wearing any. I'm wearing a dress! If I were wearing jeans, it wouldn't matter, but oh my God, Ruben!"

Sensing my stress, he comes out from under my skirt. Straightening up, I see the wheels turning in his head. "I'll ask if Carla has any jeans and a sweater you can borrow. See? Sorted."

Why doesn't he realize how embarrassed I'm going to be going out to be with his family again? I should have realized this before we stripped, but we were preoccupied. I meet his gaze and tell him, "You're a dick," as I stomp off toward the ladders. Without looking at him, I climb down, praying there isn't anyone waiting down there. If they look up, they'll get an eyeful.

We're alone, so when he drops to the floor in front of me, I continue, "How can you not realize how embarrassing this is for me? I love being with you, and the minute you touch me, I forget everything. Now, I'm going to be so embarrassed going out there to see your family again—and your mom. Oh. Oh. I can't do this. I can't go out there. You need to take me home."

"Babe, calm down. There isn't anything to be worked up about. Mom caught Michael and Sebastian with their girls, and they're still showing their faces around here. You should be glad it was Sebastian who came to find us. As for the clothes, we always play football after dinner, so that's a good enough excuse to change. Even if they know anything, they won't say anything in front of you. They'll wait until I'm alone. So don't sweat it."

He's a guy, so I guess I should expect him not to understand. But fuck! I'm wearing a sundress with no panties. It doesn't get any more uncomfortable with his family around.

"Stop biting your lip."

"I'm not," I reply, releasing my lip from between my teeth. "I'm getting hungry, so let's just get this over with. Hopefully, I won't lose my appetite from nerves now that you've ravaged me."

Ruben takes my hand, kisses my knuckles, and tugs me out of the barn. Suddenly, he stops when we come face to face with Lucien.

Unexpected.

"Sabrina sent me out with these. She thought you might need them." He looks between us, and when we don't make a move to grab the clothes, he asks, "Do you want them or not?"

"I want them." I smile at him as I take the clothes. "Sorry. I was just surprised, that's all. Tell Sabrina thank you."

"I'm sure you'll have the chance to tell her yourself at dinner in five minutes." He turns and heads back toward the house.

"Thanks, Lucien, for bringing these to me," I shout to his retreating back.

"I'm not sure what's wrong with him."

Why are men so clueless half the time? "Sabrina is what's wrong with him. She's really starting to get to him," I point out, watching as the light bulb goes off in his head.

"Ah, so you think he's coming around to the idea of Sabrina?" Ruben asks, sounding hopeful. "I hope he is. I hate seeing my brother so alone."

I walk back into the barn. "Let me quickly put these on. I hope they fit."

"They will. She's about your size. Need any help?"

"No, you stay right where you are." I chuckle, relieved that I'm going to have a bit more protection between me and his family.

13

Ruben

NOT WORKING AT KENZA FEELS STRANGE. ALTHOUGH, truth be told, I'm still working in my head and keeping an eye on things. I spend my time wondering who is messing with my club. Rosie is a distraction, though—a very nice one. Sabrina's jeans fit Rosie like a glove, and the shirt she's wearing dips really low in the front. Throughout dinner at my parents' ranch, my eyes kept wandering, prompting amused snickers from my brothers.

Rosie is a hot little firecracker. Right now, I'm trying to stay in my seat as I watch her stop to talk to Hunter on her way back from the restroom. She says he's just a friend, but I'm sure that if I weren't here, he would have made a move on her. I have no doubt as I watch her walk toward me with Hunter's eyes on her ass. *Look,* because that's all you'll ever have.

"Hey, why the scowl?" She straddles my lap and wraps her arms around my neck. "You feel good," she whispers in my ear before biting my earlobe.

She knows how to distract me.

I grab her ass and pull her tightly against my aching dick. "I don't like Hunter staring at your ass," I growl. "Your ass gives me all kinds of ideas. As it does with any red-blooded male. I don't like anyone else having the same thoughts about you that I do."

"You having naughty thoughts about me?" She grinds against me.

"Always. Why do you think I'm constantly hard?"

She smirks. "Too much Viagra."

My whole body freezes. Viagra! "What the fuck?" I pull back and look into her watering eyes. She's laughing so hard that tears are falling down her face.

"Sorry," she laughs.

"You're not sorry."

"Okay, I'm not," she hiccups. "It was worth it to see the expression on your face."

"That wasn't funny."

"Yes it was," Lucien thumps me on the back. With Rosie sitting in my lap, up close and personal with my cock, I'd forgotten that my brothers and their girl-friends are here with us.

"Mind your own business," I tell my brother. Turning back to Rosie, I say, "I think I need to keep you naked in my bedroom. I'll give you fucking Viagra."

Rosie freezes against me. "You realize I was only joking, right? There's no way you need anything to keep you up. You need something to help you stay flaccid."

I reassure her with a smug look. "I know you were joking, but babe, please don't joke about things like that. It deflates my manhood."

"Are you serious? You're hard as granite between my legs."

"Do you two mind? I don't want to hear shit like that about my brother," Sebastian interjects.

I'm not sure how he heard anything, considering how loud it is in here with the music. Even though tomorrow is a workday, Kenza is packed solid tonight, with hot, sweaty bodies rubbing against each other all over the dance floor. That's what I want to be doing with Rosie, except I'd rather do it upstairs in my apartment than have everyone see us on the dance floor. The boss dancing would probably get more attention than the usual guy. Especially since the boss never loosens up here—until now, it would seem.

As I watch my brothers—apart from Lucien and Ramon—get up to dance with their girls, I wait, expecting Rosie to pull me up as well. But she doesn't. She stays buried in my neck.

"Brother, you're losing your knack. Your woman's asleep," comments Ramon, now that the music has lowered in volume slightly, as it does when midnight hits. Romantic music plays for a couple of hours until the place clears out.

"Do you want me to open the doors to your place so you can tuck her in?" Lucien asks.

"Not yet. Have you seen anything tonight?" I hate having to rely on my brothers to figure out what's going on, but I'm not seeing it. And that pisses me off. This is my club, and I should be the one to get to the bottom of it. I'll be the one to finally figure it out. Make no mistake about that.

Lucien kicks me under the table to get my attention. "As long as you're in the club, I doubt anything will happen. They know nothing gets past you, so they'll wait to attack again when you're not here. But we will be, and so will Hunter."

"Are you sure we can trust Hunter? We don't know anything about him." I think we can trust him, but I still have my doubts. I can't decide if it's because he rubs me the wrong way with Rosie or because I don't know anything about him.

"You can trust him." Ramon sits forward. "He's helped me out now and again."

Ramon can be frustrating as hell when he wants to be. Unless he wants you to know something, he keeps his lips sealed. He's caused enough arguments over the years with his silence.

"You need to go away for a few days, or just stay away from the club. Give them an opportunity to try to pull something," Lucien suggests.

"I'm flying to Calgary tomorrow to attend a meeting for Sebastian, so I'll be away for a few days." The thought that I might not be here to solve the problem at the club gnaws at me. "I want Rosie looked after. She's been injured here before, and I don't want that to happen again. I also need to tell her that I won't be here."

"You haven't told her?" Lucien asks incredulously.

"I didn't find out until recently, and I planned on telling her when we took a walk at the ranch earlier, but we got sidetracked. So, no, I haven't told her yet. I'll take her upstairs soon. Hopefully, she'll be awake enough for me to talk to her."

"Or something else," Ramon smirks.

"I wouldn't say no to that, but she's exhausted and needs to sleep."

"Sleep sounds good, baby," she mumbles into my neck as she snuggles more deeply against me.

How the hell am I going to leave her tomorrow morning? In all fairness, I tried to get two seats on the flight, but they were sold out. In the end, all I did was switch Sebastian's name with mine.

I tighten my arms around her and bury my face in her hair. God, this girl is under my skin. She only has to smile, and my heart feels different. It's a feeling I'm starting to get used to, though, without it sending me into a total panic.

"So, what's with you and Sylvia? I thought you had different tastes," I hear Lucien say to Ramon. I've been wondering about that since this afternoon at the ranch, when I discovered that he'd brought her to the family dinner. I was surprised, to say the least.

I'm glad my face is hidden in Rosie's hair, so he can't see my grin. He's squirming where he sits. He's just like he used to be when one of us put him on the spot back when we were kids. It was so damn funny. We'd do it on purpose just to see him squirm. He never changes.

"She only has an elderly grandmother who lives in River View Retirement Village, so I kind of felt sorry for her. She's already good friends with Lily, so I thought I'd invite her to dinner with the girls." He shrugs. "It's no big deal."

It's no big deal! I've seen the way Sylvia looks at my brother when he's not paying attention. I think it's more of a deal than he wants to admit. I'm also curious about what's going on between Lucien and Sabrina. They avoided each other earlier like the plague. After Lucien brought Rosie clothes from Sabrina, they acted strangely whenever they were together.

I was about to confront Lucien to help Ramon when Rosie lifted her head and bit down on my earlobe. My earlobe is one of the most sensitive parts of my body, along with my balls and dick. Fuck! She nibbles my neck and moves back up to my ear. If she continues, I'm going to embarrass myself in front of everyone. As it is, my dick is hard, pulsing, and leaking with excitement. Whenever she's near my ears, I instantly get a boner.

"Take me upstairs, Ruben," she whispers into my ear before clamping down again on my earlobe. My whole body shudders as arousal rushes through me. God, I'm in trouble. She has me on sensory overload. I can't remember the last time I felt like I was seconds away from coming.

"Now." She presses her pussy against me while sucking my earlobe. My dick jerks. *Fuck. Fuck! Fuck!* I grab her hips and hold her down against me as I have a silent orgasm that takes my breath away. I hear her chuckle against me before she slips her tongue into my ear, causing my cock to release more cum.

I'm a mess. I bury my face in her neck, and she holds me close, allowing me to get my bearings. When I do, I silently groan. This doesn't look good. I just had an orgasm in front of the whole club!

"Don't stress. We're alone. Your brothers left after the first bite."

Thank God for that.

"Carry me to bed, Ruben, and make love to me until I can't walk."

"My pleasure."

I pray that having Rosie in my arms hides any damp patches on my jeans and shirt as I grab her ass, let her legs wrap around me, and carry her through the club toward the stairs leading to my apartment. I thank God she's my girl and I don't care who sees us.

Rosie

It wasn't the best way to wake up to find out during the early hours of the morning that Ruben was going on a two-day trip. It made me wonder why he'd left it so late to tell me. After all, we had spent the whole day together yesterday, so there had been plenty of opportunities for him to tell me. To say I'm still a little miffed is an understatement. I'm kind of pissed. Who waits until the last minute to tell their girlfriend they're leaving town? Ugh! Well, at least the chrome edging on the bar will shine by the time I'm done. Kenza has cleaners who come in to do this kind of work, but I need to burn off some anger before I take it out on the customers—of which there are only two.

Kenza opens the bar at two in the afternoon, but we keep the main part of the club blocked off until later in the evening. A few regulars come in around this time to sit back with a drink and people watch. A couple of women who work in an office building a block away have recently become regulars. I can't decide if they're here to drool over Ruben or Simon. I'm sure they're trying to catch the attention of both of them.

Ruben ignores them, offering only a polite hello if they get in his way. Simon has gotten into the habit of sitting with them for a drink and flirting with them. At least, that's why I think they always walk out with a blush on their faces. Then again, it could be the alcohol they consume.

Reaching one end of the bar, I stand back and admire its shine. It's so shiny that I can see my reflection more clearly than usual. I also notice a huge guy standing behind me who looks like Hunter.

As I turn to look at him, I lean back against the bar and smile up at him. I like Hunter, and I wish the darkness I see in his eyes would disappear, even when he hasn't hidden it behind a shield. He's a good guy, and I'm sure he doesn't deserve to fight whatever demons he has.

"I don't think Ruben would be happy to catch you looking at me like that." He smirks.

"Like what?" I ask, genuinely curious to know how he thinks I'm looking at him. When he doesn't answer, I try again, "Hunter, how was I looking at you?"

He runs his hands through his hair, a clear sign that he isn't happy with the direction of the conversation. Why do guys always tug at their hair when they're unsure how to answer? Ruben does this, and so do his brothers. It's definitely a guy thing.

Hunter leans closer and says, "You were looking at

me as though you wanted to get to know me. As in, the down-and-dirty getting-to-know-me." He laughs.

My blush has worked its way up from my chest to my face as I listen to him. I know he's only teasing me because I certainly didn't look at him that way. That way is reserved for Ruben.

I shove his chest. "Stop! I most certainly did not look at you that way! As you well know. I might have looked happy to see you, though, because I am. I'm always happy to see a friend." I place my hands on my hips, more or less telling him not to mess with me. I'm not sure it's working, though, judging by the laughter lines around his eyes, which also look full of humor.

"I'm glad we're friends, Rosie. I really am, but I'm not used to having friends, especially of the pussy variety—"

I gasp, and before he can finish, I turn away from him and head behind the bar, thinking that I don't want this conversation to continue. What the hell is wrong with me this morning?

"Rosie." He grabs my wrist and turns me around to face him. "Yeah, I'm a jerk, but I'm also a guy, and guys like me don't have female friends. But I'm willing to keep trying, okay? Hopefully, Ruben will be around soon to keep me in check." The whole time he's talking, his eyes stay focused on mine. Not many people do that. "Truce," he says after a minute, holding out his hand.

I place my hand in his, and he tightens his hold as we shake. "I also promise to stop coming on to you, although you're so sweet to tease."

I roll my eyes without thinking. There's no way he'll stop teasing me. He enjoys it too much. "We'll see how long that promise lasts, but I'm on to you now, and I'm prepared to give as good as I get, so be warned." Then something occurs to me, and I ask, "You haven't met the girls over there yet, have you?" Knowing the answer, I continue, "I'm sure they'd love to meet you. I mean, who can refuse such a sexy, tattooed guy?" I smile and stand in his space, whispering, "I mean, who could refuse someone built like you? They'd have to be blind." His eyes widen in surprise at my comments, and I gloat at my ability to tease him when he didn't see it coming—or rather, didn't see me coming.

I wink, duck under the hatch, grab a towel, and, ignoring Hunter, start to wipe down the already clean bar to keep myself busy. I enjoy giving as good as I get, but I'm not very good at it, nor at hiding my embarrassment. I really just want to be friends with him. It's been so long since I've had "real" friends, and being friends with Hunter would be different. I don't know why, but I'm positive he'd always be there for me if I needed him. I'd be there for him, too.

At least he took my mind off Ruben's absence for a little while. I'm still mad at him for waiting until the last minute to tell me, though. I wonder how I can make him pay. Withholding sex might work. But then I'd suffer too, and that wouldn't be fair. I could go back to my apartment for a couple nights after we have sex, but then again, I'd suffer with him because I love sleeping with his body spooning mine. I love waking up with him hard and inside me, stroking my walls with his thick penis.

I need to practice saying "cock." I don't know why, but I feel uncomfortable saying "cock" instead of "penis." When I think of a cock, I can't get a proper image in my mind. But when I think of a penis, I see Ruben's long shaft. He has a wide girth, and veins throb along his shaft to the crown. By the time my eyes reach that point, it is usually leaking pre-cum. My dream of licking my lips and thinking about Ruben's cock comes to an abrupt end with the smash of a glass. I realize that I'm responsible for breaking the glass.

"Don't move, Rosie. The glass is all around your feet," Hunter shouts, dashing toward me.

He picks me up, glass crunching beneath his boots, and places me on top of the bar.

"Are you okay?" He runs his hands up and down my legs. "Rosie, damn it. Are you okay?"

Shit. "Sorry. Yes, I'm fine. I didn't see it." I still can't believe I broke a glass. I haven't broken anything since I started working here, which is amazing. Well, except for the night I got caught in the middle of a fight.

"There are about three glasses here. Let me clean up the mess." More glass crunches beneath his boots as he walks over to the door behind the bar to get the broom I'd left propped up there.

I can't let him do this. "Hunter, I can do that. I'm fine. Seriously."

"You're only wearing shorts. All it would take is one shard of glass to jump up, and your gorgeous legs would be scarred."

"While you're cleaning that up, I'm going to take my girl and admire her legs in private," Ruben says, startling me. I glance over and see him beside the bar. His eyes gleam as he makes sure Hunter knows whose girl I am. The heat in his eyes momentarily distracts me from the fact that he's here and not elsewhere.

Snaking an arm around my waist, he pulls me

away from the bar, frowning at Hunter. A silent message seems to pass between them. With a nod, Ruben grabs my hand and pulls me toward his office.

Once inside, he flips the lock, lifts me into his arms, and pushes me back against the door. Before I can catch my breath, he seals his mouth over mine. His mouth is wet and sinful as our tongues meet. My core throbs the way it only ever does when I taste this man. He doesn't just kiss me—he devours me. The attention he pays to my mouth leaves me quivering in his arms. My hips start grinding against the bulge in his pants. His hands grip my bottom tighter, pushing me against him.

He lifts his mouth and, resting his forehead against mine, inhales, trying to take air into his lungs. "I fucking missed you," he admits huskily. "I got to my connecting flight and decided to do business over a conference call. I caught the next flight back here to you. I couldn't stop thinking about the look on your face when I left this morning." He trails wet kisses down my neck to my collarbone and back up to my lips. "Rosie...Jesus. I can't get enough of you. I've never changed my mind mid-flight before, but damn, I couldn't wait to land so I could get back to you."

"I've been mad at you all morning," I start to tell

him, but I have to stop when he rips my shirt and bra off.

"You have the most amazing breasts. They're not too big. Not too small either. Just the right size for my hands. I love how, the minute my eyes look at you, your nipples go rock hard, begging for my touch." He dips his head, capturing one nipple in his mouth, and laps at it while rolling it against the roof of his mouth. My back arches, pushing my breasts further into his mouth and face. He growls as he switches to the other nipple.

I'm wet and needy between my legs from Ruben's touch. I feel him growing harder—if that's possible.

When he releases my nipple from his mouth and our eyes meet, I know what I'm going to do. Even a month ago, I wouldn't have considered doing it, but this is Ruben, and he's made me feel comfortable. I still don't think I'll ever trust him enough to be tied up, but I can do this.

"Let me down," I say, smiling secretly.

He pauses.

"I want to touch you."

He closes his lust-filled eyes, opens them again, and lets me slide down every delicious inch of him until my feet hit the floor. Ruben backs up to his desk and quickly removes his clothes. He stands before me, completely naked. My breath hitches at the sight. He's magnificent. His muscular physique is coated in tanned skin. I don't think I'll ever tire of looking at him. As I stand and watch him, he takes hold of his penis—I mean, his cock. Nope, that doesn't do anything for me.

But watching him stroke it with the tip leaking is making my knees weak. If I don't do something soon, he's going to come without me.

I remove my clothes and toss them onto a chair off to the side, staying standing across the office from Ruben.

"Sit in your chair," I instruct.

He wraps his fists around the base of his shaft and looks like he's squeezing. I smirk, knowing he's trying to stop himself from squirting everywhere before we've even started.

When he turns his back to me, I get an amazing view of his firm, delectable butt. This man makes my mouth water and other parts of me uncomfortable.

Now that he's sitting in his office chair, I slowly walk toward him, rubbing my aching nipples. His gaze is transfixed on my fingers, while I stare at the huge erection jutting out—and proud—from a light sprinkling of hair on his groin.

When I'm standing before him, he places his hands on my hips.

I keep one hand on my breast, and with the other, I rub between my legs, coating my fingers with my excitement for him. His eyes glaze over, and I realize he's holding on by a thinner thread than I thought.

I drop to my knees and his hands move to my shoulders. As he starts caressing me, his eyes darken with lust. I caress his legs and thighs, moving my hands up from his ankles, and come to rest at his groin. His cock jerks, knowing what's coming next.

I stroke him with one finger, moving from between his legs, over his quivering balls, and up along his thick shaft to the soaked crown of his penis. Unable to resist any longer, I tilt my head toward his groin, and my tongue slips out between my lips to swirl around his head. I feel his fingers slide into my hair, gently massaging me and urging me to continue —to take him into my mouth.

I don't need to be told twice, and with one powerful suck, his penis fills my mouth to bursting. But I don't really care. All I care about is how he feels. Hard. Smooth. Pulsing. The more I swirl my tongue around his head, the more pre-cum he leaks. I pull back and let him slide out of my mouth, then lick him from tip to base, finally lapping at his balls. There is only a light sprinkling of hair around the base of his cock. His hairless balls make me want to sample them.

Dipping further between his legs, I lick and suck. When I press my tongue on a sensitive spot, I hear him hiss. I love having him at my mercy, knowing he's trying to hide his dominant nature from me. It makes me love him all the more.

Moaning, I take his balls into my mouth and massage them with my tongue. Then, I lap up the length of his penis and take it into my mouth again. He gently pumps his hips back and forth into my mouth. His hands grip the arms of the chair. As I look up, I see that he has thrown his head back, facing the ceiling. The pulse in his neck beats wildly.

Desperate for attention on my core, I spread my knees wider. For now, I imagine Ruben down there with his magic mouth, lapping and sucking my clit. Oh God, my clit is throbbing, and one touch is all it will take to send me into an orgasm.

I relax my throat, and Ruben's penis touches the back of it. This brings him up, cursing and swearing. Before I can think, he slides free of my mouth, puts me face down on his desk, spreads my legs, and puts his fingers inside me.

"Fuck! You're as turned on as I am. Look at your swollen nub! Oh, sweet Jesus."

"Ruben, fuck me... Ahhh... Oh... Umm..." He's inside me before I can finish my sentence.

"I need to go away more often if this is the welcome home I'm going to get, babe."

There are no more words as he slides his hands beneath me to cup my breasts, and then he starts pistoning in and out of me. His balls smack against my clit, sending shards of pleasure through me. I grip the table as his thrusts become harder, sharper, and more defined. He pinches my nipples, and my climax rips through me, squeezing down on his shaft. Ruben grabs my hips to keep me still as he slams into me once more, releasing white ribbons of his cum inside me. I feel his penis jerk with his release, which prolongs my orgasm.

Even with Ruben lying spent on top of me, I can feel small tremors traveling along the length of his penis. He'd started to shrink, but not anymore. Now, he's hard and pulsing inside me.

"Ah, Rosie. You're going to kill me." Ruben wraps his arms around me, stays buried inside me, lifts me up, takes two steps back, and drops into the chair.

"Umm, that felt good." When he sat down with me on his lap, the impact of my landing sent his penis

even deeper inside me. "I'm not going to be able to walk."

"You don't need to walk until I take you out for breakfast tomorrow morning. Or better yet, I'll bring you breakfast in bed." He moved my hair from my shoulder and kissed me where my neck and shoulder met—my favorite spot.

"I'm working tonight, and before you say someone will cover for me, know that I am the cover. So behave, and think about getting me naked when the club closes tonight."

He grumbles. "You can at least let me hold you for a bit longer."

"I'd like that." I love this man.

14

Ruben

Well, there's a first time for everything, like making love to Rosie in my office. If I close my eyes, I can still feel her wet heat surrounding my dick. She feels amazing and always gets me really excited. She worked me up so much that I thought I'd squirt all over my hand before I slipped inside her.

"Ruben, I'm heading upstairs to shower and change for work. Ruben, are you listening?"

"Um, what?" I mumble, barely catching the tail end of what she said. I have no idea what she's talking about.

Rosie grinned, stood in front of me, and squeezed

me through my jeans, causing a groan to slip out of my mouth.

"I think we need to go upstairs," I suggest, bending to kiss and nibble her neck.

She chuckles and pushes me away, but not before rubbing my dick again. I'm ready to get naked again. In fact, we don't even need to get undressed. We only have to unzip a few things, and we'll have access to the important parts.

"If you hadn't been lost in space, you would've heard me tell you that I'm going upstairs to shower and get ready for work. You can wait down here until I'm finished. I can't be late because Kenza will be packed and having only two people behind the bar won't work."

"In a few weeks, we're both taking time off, and I'm going to take you somewhere so I can have you to myself for the week." I wiggle my brows, making her laugh. But I can see from the glaze in her eyes that she'd like that. "Just you and me, naked, for the whole week. No clothes allowed." I grin, liking my idea more and more as I speak.

Rosie walks toward the door. Before opening it, she looks at me over her shoulder and gives me a smoldering look. She's driving me fucking crazy when I can't follow her.

"I'll go on this naked retreat on one condition." She watches me for my response, which I give with a nod. "The condition is that on the first night, I get to be in the driver's seat," she quickly blurts out, leaving me stunned.

Does she mean what I think she means? She can't...can she?

"Yes, Ruben. I'm going to lick and suck you until you come in my mouth, and then I'm going to ride you hard," she says, shooting out of my office door and slamming it behind her before my brain can catch up with my little brain, which is as hard as hell.

Grinning, I reach down and shove the band of my shorts over my dick to help keep it under control. Damn uncomfortable.

I never expected to be turned on by thoughts of someone else being in control, but damn, I am with thoughts of Rosie.

There's a bang on my office door before Simon walks in as though he owns the place. His attitude lately is pissing me off and making me wonder if he has anything to do with the problems going on here at the club. My brothers and I have thought about the possibility of Simon being the problem, but he's never given me any reason to suspect him. Shit. This problem at the club needs to stop soon because, until it does, everyone is a suspect. I'm close to doing an unexpected locker search, which I know will piss everyone off. I need to think more about it.

"A problem?" I finally ask, frowning at Simon.

"Depends on what you mean by 'problem.'" He sighs and sits down in the visitor's chair across from my desk. "The club's doing well, but there's a woman at the bar who insists on talking to you. She says you may know her in a carnal way, if you know what I mean. She says her name's Miranda.

Miranda. That name sounds familiar. Where have I heard it before? *Shit!* It's the woman I slept with and had a bad feeling about when I left. What the hell is she doing here? Rosie!

"Where's Rosie?" I jump out of my chair, grab my cell phone from my desk, and make my way to the door.

"She hasn't shown up yet."

Thank God.

"Okay. Let me find out what she wants." As I walk down the back corridor, I hope Rosie doesn't come down until I've gotten rid of Miranda. The last time she saw me with someone I'd slept with, it didn't go well.

Hunter spots me walking toward him and Miranda, and he doesn't look too happy. He breaks away from her, passes me, and says, "You better hope Rosie doesn't see her." He points over his shoulder. "She doesn't need that shoved in her face."

He walks away before I can respond. My fists clench at my sides, wanting to hit something or someone. But, in reality, he spoke the truth, and I know I need to get Miranda out of there quickly before Rosie appears.

Miranda's perfume is overpowering and unpleasant, so I take a step back to try to get rid of the stink. What the hell was I thinking when I slept with her? Well, I wasn't really thinking—or rather, I was, but with a different part of my anatomy. The hair reminds me of Rosie's. Thinking of Rosie makes me take another step back, standing behind Miranda.

I tap her on the shoulder to get her attention away from the guy she's flirting with, letting her see my impatience. "What are you doing here?"

She grinned. "Ruben, that isn't very polite, considering how well we know each other."

"We don't fucking know each other. Now answer my question." I'm practically vibrating with suppressed anger, though I'm not sure why. I'm usually a laid-back kind of guy. I only get intense around Rosie.

"Hmm. I thought we could go get coffee and chat

about your club." She reaches out and runs her finger down the front of my T-shirt. She doesn't get too far, though, as I grab her hand and hold it down at her side.

"Keep your hands to yourself."

"All I want to do is get coffee and tell you what I've overheard about your club and who I've heard is involved from your staff. But if you don't want to know, then I'll leave and won't bother you again."

Miranda turns to leave, but I grab her wrist. "Wait. I'll go with you, but it better be good."

"Oh, it is."

As I start to follow her toward the club's exit, I catch sight of Rosie talking to Hunter. She has her back to me, so hopefully she missed the discussion I just had with Miranda. However, I need to tell her that I'm going out for coffee because I'm not prepared to mess up our relationship again. I don't want any misunderstandings between us. With this in mind, I pull Miranda up short.

"I need to talk to someone first. I'll meet you across the street in five minutes."

She doesn't look happy, but I watch her exit the club before turning and walking toward Hunter and Rosie, wondering what they're talking about.

Coming up behind Rosie, I slide my arm around

her waist and pull her against me. The scent of her freshly showered hair wafts up, filling my nostrils with strawberries and my girl. Rosie is the only one who turns me on just by smelling like herself. I could stay wrapped up in her forever and never get tired of it.

She turns in my arms and wraps her arms around my neck. I notice Hunter slipping away as my hands land on her bottom. I press her against me and nuzzle her neck and hair, which she hasn't pinned up for work yet. "Ruben. What's wrong? What did that woman want?"

I freeze at her words, and all the lust I'm feeling disappears. I'd hoped she hadn't seen me talking to her, but I suppose that was too much to hope for. At least she's still holding me tight.

How the hell do I explain Miranda? Taking a deep breath, I try, "She's someone I met a while back, before we got together. For the sake of full disclosure, yes, I had sex with her once, and only once. I haven't seen her since, until she showed up here tonight. Apparently, she knows something about the trouble the club's been having, and she wants to go for coffee to discuss it. I'm going. But I promise I don't have any feelings for her whatsoever." She stays silent in my arms, and for the first time, I can't read her thoughts.

Usually, her thoughts are written all over her face, but not this time. "Rosie, please. I need to know what she knows. I have to go."

Just when I think I may have lost her, she looks up at me, smiles, and kisses me as though she's never going to get another chance. This sends blood rushing south to my already growing erection. Then, she squeezes my junk with her hand. Then, after patting my balls, she saunters away, blowing me a kiss over her shoulder. Fuck me! She really does have me by the fucking balls.

Rosie

I blow a kiss over my shoulder to Ruben and try to maintain a sultry expression so he won't notice how worried I am. I have no doubt that he told me the truth about his past with her, but I can't help feeling insecure. My relationship with Ruben is so new, and it went from zero to fifty in a very short time. He's a hot guy, and I know he attracts female attention everywhere he goes. I just need to accept that he's mine, at least for now, and hopefully for longer. The bigger question, though, is whether I trust him. Given how I grew up, I once said I'd never trust anyone again. However, Ruben has really gotten under my skin, and I trust him. I trust him to be true to me. It's difficult for me, and I'm not sure if I'll ever be able to let him use restraints. So far, though, he hasn't even hinted at using them, and he seems to get aroused quickly enough without them. Good God, he gets aroused easily, especially around me. Whenever I rub against him, he gets hard in all the right places.

My concentration is playing hell with my work tonight. He's only been gone five minutes, and I've already messed up two drink orders. I'm just about to mess up my third when a hand covers the glass and grabs the bottle of scotch in my hand.

"Jameson," Hunter reminds me.

"Shit." I snatch the bottle from Hunter and slam it back into place on the shelf before grabbing the Jameson beside it.

"Rosie, you need to concentrate. Ruben isn't going to do anything stupid to mess things up with you. Anyone can see that. So focus on what you're doing, and he'll be back before you know it."

I glared at Hunter as I over-poured the whiskey. The guy waiting had no objection, though, and threw cash on the bar before grabbing his drink.

While I'm trying to hold Hunter's gaze, I see movement just over his shoulder. Simon and that guy.

"They're back," I mouth to Hunter, who glances above my head to see their reflection in the mirror running along the top of the bar.

"Stay away from them, Rosie."

I have no intention of going near them, but I'm not sure staying away will work, considering I work here. Simon knows that the guy he's with makes me nervous, so I bet he's going to ask me for drinks again to force my hand. He's a jerk, and I really hope Hunter or Ruben find something on him soon so they can fire him.

Simon has worked here since the club opened, and I don't know why he'd turn his back on Ruben, who is the manager. Ruben pays all his staff well, and as the manager, he must make a small fortune, so why would he do something illegal? He's a greedy idiot, and I hope one of the guys gets the chance to knock some sense into him.

"Rosie? Are you listening to me? Stay the fuck away from them. If you're asked to get drinks or anything, come find me, or ask Lucien to go with you."

"I'm not deaf. I hear you."

He lets out a breath before turning and heading

off while muttering to himself. I can't help but smile at him. Watching him walk away reminds me of one of the characters from J. R. Ward's Black Dagger Brotherhood books—muscular, dark, and lethal.

"Here you go, Lucien." I put his usual whiskey on a napkin in front of him and notice how tired he looks. "You okay?"

He downs the whiskey in one gulp and stays silent while I pour him a refill.

"I've been a lot better." He takes a slower drink this time. "How are things with you? Is my brother still treating you right? What was that about with Hunter?"

He's on a roll tonight. Lucien isn't usually so talkative, unless it's about his niece or nephew, of course.

Leaning across the bar, I answer, "I'm fine. Ruben is treating me well, but Hunter told me to stay away from Simon and the guy he's drinking with. They give me the creeps."

"Rosie," he hisses. "What the fuck is going on?" He puts his hand to my mouth. "I know you're aware that something is wrong at the club, but what does Simon have to do with it? Who is Hunter? We don't know him. My brothers vouch for him, but why is he warning you away? What does he know?" He wraps his hand around mine, though I don't think he realizes it.

"Calm down. I'm not sure where Hunter's from, but he's a friend who's only looking out for me. I don't know what's really going on here, or what he knows. You'll have to ask him. All I know is that Simon and the man give me the creeps. Don't get bent out of shape over it." I pull my hand from his, pat him on the shoulder, and serve a couple more customers. Unfortunately, my peace doesn't last long.

"Rosie?"

Fuck!

"Yeah, Simon." He doesn't say anything, so I look up and meet his hard stare. He's angry about something. I take a quick glance at the guy next to him, who has a smirk on his face. I realize that all isn't well between them, and my stomach fills with dread.

"Two lattes in my office."

Bastard!

"Simon," Lucien interrupts. "I don't think I've met your guest." He holds out his hand to the guy and says, "I'm Lucien McKenzie."

The stranger hesitates before reaching out and clasping Lucien's hand. They size each other up, but I can't read the hardened look on Lucien's face. He doesn't look happy.

"Joe Abatangelo."

Within seconds, Simon is ushering Joe toward his office.

"Don't forget the coffee," he shouts over his shoulder.

"I'll take it," Lucien finally says, looking at me. "I agree with Hunter. You need to stay away from them." He rubs his neck. "Make the coffee, please, Rosie."

Ugh! What is it with men and their demands? Where the hell has Ruben gotten to? It shouldn't take this long to have a quick chat and find out what's going on. All he needs to do is be here, and he'd probably find out.

With the coffee ready, I put out a plate of cookies and signal to Lucien that they can be taken in.

I'm annoyed that someone else is doing this, but I'm also relieved that I don't have to face them. Why can't everyone else see that something is going on between the two of them? I know Hunter knows, and perhaps now Lucien does too.

"Where'd Lucien go?"

"Taking coffee to Simon's office. He insisted on meeting 'Joe Abatangelo' and suddenly decided to get on my case as well."

"You're distracting me. Stop standing like that," Hunter mumbles.

"I'm not standing like anything." My hands are on my hips as I frown at him. "You want to elaborate?"

He smirks. "Standing like that makes your shirt gape where the two missing buttons would be, giving me and everyone else a glimpse of your smooth skin and your sexy, pink, lacy bra."

I quickly hold my shirt together and say, "Hold down the bar while I go change," not giving him time to refuse.

I dash out from behind the bar and manage to get into the staff locker room without being noticed. The room isn't big, with lockers down one wall and a few benches. There are two individual shower rooms that aren't used that often, except by the female staff to change. The guys tend to wear their uniforms to work, but I prefer to change here.

As I'm about to step out of the shower room, I hear the main door bang open, followed by some shuffling. I freeze to the spot.

"What the fuck, Simon? You're not going to back out now. No fucking way."

"I didn't say I was backing out. I said we need to change the way this goes down. I don't trust Hunter. Ruben asked him to hang around the bar and keep an eye on the female staff, especially his girl. But I have a feeling that isn't the only reason he's here. Then, when Lucien brought the coffee in, he was giving off bad vibes."

My heart pounds as I hear them both. But, fuck, I'm stuck in here, and I can only pray that they won't discover where I am and that Hunter won't come looking for me. *Shit. Shit. Shit.*

"You're freaking out for no reason and you're going to give yourself away. If anyone asks how we know each other, say that I'm trying to convince you to move to New York and manage a club that I'm opening. Our story needs to be consistent. I'm leaving, and you need to go back to your office, have a drink, and stop messing everything up."

What are you going to screw up, Simon?

I hear some shuffling, and I'm sure they're in the shower room next to me.

"Mind you don't break the fucking tiles, and how the fuck doesn't the stuff get wet in there?"

"It's sealed really well. And stop getting in my space before I drop it," Simon grumbled.

Oh God! What if they plan on coming in here next? I need to leave. But how?

I take off my shoes and, without making a sound, slowly open the door and peer out, praying they're still in the other shower. When I don't see anyone, I quickly dash for the door. But as I pull it open wide enough to pass through, it makes a creaking noise. *Crap!* I'm almost home free.

I slip out and dash down the corridor, hoping I have enough time to get away. As I burst through the door into the main part of the club, I look back just in time to meet Simon's gaze.

15

Ruben

ON MY WAY BACK TO KENZA, IT STARTS RAINING. BY the time I reach the other side of the road, I'm completely soaked. Great. Just fucking great. What a shitty end to a pointless coffee with Miranda. All she wanted was to rekindle the night—or rather, the hours—I'd spent with her, but that's not happening. Even if I didn't have Rosie, nothing more would have happened with Miranda. But now Rosie's my girl, and I'm going to do everything I can to keep her.

With Rosie on my mind, I dash down the street to the front of the club to escape the rain. The front entrance is rarely used by staff or me, but I'm soaked to the bone. I hope Rosie is around so she can warm me up.

I smile as I enter the club and shake like a dog, which doesn't go over well with some of the women standing around in their skimpy outfits, taking shelter.

Grinning, I say, "Sorry, ladies," and continue into the club. I head toward the bar but don't see any sign of Rosie. Where is she? It isn't even midnight yet. Looking around the room, I spot Lucien propping up the bar at the end. I make my way over to him. He does a double take when he sees me standing beside him.

"What happened to you?" he slurs.

"It's raining. What do you think happened to me? And why are you getting drunk in my bar?" The minute the words leave my mouth, I realize that this is the first time I can remember Lucien getting drunk —or even close to it—since the accident. "Why are you getting drunk?"

"I'm not drunk yet," he replies, struggling to form his words, probably three seconds from passing out.

"You're drunk, brother, and if I have to guess, I'd say it has something to do with Lily's sexy friend."

With a sigh, I take him by the elbow. Shoving my problems to the back of my mind for now, I drag him to the back of the club, intending to take him to my apartment. But we're met by a disheveled Simon.

"What's wrong with Lucien?" he asks.

"Too much whiskey. What's going on?" Something is off. Simon never has a hair out of place, yet his hair is sticking up everywhere, his clothes are marked, and his shirt is hanging out of his slacks.

"Everything's good. There was some trouble out back, but it's been taken care of and they've left."

"You sure?"

"Yeah, I'm just going to finish some paperwork before the club closes." He walks to his office and turns back to me. "And before I forget, Rosie left. She's okay. She was just asleep on her feet, so Hunter took her home." I watch him disappear behind his closed door, wondering why Hunter took Rosie home. She seemed fine when I left for coffee. What happened between then and now?

"I think I'm drunk," Lucien whispers, reminding me that he's beside me.

My heart tells me to go after Rosie, but my head tells me to take care of my brother first. No matter what anyone tells me, I know that Hunter has eyes for Rosie, but I'm going to trust her. I also feel guilty for keeping her awake on and off during the nights. I can't get enough of her. It's odd, though, that she'd head back to her place without saying something to me. We haven't slept apart since we got together. Is something else going on? Ugh! I need to stop imagining problems when there probably aren't any.

"I think I'm going to hurl," Lucien blurts out, bringing me back to the present.

"Not out here, you're not." I quickly punch in the security code and shove him through the door.

Luckily, he makes it to the bathroom in time to pray to the porcelain gods. I leave him to it and head into the kitchen, grabbing him a bottle of water from the fridge. While I'm at it, I send Rosie a text to make sure she's okay.

"That for me?"

Lucien takes the water from my hands, takes a long gulp, and drops down onto the sofa. Shaking my head, I search a cupboard for the bottle of Tylenol, shake out two pills, and pass them to Lucien, who is nearly passed out.

It's surprising that my levelheaded brother is drunk, and it makes me wonder what happened or between him and Sabrina. We all know he's fighting an attraction toward her, and vice versa. What I can't understand is why he isn't doing anything about it. Well, I can understand it from his screwed-up way of thinking. She's a beautiful young woman, and half the time, she looks lonely, though she tries to hide it. Mom has noticed this, which is why she tries to mother Sabrina and include her in everything we do as a family.

Glancing at Lucien, who has decided to sleep on my sofa, I kick his feet, startling him. "What's going on? And don't give me shit."

"Can't you leave a guy to drown in his sorrows?"

"You're not just a guy. You're my brother, so the answer is no, I can't."

I sit down opposite him in my recliner and hold his glare. I keep my sigh of relief to myself when I see him give in.

"She's on a date." He sits up, leans forward, and rests his arms on his thighs. This gives me a minute to take in what he just said.

I'm surprised because I thought they were gradually getting to the point where something would happen between them. I knew the possibility of someone else coming along for Sabrina was high if my brother didn't make a move.

"She looked hot, sexy, beautiful," he whispers, covering his face with his hands. "I watched her meet him at the restaurant. He kissed her, and she let him." He leans back into the cushions, resting his head on the back of the sofa with his eyes closed. "I've never felt like this about anyone before. Seeing her with someone else is killing me. I can't have her, so it isn't fair to expect her to stay alone. But it's eating away at me."

He keeps saying that, using it as an excuse. "Why can't you have her?"

His eyes snap open. "Look at me." He holds his arms out to the side, leaving himself open.

"I am you, bastard," I reply, feeling my anger start to build. "Stop using your scars as an excuse. I've seen the way she looks at you when you aren't looking, and I'm telling you, she doesn't give a damn about them. She sees you. The way you think is starting to really piss me off. What are you afraid of? Tell me." He's frustrating the hell out of me.

"I can't give her what she needs. What any woman needs from a man," he says so quietly that it takes me a minute to realize what he said. But I'm confused.

What the hell is he talking about?

"What? I don't understand. Explain it to me?"

"Fuck! Are you really going to make me say it out loud?" He wiped his hand down his face in a weary gesture. "I can't get an erection."

I just stare at him. "What?"

"Fucking hell, Ruben. I can't get an erection." All the anger drained from him as his words hit me.

"Since when?"

"The fire."

He left me stunned. None of us had any idea that this was the reason he'd stopped dating. We all just assumed his scars were what he was hiding. How wrong we were! I honestly don't know what to say to him. I can't imagine going years without having an orgasm, yet he's done just that.

"Well, that shut you up," he observes.

"I don't know what to say. I mean, are you sure?" I ask, then start to laugh. "Sorry, of course you are."

The doctor said he's eighty percent positive that I'll always be like this from now on. But..."

"But what?" I ask, but he cuts me off mid-speech.

"It doesn't matter."

"Like hell! Spit it out, Lucien."

Oh, this is going to be good—he's blushing! "Sometimes around Sabrina, I, well, you know." He sighs.

I chuckle and ask, "Know what?" refusing to let him off the hook.

"Jesus Christ... I get aroused. I feel something in my dead dick. Okay, happy now?"

Not wanting to delve further into my brother's problem, I stop asking questions, holding back my laughter. God knows what other things he'll reveal.

Shuddering at the thought, I remember to check my phone for a reply from Rosie. I could use hearing her voice, but I won't talk to her without privacy.

Lucien's breathing has evened out, and he looks like he's gone back to sleep, so I pick up my phone from the table and read Rosie's message. She says she's fine, in bed, and about to go to sleep. She'll see me in the morning, once she's fully rested.

I'm not happy about sleeping alone tonight, but I suppose she thinks she'll sleep better if she's alone at her place. Tomorrow, I'm going to show her that I can leave her alone when she needs rest. She's my woman, and I don't like her thinking otherwise.

As I hold my phone, it starts to vibrate with an incoming call. For a split second, my heart accelerates, only to thud in disappointment when I see Ramon's name flashing on the screen.

"What do you want at this time?" I grumble into the phone and quickly move to the kitchen so I don't wake Lucien. He's slumped over so deeply that a train could probably run through the apartment and he wouldn't wake up.

I pour myself a glass of water as Ramon asks, "Have you seen Lucien? I'm supposed to be his ride home."

"He's passed out on my sofa. Head home, and I'll

get him tomorrow," I say, rubbing my temples as a headache is starting.

I shake out two more Tylenol, this time for myself, and knock them back with the cold water. I drain the glass, not realizing how thirsty I am. It's the damn latte they make across the street. I'm sure they add salt or something. I really need to stop going there.

"Okay." He hesitates, as though he wants to say something else. "I think something went down tonight."

"Say that again?"

"I said—"

"Never mind," I cut him off. "I heard you. But what do you think happened?"

My head pounds as I back up into a chair and sit down. I need sleep, and I need this shit to stop at Kenza.

"I overheard two guys talking while I was taking a leak, and they'd just scored some 'brown sugar.' You know what that is, right?"

"Are you fucking me? Of course I know what brown sugar is." I try to calm down because getting pissed at Ramon isn't going to help. "Did you hear them say where they got it?"

"Yeah, I did. In fact, you already know."

"Fucking hell." I slam my fist on the table beside me. "Who the hell is doing this?"

"Someone who works at the club. I didn't catch their name or gender. They left. That's all I know. Look, I'll be around with breakfast first thing tomorrow, and we can hash out a plan then, okay?"

"I'll see you then." I hung up the call, wanting to go downstairs and find the staff responsible for this.

When I find out who's behind this, I'm going to have the last laugh. They'll be behind bars, and their fucked-up operation at my club will be over.

Rosie

I'm really not sure how Ruben will take the fact that I spent the night in Hunter's hotel room. Nothing happened, and I didn't expect anything to. However, after he saw the look on my face when I returned to the club, he made me tell him what had happened. As soon as I did, he took me on his bike to his hotel room before I could say anything else.

He's more like a big brother to me than anything, and last night, he held me while I slept. It should have felt awkward, but it made me feel safe. He made me feel safe.

At first, Hunter suggested we report what I'd seen to the police, a friend of his, but I wasn't too keen on the idea. Then they'd know I was responsible, and I was afraid they'd come after me. I told Hunter what I heard in the locker room. He thinks it will be sealed up by now because Simon knows I saw or heard them. Still, he'll check it out and keep an eye on Simon now that he has more information. Hopefully, they'll catch him red-handed so they won't need me. I can hope anyway.

Against my better judgment and Hunter's advice, I'm heading to Kenza this morning to talk to Ruben. I need to tell him what I saw last night and explain why I can't be around the club anymore until the trouble is gone. I practically quiver in my boots at the thought of bumping into Simon again. However, it's where Ruben lives, and he isn't answering his phone, so I don't have much of a choice. I sigh in relief, though, when I spot Hunter's bike parked against the wall outside the back doors of the club.

After taking a deep breath, I open the club doors, and, for the first time ever, I'm met with silence. What's going on? Usually, the cleaning crew is in by this time, and the humming of the floor buffer would hit me the minute I stepped inside. But not today. Today, I'm greeted by silence, which worries me.

As I move toward Ruben's office, I hear muffled voices through his door. It sounds like there is some sort of meeting going on. I can't make out their words, but if I'm not mistaken, Lucien and maybe Ramon are in there.

Instead of pussyfooting around outside the door, I need to go in there before I run into Simon. On that note, I raise my hand and knock on the door rather than barging in, which is what I would normally do.

"Come in," Ruben roars, making me practically jump out of my skin. He doesn't sound like he's in a good mood today. Hopefully, it isn't because I left the way I did last night.

I push the door open, but the smile on my face slowly fades when I meet the anger in Ruben's eyes. The room is quiet, with Ramon leaning against the back wall and Lucien slouched in one of the chairs opposite his brother's desk. He doesn't look too good.

"Um," I say, swallowing, which is difficult because my mouth is as dry as sandpaper. "I can come back later."

I need to find Hunter. Surely he hasn't told Ruben where I spent last night. It was completely innocent.

As I start to back away from him, he jumps up and

shouts, "No!" startling me. I freeze with my hand on the doorknob.

"This is about you. I want answers," Ruben states.

I frown and meet his gaze, and my heart starts to shatter. All I see behind his eyes is anger, nothing more or less. I haven't done anything to warrant that look. My thought process has shut down. I don't know what he wants me to say or do.

"Why, Rosie? Did they tell you to distract me by sleeping with me?" He snarls.

"What?"

"I don't know—" He cuts me off.

"Oh, come on," he says, standing up and walking around his desk. He clenches his fists and whispers into my ear, "We know."

His cologne wraps around me, and all I want to do is wrap myself around him. I hold on until he tells me it's all a joke.

"We found the sugar, Rosie," Ramon tells me.

"Sugar? What sugar? I have no idea what you're talking about."

I reach out to Ruben, sliding my fingers between the buttons of his shirt, but he abruptly knocks my hand away. "Don't touch me," he snaps, walking back behind his desk, out of reach.

My wrist starts to throb from how roughly he

pushed me away, so I cradle it against my chest with my other hand. That's when I catch a glimpse of my Ruben—the flick of concern in his eyes. It doesn't last, though.

I'm starting to get angry myself. I have no idea what this is about. I have no idea what "sugar" is supposed to mean. This is ridiculous. My emotions are all over the place right now. I feel like a child who wants to stamp her feet.

"Okay," I start. "For some reason, you all think I know what you're talking about. But newsflash. I don't have a fucking clue. It's obvious that you're accusing me of 'fucking you' just to distract you. You know me better than anyone, so to say that..." That comment really hurt me, so I take a few seconds to pull myself together. "And what the hell is 'sugar?'"

I swipe at the tears that escaped and wait for one of them to answer, directing the question at all of them.

"Rosie," Lucien says. "We did a locker search this morning, and we found a small bag of heroin inside yours. Sugar or brown sugar. It was stuffed inside the toe of one of your sneakers."

I gasp in shock. How the hell? Slumping against the door, I try to process what Lucien has just told me. I've never done drugs, and being accused of this by the man I love is more than I can take.

The tears I've tried to hide flow down my face as I watch Ruben watching me.

"Why, Rosie?" he asks, resting his arms on the back of his chair.

I shake my head and keep my mouth closed. Why waste my breath? He already thinks I'm guilty, so nothing I say will change his mind. It's all because Simon knows I overheard what was going on last night. He's the one who's guilty, and he's the one who put the drugs in my sneakers. He's the manager, so he has access to the pass keys. Why can't they see that?

Ruben is standing in front of me, looking disgusted, as my tears continue to flow. "I can't look at you anymore. Here's your stuff." He thrusts a bag at me, which I grab with my good hand. I sling it over my shoulder, and shock seeps through my body. I stare at him numbly as he continues, "I never want to see you again. I haven't called the cops yet, but I will."

This isn't a joke. The man I love—loved—has just torn my heart to shreds.

"Go. Get out," he said in a hard voice.

As I fumble with the doorknob, Ramon asks, "Do you have anything to say, Rosie, before you leave?"

I have the door open now. Hunter is looming over

me with a concerned expression, but when he spots the three McKenzies in the room behind me, his features tighten, and he suddenly looks like a gladiator ready for battle.

Before he can do or say anything, I place my uninjured hand on his chest and turn to face the room. "Yes, I have something to say," I say, trying to slow my breathing in hopes that it will stop the flow of my tears enough for me to see. "You all know me. I've been treated as part of your family. I thought I loved you, Ruben. What hurts the most is that not one of you bothered to ask me if I was guilty. You all just assumed."

I step out of the room and into Hunter's arms, letting the door slam shut behind me as I cry on Hunter.

"Fuck," he curses, picking me up into his arms. "What the hell happened back there?" he asks, kicking the back door open.

"They found 'sugar' in my sneaker, which was in my locker." He placed me on the back of his bike. "I didn't know what it was, but they spelled it out for me." I hiccup. "Hunter, I swear I—" He covers my mouth with his hand.

"I know you had nothing to do with that. I would have known that even if you hadn't told me what happened last night." He puts a helmet on my head and fastens it. "Ruben's a bastard for doing that to you. Once I've taken care of you, I'm going to have words with him. There are a few things he needs to know."

"I don't really care what happens, but can you take me back to the hotel? I don't want Liz or Ed to see me like this."

Without Hunter, I'm not sure what I would have done. It's been so long since I've had someone to rely on in times of need. I thought I'd always have Ruben by my side, that he'd always be there for me, to kiss away my worries. But not anymore.

On the way back to the hotel, I cried silently while clinging to Hunter. I hope I'm not cramping his bachelor status by staying here with him. Contrary to what he may think, I'm not blind to the glares we get as we walk through the lobby. He shrugs it off. The life of a true bachelor. Love 'em and leave 'em.

"Forget it. I wouldn't touch one of them if you paid me. They aren't impressed with you because I've always rejected them."

He pulls me back toward his chest. "Rosie, I'm not going to let anyone hurt you, okay? I need you to know that. I'm not going to defend Ruben because what he did was wrong. But one thing I will say is that deep down, he knows you aren't guilty. He's using this excuse because you have him running scared." He brushes his fingers through my ponytail. "I bet the bachelor who is always used to being free has suddenly realized he can't act like he used to."

I shake my head. "No, he told me he was going for it with me, and he was tired of pretending he didn't want to be with me. Thanks for trying to make this easier, but the fact is, his heart wasn't involved with me like mine was with him." As Hunter goes to say something else, I stop him. "Can we please talk about something else, or nothing? In fact, I could use a rest. I didn't sleep well last night, and with everything that happened this morning, I'm exhausted."

"That's good," Hunter says, ushering me toward his room. "Because I want to leave you here for a bit."

He's going back to Kenza.

"What are you going to do? Please don't get in any trouble."

"I won't. I promise," he says, kissing me on the nose. "Get some rest. I'll bring food in a couple of hours." Then he notices my wrist. "What happened?"

"I grabbed for Ruben, and he knocked me out of the way." I'll take some Tylenol and go to sleep. I'll be fine. Don't worry."

"Okay, if you're sure."

"I am."

I leave him checking his computer and head to the bathroom. When I'm done, I kick off my boots and climb into bed. Hunter comes over and tucks me in. At least he makes me grin.

"That's better. Now, get some sleep, and don't worry about anything."

I watch him leave and pray that he won't get arrested on my behalf.

16

Ruben

"WHAT THE HELL HAVE WE DONE?" LUCIEN MUMBLES from behind his hands, his face buried in them. "There must have been another way to go about this. That was brutal. Did you see her face? She's not even my girl, but I still wanted to pull her into my arms and tell her the truth."

Since Rosie left, I've wanted to find Simon and beat the shit out of him. I trusted him. I gave him a job when no one else would, and he betrayed me. He stabbed me in the back.

After Hunter called me last night and told me everything that had happened, I wanted to grab my keys and go to Rosie. But Hunter had a better plan.

It's one that I'm still having trouble dealing with. It took him a while to convince me that the plan would work.

Seeing Rosie looking so heartbroken has torn me in two. It feels like my heart has been ripped out of my chest. And her wrist. I was angry that I had to do this to protect her. I never meant to hurt her, physically, that is. I intended to make her hate me so she'd leave and stay away from all of us until this is over. But seeing that I'd hurt her nearly made me cave and take her into my arms and show her how much I love her. Because I do love her. She has my heart, even though I just crushed hers. Hunter promised to look after her and keep her safe, and he better do that.

"I need a drink," I say to the room in general.

"It's not even noon," Ramon informs me.

"Yeah, well, it's not every day I get to crush the woman I love, is it?"

Hunter walks through the door. "She's sleeping. What the hell did you do to her wrist?"

I drop into my seat and bury my head in my hands. I'm not cut out for this.

"How is she? I know you said she's sleeping."

"She's doing about as well as you'd expect. She has a broken heart and a swollen wrist."

"Fuck! I knocked her hand away. Please tell me it

isn't broken." I couldn't bear to have hurt her that badly. Hurting her enough to cause her wrist to swell is killing me, but hurting her enough to break a bone would be too much.

"It isn't. Probably sprained." Hunter sits in the chair next to Ramon. "I have a friend keeping an eye on the hotel. She's safe for now. Have you called Simon?"

"Not yet."

Calling Simon will set the whole thing in motion, and I hope it won't backfire. Hopefully, Simon and his friends will show up at the club now that Rosie isn't around. Then, I can tell Rosie that I never believed she had anything to do with drugs. Hopefully, I'll get the chance to tell her that when we found the drugs in the locker, none of us believed she was responsible. We decided to use that as an excuse to try to keep her safe. We hoped we'd catch Simon with his guard down.

"You need to do it now. Just like we agreed," Hunter said, sitting back and looking relaxed. His right ankle rested on his left knee, and his hands were behind his head. He's trying to look relaxed, but he's not quite pulling it off.

"I'll do it." I might as well get it over with, although it makes me sick to my stomach. "You promise me that Rosie has someone looking out for her." I point to Hunter.

He sighs. "Look, I like Rosie, so there's no way I'd leave her at the hotel alone without someone keeping an eye on things. Just make the fucking call. The sooner you do this, the sooner it'll be over, and you can go get your girl."

"I'm going into the bar to see if I can rustle up some coffee," Lucien says, standing and stretching. "You can come with me," he adds, looking at Ramon.

"What are we, a bunch of girls who have to go in pairs?" Ramon mumbles, following Lucien out the door.

"Ruben."

"Fuck! I'm on it." I pick up my cell and find Simon in my contacts. I dial him, half hoping he won't pick up.

"Ruben," he answers.

There goes that wish.

"I've fired Rosie."

"What?"

"I did a locker search this morning and found drugs hidden in her sneakers. I trusted her, and she betrayed me and the club." I spit out the words, wanting to reach through the phone and strangle him. But, catching the shift in Hunter, I continue, "I wanted to let you know before you came down here. I also don't trust Hunter, so watch out for him. It wouldn't surprise me if he had something to do with all this. Maybe he's the one who got Rosie involved."

My anger flares up again as I talk to him on the phone. He stays silent while I tell him everything we want him to know. Hopefully, we can keep Rosie safe at the hotel while some of Hunter's friends come to the club tonight to try to find the guy supplying Simon. He's the man responsible for all the shit going on at Kenza, and, from what Hunter has told me, at other clubs around the area and even out of state.

"I'll be there in a couple of hours. I've got some errands to run. Thanks for letting me know." He hangs up.

I throw my phone across the room and watch it hit the steel bar running from one side of the room to the other before shattering.

Does that make me feel better? Hell no!

"What now?" I ask Hunter, who has gone across the room to retrieve my broken phone.

"That was a good idea," he says, his voice thick with sarcasm.

I ignore him and start pacing behind my desk. Not being with my girl at the hotel is making me anxious. She's there, and from what Hunter told me, Joe

Abatangelo isn't someone to mess with. If this back-fires and they stay away from the club and go after Rosie instead, I'm not sure what I'll do.

Hunter thinks they'll ignore Rosie for now, thinking she's out of the way. What I don't think he's telling me is that they'll eventually go after her. Joe isn't someone to mess with, and he won't leave any loose ends. That's why a friend of Hunter's is babysitting Rosie at the hotel, just in case we've underestimated them and they show up there first, having tracked her down. The more I think about her, the tighter my fists clench.

They need more evidence than what Rosie witnessed to arrest and charge them with drug-related offenses. Fuck! I need to be with her. I should let Hunter and my brothers deal with the problem here, but I can't. It's my club, so it's my problem.

Screw this! I grab my keys from the desk drawer, tell Hunter, "I'm leaving," and make the decision to go to her.

He sighs and follows me out of my office and through the club to the back, where our cars are parked.

"What do you intend to do when you get there?" Hunter asks, grabbing my arm.

"I'm not letting anyone get near her. I shouldn't

have listened to you in the first place. If anything happens to her because of me." I shake my head, unable to continue. "I love her."

I turn away, not wanting him to see the emotion I'm trying to hide. This is so screwed up.

"What's your friend going to do to prevent anyone from getting to Rosie?" I ask Hunter, catching sight of Lucien and Ramon walking toward us.

"You can't go in there and mess everything up. She's going to be pissed when she finds out you lied to protect her. The fact that we have someone watching her isn't going to go over well either. I know the guy watching Rosie. He won't let anything happen to her. He'll do whatever he's trained to do to protect her. I wouldn't have left her there if I didn't trust him."

"There isn't anything wrong with going to 'observe,' is there?" I open the door to my SUV, jump in, and start the engine.

"This is a bad idea," Hunter mumbles before jumping into the back with Ramon. "But you're not going without me."

"As long as you keep your hands off my girl, we'll be cool."

"We're seriously not doing this again. *You're* like a fucking girl."

I let Hunter's comment slide, as well as the fact that my brothers seem to be enjoying themselves at my expense. On any other day, I would have shut him up, but I can't think about anything else until I have my girl in my arms.

The drive to the hotel should only take five minutes, but fifteen minutes later, we're still crawling in traffic. This is ridiculous.

"Cut down the side street when you can," Ramon offers.

"You sure about that?"

"Totally."

When there's a break in traffic, I turn down the street, following a couple of cars that have had the same idea. Eventually, we arrive at the back of the hotel. After reversing into a parking spot, we sit in silence for a few minutes.

"Well, Sherlock, what's the plan?"

I glare at Lucien.

I really want to rush up to Rosie's room and beg for forgiveness after explaining why I treated her the way I did. But, as much as I want to do that, I don't want to mess up the operation.

"Hunter, call your friend." I turn to look at him. "I need to know she's okay."

"I can do that."

Within seconds, he puts his phone to his ear, says one word—"Julian"—and stays silent.

The man is like a robot. No emotion shows on his face, so I can't tell if my girl is okay.

Hunter finally hangs up and glances through the window without saying a word.

Something's gone wrong. Either that, or he's trying to piss me off. And succeeding.

He climbs out of the car and opens my door. "Simon's in the room with her."

What the fuck?!

He stands back and lets me exit, but I block his way. "What is going on?"

"My contact."

"Julian," I interrupt, and Hunter confirms with a nod.

"Julian is monitoring the conversation. Simon hasn't harmed her."

"Yet," I roar, pushing him up against the wall with my arm covering his windpipe. "You said she would be safe."

"Ruben, this isn't helping," Ramon says as Lucian helps him pull me off Hunter.

"You need to get your shit together, and then we'll go inside. Julian is in the room next to mine, and there's an interconnecting door."

I shake my brothers off and, ignoring everyone, run toward the back entrance of the hotel, needing to get close to her. I'm not going to mess this up, but if it sounds like he's hurting her, then everyone can go to hell and all bets are off. I'll get my girl.

Rosie

My head is pounding, and it pounds harder the more Simon sits in the corner, glaring at me and hardly saying anything.

I cried myself to sleep and woke up suddenly when Simon shook the bed. He had a passkey for the room, which he showed me once I'd woken up enough to realize that this wasn't a dream, but rather a nightmare.

Not only did Ruben throw me away, but I also got the bastard who set me up, and there's no help coming from any direction.

I grabbed my phone and cradled it to my chest before falling asleep, hoping Ruben would call me. But he never did.

After I got over the shock of being woken up so

abruptly, I remembered my phone was still under the covers. Ruben is on speed dial three, so I felt my way to the volume button, keeping my finger pressed on the minus button and hoping the volume was going down. I press three for a few seconds before releasing the button.

I love Ruben. Even after everything he said to me. I still love him. I'm not even sure he'll accept the call if he sees it's from me. That thought breaks my heart all over again.

"He isn't coming," Simon sneers. "He believes you're the guilty party. The one thing Ruben hates is drugs. So it's a pretty good setup, if you ask me. It was Joe's idea, mind you, but I chose the sneaker. I honestly thought it would all backfire. I thought Ruben wouldn't believe the evidence in front of him, but he did. It says a lot about how he feels about you."

I swipe at the tears sliding down my face and glare at him. "I don't give a shit anymore, Simon. People like you always get found out. Whether it's today or tomorrow, the cops aren't stupid, and they'll figure it out. In fact, there's already someone at Kenza who's on to you, and I know they'll come after me, regardless of what Ruben chooses to do."

Ruben may have turned his back on me, but I know for sure that Hunter won't. I just wish he had stayed with me so that I wouldn't be alone with Simon.

Simon has always been a bit weird, but never like this. He frightens me with the knife he keeps sliding up and down his jean-covered thigh. Every time I move, he stops and slowly points the knife at me. I'm grateful that he hasn't bothered to tie me up yet, but that's as far as my gratitude goes.

I know he'll use the knife. If you'd asked me last week if I thought he was capable of stabbing some-one, I'd have said no. He was odd, but not life-threat-ening. Now, it's as though a switch has been turned on, and I believe he's capable of anything—and that is the most frightening thing of all.

I'm sitting with my knees drawn up in front of me, wrapped in my arms, with my head resting on top of them. I'm not sure what we're waiting for, nor do I know why he's just glaring at me. I hope Hunter returns before Simon takes me out of here because I have no doubt that's his intention.

"You mean Hunter?"

My head shoots up, and I meet his stare.

"Oh, I know Hunter and Ruben are all up in my business, but my tracks are covered. There isn't anything left to find, thanks to the little distraction I arranged for Ruben with Miranda. My girl is damn good." He laughs. "You're just going to hang out here with me until Hunter returns. Then you two are coming with me."

There's no way Simon can get one over on Hunter. Hunter is much stronger than him. What isn't he telling me?

I frown.

"Oh, don't worry that pretty little face." He jumps up from the chair and pins me against the bed. He pushes me into the mattress with the weight of his body. His aroused body. I struggle to get a knee up to hurt him in the groin, but his legs pin me down, and his hands hold my wrists above my head.

My heart pounds in my chest as I struggle to get free. I feel my skin go cold and feverish. I can handle almost anything, but being handcuffed is something I'll never be able to handle well.

Simon moves one hand to my waist, slowly creeping it up inside my shirt and tank top until it comes to a stop over my left breast.

"No bra." He presses his erection against my hip. The solid length is more swollen than it was a few minutes ago. "I like a woman who doesn't wear underwear." He squeezes my breast as I squeeze my eyes shut, not wanting to see him. I wish I couldn't feel him.

"Are you wearing panties?" He nibbles my neck while his hand slides down my body.

I shudder in fear.

He straddles my legs, pinning me to the bed, and starts undoing my jeans. "No." I thrash around as much as I can, but I'm not strong enough to get him off me. "You bastard! Don't touch me! Get off!"

As I open my mouth to scream, he quickly reaches behind his back, bringing the knife to my face. He presses the cold tip into my cheek.

I whimper.

"Shut the fuck up! You sound like a wounded fucking animal. I haven't even started with you yet."

He drags the knife down the side of my face. It hurts so badly. He hasn't cut deep, but it stings. Then, he licks the cut he just made. My face stings, and my tears overflow, making my face hurt even more.

He lifts off of me and moves back to the chair, so I scramble back into the headboard. Grabbing a pillow, I take the case off and hold it to my face, quietly weeping into it.

If Ruben had answered my call, he would have been here by now. He isn't coming. He really doesn't care what happens to me. I always end up with someone who doesn't give a damn. My parents didn't, and neither did the few boyfriends I've had. They were only interested in getting into my panties. Liz and Ed will miss me if I don't get out of this mess. Hunter is my only hope.

Simon said we're waiting for Hunter, but how does he plan to subdue him? Hunter isn't the kind of guy who will go down easily without a fight.

As I watch him, his lip curls in a snarl, and he brings a nasty-looking gun up out of his boot. He rubs the barrel against his thigh, slowly dragging it against his groin and straining erection.

He's sick, and watching him play with the gun—which is obviously getting him more worked up—I realize that I probably don't know just how sick he is. Who gets turned on by playing with a gun? Especially around where he's playing with it?

"It has a silencer," he whispers. "As soon as Hunter walks into his room, I'll point the gun—Bang! Bang! —No more Hunter. No more getting into my business."

I'm sure the shock is evident on my face. "You're going to rot in jail."

He laughs. "No chance of that, little Rosie. I have plans. Big plans. And I'm beginning to think they could include you. I can see you in a string bikini, rubbing oil all over my body. Every inch of it." He rubs his crotch again.

"I'm going to hurl if you don't stop talking and rubbing that thing in your pants."

He grins.

This isn't good.

"I'm hard knowing you don't have any underwear on. Knowing there's only a thin scrap of material between your pussy and my cock. Hmmm," he moans, pressing his hand against himself. "I'm imagining your wet pussy sucking me inside you. Delicious."

17

Ruben

"Enough," I say, trying not to shout. The longer I'm in the room next to Rosie, listening to that sick bastard with her, the more I itch to bust through the door and kill him. "We have to get her out of there," I say, pacing back and forth. "This is wrong. You've heard him talking. He's going to rape her unless we do something. To hell with getting evidence. Get it some other way. You're not using my girl anymore." I walk toward the interconnecting door, not quite sure what I'm doing. I have no weapon, and we know he has at least a knife and a gun. All I know is that I can't leave her with him any longer.

When we walked in, Hunter's friend Julian had to hold me back when I heard Simon talking about her lack of underwear.

For once, Hunter looks undecided. Up until now, he's been determined to get Abatangelo, but now, I can see in his eyes that he's worried about Rosie. About what the bastard in there is capable of.

I clench my fists at my sides and tell them what's going to happen, "I'm going in there to get my girl. You can sit here and pretend nothing is happening next door, or you can help me. But there is no way I'm staying here any longer, letting him put his hands on her."

"We'll help. I'll cause a distraction by going in through the door to the room. After all, he's expecting me to come from that direction. What he won't be expecting is for anyone to come through there." He points to the interconnecting door. "Julian will go through. You and your brothers need to stay put and let us bring Simon down first. You'll be no use to Rosie if you get shot—or worse."

I nod my head, not really liking his idea but knowing he's right. I drop down onto the bed and put my face in my hands.

"She'll be fine," Lucien says, sitting down beside

me. He reaches up and massages the back of my neck, showing brotherly love and support.

"Julian, as soon as you hear my key in the lock, count to five, then join the party."

"Got you."

I lift my head and watch them both arm themselves to the teeth. Then, Hunter starts to slip out through the door, but Julian stops him. "Let me check his position."

He plugs a wire into his laptop, pushes the end slightly through the keyhole, and part of the next-door room appears on the monitor.

If he had this all along, why wasn't he using it?

"It wasn't a good idea to use it before," Julian says, clearly reading my thoughts. "You would have charged in without regard for your safety."

I run my hand through my hair and admit, "You're right."

"He's sitting in the chair in the corner of the room with the bed against the wall. I can't see Rosie." He removes the feed. "But, from listening to them, I'm going to assume she's on the bed. Maybe against the headboard. I'm not going to push the wire through any further in case he sees it."

"Okay, I'm going in." Hunter leaves the room.

"Trust him," Julian says, taking hold of the door-knob with one hand and brandishing a gun with the other.

Lucien, Ramon, and I stand near the entrance to the room, out of the line of fire.

My stomach turns, and my heart is in my mouth while I wait. I won't consider the possibility that Rosie won't want me with her. I broke her heart earlier, so my only hope is that she'll listen to my explanation and understand that I didn't mean for her to get hurt. Someone was watching the room. I'm not sure how Simon slipped inside with her, but I'll find out when this is over.

I'm abruptly brought back to the present when all hell breaks loose.

Hunter and Julian have opened the doors and entered the room. I hear someone shout, "He's down!" at the same time I hear Rosie start screaming, which gets me moving.

Shoving my way into the room, I quickly see that Hunter and Julian have Simon under control. I whip my head to the side and see Rosie crouched up against the headboard, covered in blood.

What the fuck?!

"Rosie," I whisper, slowly crawling onto the bed

toward her. I don't want to scare her, but I also need to hold her. I need to make sure she isn't seriously injured. "Rosie, please look at me."

She slowly lifts her head, and within seconds of our eyes meeting, she throws herself into my arms and wraps herself around me. If it weren't for Ramon behind me, I would have fallen off the bed from the force of her body coming into contact with mine.

"I thought you hated me," she sobs into my neck, trying to climb onto my lap, breaking my heart.

"Is she okay?" Hunter asks.

"She will be," I reply before whispering to Rosie, "I could never hate you. Hang on, baby." Holding her tightly, I back away from the bed, carry her into the other room, and try to put her on the bed, but she clings to me.

"No, don't leave me." She starts to shiver in reaction to what's been going on in the other room.

Lucien drapes a blanket from the closet around her shoulders.

"I'm not leaving you. I'm never leaving you again." He sits in the chair and lets her curl up in his lap. "But I need to make sure you're not in pain anywhere. Please, Rosie. Please let me check you out. There was a lot of blood on the pillowcase."

She shakes her head against me. "It's okay. I think it's stopped bleeding, but it stings a bit." I raise her head and brush the hair back from her face to see the cut. It starts beside her eye and travels down her jaw. The bastards hurt her. Marked her.

"I'll kill him." I start to rise.

"No, he isn't worth it," Rosie whispers.

"He did this to you because of me."

"This isn't your fault, Ruben." She rests her head against my chest. "I'm just glad you're here, although I'm not sure what to make of it, considering what you said to me at the club."

I knew I'd have to explain myself, but I'm conscious of my brothers hovering in the background and the movements from next door.

Sighing, I tell her the truth, "I knew from the moment we found the stuff in your sneaker that you'd been set up. Hunter convinced me to blame you, to push you away from Kenza and me, so you'd hopefully be safe. He thought that, since Simon had seen you running from the restroom while he was in there with Joe, he might leave you alone temporarily and slip up at the club somehow. Obviously, that didn't work out too well." I leaned forward and pressed my lips to hers in a gentle kiss. "It broke my heart doing that to you. I wanted to do it in private, but Hunter thought I'd mess up and tell you the truth.

"He'd have done that all right," Ramon comments.

"Haven't you two got something better to do?"

"No," they reply together. "Nothing's more important right now than making sure you and Rosie are okay."

Well, hell!

I turn back to my girl. "I love you. I promise I won't ever lie to you again. I promise." I see the shock on her face slowly turn into a grin. But then she flinches in pain and reaches up to press her palm against her face.

"Nice going, brother. Just blurt it out! Whatever happened to romance?"

"Let me find something for your face," Ramon comments, rooting through one of the knapsacks thrown on the floor.

"You know, arranging a nice meal by candlelight and all that," he continues. He pulls out a medical kit and walks back toward us. "Let me see your face."

Rosie turns to face him as I wrap my arms around her waist to keep her close. "She can have anything she wants as soon as we leave here. Just hurry up and sort her out."

"This is going to sting," he tells her before dabbing the antiseptic wipe along the cut.

She hisses through her teeth. "Ouch! That hurts."

"Sorry, but you don't want it to get infected. I'm going to cover it up. I'm just not sure what to use, though. It's in an awkward place." He roots through the medical kit but comes up empty.

"It's okay. I'll be fine. I just want to go home."

"It needs covering," Julian informs us. "I'll do it."

Rosie pushes back against me. "Who are you?"

He smiles and holds out his hand. "I'm Julian O'Reilly, ma'am. U.S. Marine."

She places her hand in his and says, "Thank you for saving me."

"All in a day's work." Releasing her hand, he crouches down in front of us. "Now, let's get something on that so you can get going."

"Hunter?" she asks.

"Hunter's fine, but he's going to have to stay here and sort this mess out, so don't expect to see him anytime soon. The paramedics and the cops are on the way." He places strips of gauze that he has just cut onto Rosie's face and tapes them into place. "That should hold you, but go get a shot just to be safe." He stands up and quickly packs his things. "I need to get going before the cops show up. I'm not supposed to be here."

"Okay. Thanks for everything." I shake his hand, then wrap Rosie back up in my arms. I watch him quickly shake my brothers' hands before exiting the room.

"How are you feeling, babe?" I whisper into her ear, feeling her shudder in my arms. I tighten my hold on her.

"Exhausted." She turns so that our lips are mere inches apart. "Will you take me back to your place? I just want to be with you." Her eyes fill with tears. "I need you to hold me and never let me go."

"I can do that." She has me all choked up. I don't deserve her forgiveness for what I said and did to her. But, based on what she's saying, it sounds like she forgives me. I just hope I'm not being wishful thinking.

Rosie

"Ruben, please stop," I snap, unintentionally, but he really is becoming annoying. He pauses beside me, so

I take his hand and apologize. "I'm sorry. My face doesn't hurt anymore, and I'm okay otherwise." I pull him down to sit on the bed. I've been sitting on this bed since he brought me back to his place six hours ago. "Since I woke up, you've done nothing but fuss over me. You've been going back and forth the whole time, when all I want is for you to lie next to me and hold me."

He turns, climbs over me, and spoons in close. He holds me tight, buries his face in my hair, and inhales, shuddering when he exhales. "I didn't think I'd get this chance again—to hold you in my arms. Not because something would happen to you, but because of what I said to push you away. God, that just about killed me. Do you…do you forgive me?"

Wanting him to see my face when I answer, I struggle to turn over. As soon as I do, though, I snuggle into him again. "Yes, I forgive you. You broke my heart because I thought everything was real, not just an act." I lean in and kiss him. "I love you, Ruben. That hasn't changed."

"While you've been asleep since I brought you home, I've hoped that you really did forgive me. I'd hoped even more after Hunter called with your cell, which he found in the room. He told me that you tried to call me while you were in the room with Simon."

"Didn't your phone ring?" I ask, slipping my hand inside the back of his sweater to stroke the skin there. Unable to behave, I slip my hand into the back of his jeans.

"Rosie," he growls. "I can't think with your hands on my ass. What did you ask? Oh, cell. It broke. I threw it across the office after you left."

"Hmmm," I hum into his ear, sending goosebumps over his skin. In turn, he throbs against my thigh. His breath hitches in his throat.

"You need to rest." He groans when I press against him, rubbing side to side. "Rosie," he warns when I slip my hand into the front of his jeans and wrap my fingers around his throbbing penis. I rub my thumb over the sensitive head and feel how wet he is. I want to taste him.

"Ruben, will you let me taste you?" I push him onto his back.

"Um—"

"And don't even think of telling me to rest. My knee's in a sensitive area, not to mention my hand." I stroke down to his sac, feeling him lengthen and twitch at my touch, and slowly caress him to the head of his shaft.

To my disappointment, he removes my hand. "I want nothing more than to be naked with you and let you have your way with me, but I want to talk first." He places a finger over my lips. "I know I'm about to kill the mood, but this is important, and I don't want to put it off any longer. Okay?"

I dread to think what he wants to talk about. I have a feeling that, since he mentioned "killing the mood," it has to do with my past. It's a past I'd really prefer to keep buried.

I lie in silence with him and tell him more of my story, "When I was a child, my parents would tie my hands together and tie me to a chair in my room whenever they thought I'd been naughty. Leaving an item of food on my plate was enough to warrant that punishment. I soon learned not to leave anything, even if it made me sick later." I give a bitter laugh. "They wanted a servant and got me."

I sit and draw my legs up in front of me. "They were both killed in an accident when I was fourteen. I was put into the foster care system until I was old enough to leave. I've bounced around from job to job, and I've worked at Kenza longer than anywhere else. So now you know." I turn my head to look at Ruben, feeling as though a weight has been lifted from me.

In the back of my mind, I knew I had been

worried about telling him about my past because he has such a close, loving family. I'm not sure why I was apprehensive about telling him. I also didn't think it would be as easy as it was and that I'd manage it without crying. I haven't admitted it to more than a handful of people, and the last time I told someone, Liz, I cried myself to sleep.

"Baby, I don't know what to say."

"You don't need to say anything. I told you at the picnic about being tied up as a punishment. My family was messed up, and because of that, I'm not sure I'll ever be comfortable trusting you to tie me up. It isn't about trusting you. I need you to know that."

"Rosie, Rosie. Don't you know by now that I'll take you any way I can?" He pulled me down into his arms and protected the injured side of my face. "When I told you that I loved you, I meant every word. There aren't any strings attached to those three powerful words. Those are the three words I've never spoken to anyone before, other than family, that is."

I smile. He's so cute. Not that I'd ever admit that to him, though. He's a guy, after all.

"I'm going to shower, and you're going to stay right here. On this bed. But feel free to strip."

I roll off the bed, grab the bag Carla brought with her when we arrived, and head for the shower. Before closing the door, I look back and say, "I'm going to show you how much I love you when I'm finished," and shut the door on his startled but excited face.

AFTER FINISHING MY SHOWER, I DRY OFF AND PUT ON the purple and black panties from the goodie bag Carla gave me. They feel delicious against my skin and make me feel naughty. After putting on the bra and fastening it, I put on thigh highs and the spiked purple high heels. I'll be lucky if I don't break my neck in them.

After fluffing my hair, I turn to look at myself in the full-length mirror on the bathroom door. I can't believe the sexy siren staring back at me is real. That it's me. Do I really look like that? Wow. I hope Ruben likes it. I'd look better without the gauze covering one side of my face, but my body! I smile. I take a deep breath, open the door, and walk toward my guy.

Ruben does a double take when he sees me, his jaw going slack. He's under the covers, and his clothes are on the chair next to the bed. So he's naked. Delicious. The throb between my legs intensifies as we gaze at each other.

Then, I take our arousal up a notch. "You like?" I ask, caressing down over my chest toward my panties. I dip my hand inside to tease him.

He nods and gulps. "Fuck, baby. You are by far the sexiest girl ever." He strokes himself through the sheet. My eyes widen as I realize how aroused he is. He's huge, and the sheet is tented when he moves his hand away.

However, his hand goes back, and as he wraps his fingers around his girth, he says, "This is all for you, baby. Only ever for you."

I take a few steps toward him, careful not to wobble in my heels. Standing at the foot of the bed, I watch him caress his length with his hand, his eyes never leaving mine.

"Will you lie there and let me touch you?"

He arches his back slightly from the bed. "Yeah," he agrees in a rough voice.

Smiling, I take hold of the sheet at the foot of the bed and pull it completely off his body. He doesn't move, but as I slowly move my gaze up his naked body, I briefly meet his lust-filled eyes before looking back down at his pulsing shaft. It seems to have a mind of its own.

"Tie my hands to the headboard."

Did I hear him right?

"I've never had that done to me, Rosie. I'll never do it to you, but if you're okay with it, I want you to do it to me. I'm giving you complete control over me."

Can I do that? I could have him tied up when I can't. Oh yeah!

"My ties are in the closet," he suggests, taking his penis in hand. It's hot and arousing as hell watching him pleasure himself. "Rosie? Ties."

"Yeah."

He chuckles at my distraction as I kick off my shoes and run to get the ties from his closet. There's a red one and a blue one. Both feel like silk.

I rush back to the bed and crawl onto it at Ruben's side. My hands itch to touch him. Ruben removes his hands from his aroused body part and reaches over his head with both hands to hold onto the headboard.

"I'm all yours, baby."

I can do this.

With a wicked grin, I straddle his hips and press down onto him. My eyes roll back in pleasure as I feel him against my throbbing core. Unable to resist, I roll my hips back and forth a few times.

"Jesus," Ruben moans, arching into me more. "Your panties are wet. Take 'em off."

I roll my hips again.

"Please..."

If I take my panties off, I won't be able to tease him as much because I'll want to slide him inside me.

"Rosie, I want to feel you. Please."

I quickly stand and remove my panties, watching as he closes his eyes after looking at me.

"I'm going to come without you touching me at this rate."

I snicker. "We don't want that, do we?"

I climb back onto the bed and rest against his leaking shaft, rotating my hips again without a barrier between us.

"You feel so good... Oh God, Rosie."

My big, handsome guy is so ready to release, and we haven't even started yet.

I pick the ties back up from the bed and wiggle up his chest, feeling him quiver beneath me.

My pussy throbs and gets wet against his chest as I take each of his wrists in turn and attach them to the headboard. He can get out of them if he needs to, but hopefully, he'll show some restraint.

Before moving back down his body, I remove my bra. Cupping my breasts, I massage them, rubbing my nipples between my thumb and finger until they harden with arousal. I position them over Ruben's face, and he laps at my nipples.

He has beautiful lips—lips I've fantasized about too many times to count.

Moving my bottom further down his chest, I feel his penis prod me at the same time he hisses through his teeth. Rising up slightly, I let him slip between my wet folds. I lean down and kiss him.

It's strange at first, me being in charge. I'm used to Ruben holding me when our lips meet, but this time, I'm in control. I get to decide how deep to take the kiss and when to stop. But, as my tongue wraps around his, I'm not sure I'll be able to stop. Tangling with him, I pull his tongue into my mouth and suck, showing him what I intend to do with his expanding cock. Cock! I just thought it without cringing.

Needing air, I pull back, and the love I see in Ruben's eyes brings tears to my eyes.

I move to nibble his earlobe and whisper, "I love you."

"I love you so much, Rosie. But right now, you're killing me."

Smiling, I lick down his neck to his collarbone. I kiss my way across to the other side before moving to his erect nipples, which match my own. Mine ache as I rub them against his stomach while licking his nipples, alternating between them.

His cock rests, or rather twitches, against my

stomach, and judging by how wet my stomach feels, I'd say he's leaking with excitement.

I leave a wet trail with my mouth down to his navel and dip inside with the tip of my tongue, my chin bumping against his straining erection.

"Oh, Christ," he moans when I lift my head, look at him, and meet his eyes. "I'm not going to survive this."

"You'll survive. You may need a week to recover."

I settle between his spread legs on my knees and push his legs wider to get an amazing view. He's the only man I've seen who shaves down there, and it's so damn hot. I can see everything.

Lying on my stomach, I use just the tip of my tongue to lick from beneath his sac, over his balls, and along the length of his penis. I witness more pre-cum leaking from his slit as his whole body quivers with suppressed need.

"You liked that," I say, swiping my tongue around the stretched, tight head. He doesn't answer, but then again, it wasn't really a question. He usually can't keep his mouth shut, though. Before traveling back down his length, I glance up and see his head thrown back and his jaw clenched tight. Good.

He's so big that, as I lick him like a Popsicle, I wonder if he'll fit in my mouth. He has before. There's only one way to find out.

Back on my knees, I massage his tight balls as I slowly take him into my mouth. His taste explodes on my tongue. Groaning around his length, I suck him in as he arches into my mouth while his legs twitch. He's going to come in my mouth.

I love that I can make this guy lose his cool with my body. I move my hand between his legs and start rubbing him there. Apparently, guys have a really sensitive spot between their balls and anus that becomes more sensitive during sex. I want to find that spot.

"Ahhh...Jesus...Fuck!"

I think I found it!

"Rosie. Stop. Please."

I do.

"You don't like what I'm doing."

He growls. "I love what you're doing, but I want to be inside you when I come."

"You were in my mouth."

"Let me be more explicit. I want to be buried deep inside your cunt when I come. I want to feel your muscles clamp down on my cock when you climax."

The more I listen to him, the more aroused I become. I squirm, trying to ease the ache he's created, but nothing works.

"Bring your bottom up here, baby. Let me taste you while you're tasting me."

Does he mean what I think he does?

"Yes, I do," he says, grinning like the cat who got the cream.

With the grin still on his face and his eyes alight with lust, he pulls his hands free of the loose ties and waits for me to make the first move.

Uncertain of what to do, I straddle his waist again, facing his feet, and slowly push my bottom into his face. That's when I feel his hands on my hips. He arranges my knees on either side of his face, then plants a kiss on my wet pussy. My head drops into his groin, overwhelmed by the havoc he's creating with his mouth and searching tongue.

"I'm starving for you, baby."

I don't reply. I just lift myself up onto my elbows, rest my arms on his groin, and suck him into my mouth. I clutch his sac with one hand, massaging it with my thumb. With my other hand, I grip the base of his shaft, bobbing my head up and down. He's hard as hell in my mouth but also hot. It's difficult to focus on what I'm doing to him because of the pleasure he's creating inside me. Then, it completely overwhelms me when he inserts two fingers inside me while lapping at my clitoris.

My climax rushes through me, curling my toes. The intense pleasure drags a moan from deep within me around his shaft, which I have clamped my mouth around.

Before I can think, Ruben has me lying on my back with him looming over me as he slides his penis all the way inside me.

He gives me a quick kiss before sucking one of my nipples into his mouth, nibbling and sucking while pinching and rolling the other with his finger and thumb. My pussy is hypersensitive from my orgasm as he slowly withdraws to the tip of his shaft before slowly entering me again.

Every muscle in his body strains over me as he tries to contain the passion running through him, keeping his hips rocking in slow motion. He was so close to coming, so holding back must be killing him now.

I wrap my legs around his waist, reach down, and massage his sack.

"Fuck," he curses, and starts thrusting into me harder. After one final rub, I bring my arms up and wrap them around him.

Another orgasm starts to build inside me, and, as I feel it start to explode, I bite down on Ruben's shoulder. He thrusts up into me one last time, then holds me down. His cock twitches with his release inside me. My climax follows, clamping around his shaft and pulling him deeper inside me. I writhe under him in the pleasure of our joint release.

Ruben collapses on top of me, and my legs go slack around him.

When he tries to roll off me, I tighten my grip on his shoulders. "No, I want you to stay."

"I'm not going anywhere. But I'm too heavy."

He slides a hand beneath me and, clutching my bottom, rolls us over so that I'm sprawled on top of him, his cock still buried deep.

"I don't have the words to describe that. You are so fucking hot, baby. I want you to wear these only," he says, sliding his hand inside the top of my thigh highs. "Nothing else. Just these sexy pieces of silk."

"Anything for you." I squeeze my internal muscles and smile when I hear a hiss escape between his lips.

"Babe," he says, pressing me tight against him and thrusting up into me. "You have to stop doing that. You've taken it out of me. I need about twenty-four hours to recover."

Chuckling, I do it again. "Yeah, right. I can feel you inside me, enlarging. Your recovery time is more like five minutes." I wiggle on him and feel him grow even bigger.

"Oh, baby, that feels good. But we have to get ready. Are you feeling up to it?"

I raise a brow in question.

"We're supposed to meet Sabrina, Carla, and Sylvia downstairs. Thirty minutes ago. I texted Ramon and Lucien to meet us as well."

I start to laugh. "Are you matchmaking?"

"Don't be silly. Guys don't do that."

I place a gentle kiss on his lips and say, "Maybe not, but guys who care about their brothers might. For what it's worth, I think it's sweet. It makes me love you all the more because of the love you have for your family and how you show it." I kiss him again. "And don't say anything cocky to ruin what I just said."

He gives me a crooked smile. "I wouldn't dream of it, baby. Besides, I'm hoping you'll call them your family one day soon. Of course, for that to happen, you'll have to marry me first."

I blink a few times, wondering if I heard him correctly. Did he just propose to me indirectly?

"Um."

"Baby, I'm dying here. Will you answer the question?"

"You didn't ask a question," I reply, my grin spreading across my face.

His eyes widen in surprise, and then his grin matches mine. "I love you. Only you. Will you make an honest man out of me by becoming my wife? Will you marry me, Rosie?"

There is only one answer I can give him. "Yes, I'll marry you."

With those words, the others are forgotten, and we celebrate our engagement as only two people in love can.

THE END

KENZA

DEAR READER

Thank you for reading *Playing with Desire,* and thank you for your reviews! It's really appreciated.

Subscribe with your email to be alerted about new releases, sales, and events.

http://lexibuchanan.net

ONE OF SIX
A DARK ROMANCE

Six brothers

Six heartbreakers

Six Den Hollows

Essex Redd, the youngest of six brothers at the age of nineteen. My father

was murdered four years ago, and we know who did it. What we don't know

is why. Things get complicated when I fall in love with the killer's daughter.

As the truth begins to unravel, I realize that Bea and my family are in more

danger than anyone thought.

My name is Beatrice Alexandria Lincoln. I prefer to be called Bea. I live in

the town of Mount Sterling, which is known for its old-fashioned charm and

Southern hospitality, and residents like my parents keep those traditions alive.

I long for a life of my own choosing. When my mother dies suddenly, my

eyes are opened to the harsh reality of what it truly means to be a Lincoln.

My father has no idea what I will do to protect the people I love.

Available Now!

ONE OF SIX SNEAK PEAK

Chapter One - Beatrice

Beatrice Alexandria Lincoln. This has been my name since the day I was born eighteen years ago. My parents, Richard, and Elisabeth are patrons of the town of Mount Sterling in the Deep South. Sweet tea, served with a side of sweet fancy, is the official offering to visitors to the house.

I often wonder if anyone else would appreciate my life more than I do. My father is the one who bought and paid for my entire existence.

We live in a white mansion, a five-minute walk from the edge of town. It's where the wealth is. Lush gardens, sleek and shiny vehicles, designer flower beds, and fake people. The town of Mount Sterling is known for its old-fashioned charm and Southern hospitality, and residents like my parents keep those traditions alive. Despite the material wealth that surrounds us, I sometimes long for a simpler life. My father is the mayor. My grandfather is the judge, and my uncle is the sheriff. You see what I mean?

The residents want to be in my parents' circle of friends. They push their offspring in my direction, hoping that being my friend will bring them recognition. I don't bother anymore. I have one friend and she's enough. It can be lonely living in a community where people are more interested in your family position than who you really are as a person.

I feel like a robot. A Stepford wife. Every waking moment is planned, even more so since I graduated from high school. I want to go to college. Not that I am interested in any field, but to get away from my family. I'm not sure that is going to turn out to my advantage, as my parents are against it. If my parents hadn't been on my back all the time about grades, maybe I would have fought harder. But now it's too late.

My skin itches against the cotton fabric of the dress I wear. The humidity makes sweat run between my breasts and down my back. The weather makes me sleepy as I listen to the drone of my mother and her three closest friends. The suffocating feeling of being trapped in this picture-perfect life is overwhelming. I long for freedom, for a chance to discover who I really am beyond my family's expectations.

Today's meeting is for them to decide which of their sons I will date first. I don't want to date any of them. I have no choice. Richard Lincoln has spoken. I feel like a pawn in their game of social status and tradition, with no say in my own future. The weight of their expectations crushes me.

I smile in all the right places, only half listening. A loud vibration shakes the China on the dining room table. My eyes wander out the window as a slight smile appears on my lips. Motorcycles roar past the house. The men who ride them live across the railroad tracks in Den Hollows. There are no white mansions with manicured lawns in Den Hollows.

I want to be free like them. Free to ride like the wind through the town without a care in the world.

Seconds later, my dream shatters as the sirens announce the arrival of the sheriff's deputies. I sigh, wishing my uncle's deputies would leave the men alone.

They are real men. No tailored three-piece suits covering their pasty white—sometimes overweight—bodies. Jeans and T-shirts cover their muscular frames. I imagine it's one of them every time I use my vibrator.

A blush covers my cheeks as I turn my attention

back to my mother. I wish I'd paid more attention, because ten minutes later they agree on something I missed.

As mother walks them out, I go to my bedroom and close the door with a huge sigh of relief. I throw the clothes off and into the hamper. In the shower, I scrub my hair to get the hairspray out, which Mom insists on before I scrub my body until I'm red and clean.

When I'm done, I brush out my red hair and put on shorts and a vest. I go downstairs barefoot and follow the sound of my mother's voice into the kitchen.

She gives me a scathing look, her mouth tight. "Beatrice, I asked you to be polite. I didn't expect it to be so difficult for you."

"I was there. I served the sweet tea and the fancies. I smiled and spoke when spoken to. What did I do wrong?" I clench my fists behind my back, angry at the words I force from my lips when I want to say so much more.

"Honestly, child." She grabs my arm and drags me through the house. "My friends noticed when you were distracted by the window." Her eyes narrow. "Those Redd boys and their gang of thieves."

"They're not thieves, Mom." The second the words are out of my mouth, I feel a sharp pinch on my arm. "Ouch."

"You watch what you say to me!" she snaps. "Your father was right. You need a man to keep you in line."

"I'm eighteen. I want to go to college and get an education." I pull my arm free, feeling the bruise already marking my skin. "Dad said he would think about it."

Mom sits down. "Yes, well, your father has thought about it. You are going to get married. We can keep an eye on you here until that happens. Make sure you stay pure for your husband."

My mouth falls open.

"Oh, Beatrice, stop catching flies." Her eyes sweep over me in disgust. "You have a date with Jason Greenwood tomorrow night. You will behave like a lady or face your father. Do I make myself clear?"

"Jason? Isn't he old?"

"He's a respectable lawyer in town. He just turned thirty." Her eyes narrow. "Didn't I ask you a question?"

"Yes, Ma'am," I say. "I'm clear." Inside, where no one can hear me, I scream.

"Instead of sulking around the house, go to the store and buy some milk."

It's on the tip of my tongue to tell her to go get it herself in her nice, air-conditioned car. But I don't. My dad's hand hurts bad.

I take the ten dollars she hands me. "Get yourself something to drink so you don't faint on the way home."

As soon as I slip my feet into a pair of ballet flats, I step outside, and the heat envelops me. This summer is hot.

The houses I pass make me sick. None of the people who live in them deserve it. They don't care about anyone but making more money for themselves and kissing my family's ass.

I walk through the gates that are supposed to keep others out, wondering which guard will lose his job because the men from Den Hollows rode through. The men ask for trouble by doing what they did today. Part of me doesn't blame them. If I was told to stay away from somewhere, I'd want to go. The only difference is that I wouldn't have the courage to do it.

I walk through the pretty town, past the barber shop, the post office, and the library on the corner. I cross the street and pass a few restaurants and the sheriff's office. I turn right and walk towards the big grocery store.

The store is quiet as I enter, and I take a moment

to stand under one of the air conditioning units in the ceiling. My eyes go wide when I catch my reflection in a mirror. My red hair is completely dried and sticks up everywhere. There is no rhyme or reason to it.

"Beatrice, how are you?"

"I'm fine, Mr. Gleeson. Mama sent me for milk." I sound like my ten-year-old self. "And a popsicle." I like the owner of this store. He has always looked the same—slim, with a head full of white hair, a big nose, and dark eyes that miss nothing hidden behind large black specks.

He smiles warmly, revealing a row of perfectly straight teeth. "You always liked the popsicles."

"I deserve two today. Or maybe three."

"You know where everything is." He smiles. "I'll ring you up when you're ready."

"Thank you." I move away but pause. "Mr. Gleeson?"

"Yes, Beatrice."

"Did you see Den Hollows come through town?"

Mr. Gleeson's smile falters slightly before he answers. "I'd have to be dead not to know when they ride those bikes." He winks. "The sheriff's men chased them right back out of town."

"Oh!" Disappointment settles in my stomach, and

I'm not sure why. It's not like I know how to talk to them. If I did, I would feel my father's hand afterwards.

I walk over to the popsicles, pick out a pink one and bite into it with my teeth. As soon as the popsicle bursts it's wrapping, I lick it slowly, savoring the taste. I close my eyes and sigh with pleasure. I wrap my tongue around the ice before taking it into my mouth. It tastes so good.

The sound of a growl makes my eyes open wide. My heart stutters in my chest. The Redd brothers stand on the other side of the store with all eyes focused on my mouth. It has been a long time since I have seen one of them. I don't think I've ever seen them all together— Atilio, Nico, Boone, Galen, Ridge, and Essex. Six brothers. Six heartbreakers. Six Den Hollows.

Chapter Two - Essex

My eyes focus on the girl with the brightest hair I've ever seen. I know who she is. Everyone does. Beatrice Lincoln. The mayor's daughter.

My instant response to her has nothing to do with her parentage, but the girl herself. Curves to make a guy's mouth water. Curly hair that falls in a mess around her face and down her back, over her breasts. It's more orange than red. Fiery.

What freezes me and my brothers to the floor is the way her tongue curls around the popsicle in her hand. The way she licks with her pink tongue, and then heat slides through me when her mouth wraps around the ice.

My dick is so hard that I need to pound something. Preferably into her sweet pussy.

She lifts her gaze and sees the six of us standing watching her. When her eyes land on me my dick jerks behind my zipper. I have never had such a visceral reaction to anyone before and it makes me angry.

Just my luck it's the one girl none of us can touch. Probably one of the only virgins to graduate high school.

I glance at my brothers and wonder what they're thinking. How can one innocent girl bring the six of us to a stop.

Ridiculous.

Still, no one moves.

"Gleeson," I shout. My brother to the right jumps, but I bring us back to the present and the reason we are here.

The girl grabs up two more popsicles, turns, grabs some milk and then high tails it toward the exit.

I feel like I can finally breathe.

Chapter Three - Beatrice

Mr. Gleeson runs toward me as I head for the exit. I toss him the ten dollars and head for the door. I stop. What if Mr. Gleeson needs help?

I'm not sure how long I stand in the doorway, but the next thing I know I'm being grabbed from behind. I don't even struggle when I look down and see strong hands leading to leather-clad arms around my stomach. When I inhale, the man behind me even smells wonderful. I'm tempted to turn my face to his neck and take another whiff. He'd probably think I was crazy if I buried my nose there.

"Aren't you going to fight me, little girl?" His rough voice breaks me out in goose bumps.

"Atilio," Mr. Gleeson's voice makes him turn around so we're both facing the shopkeeper. "Please put Beatrice down. She's a good girl. Not like..." he winces.

The tall man is the oldest brother, only twenty-six. He was born Atilio Junior, but when his father died four years ago, he dropped the Junior. At least that's what I heard. I may not see the Redd men, but I know all about them. I'm good at listening when others think I'm not.

"I like it in his arms." He starts to move and Mr. Gleeson winces as we pass him. "Make sure the doors are locked."

He carries me to the back of the store where his brothers are waiting. They are all handsome men with a mixture of dark and medium brown hair.

"She's checking us out," another brother says with a grin on his face and amusement dancing in his bright green eyes.

I narrow mine. "I wonder who I should kick in the balls first," I reply.

His eyes go wide, and he moves in front of me. "I can assure you that if you ever get near my balls, you will either be on your knees sucking my dick or on your back with your legs spread."

"Dipshit!" one brother slaps the younger one on the back of the head.

"Excuse Ridge, all his manners were knocked out of him years ago when Atilio dropped him on his head."

"Fuck you, Boone!"

"Guys," Mr. Gleeson appears. "Leave them alone.

Atilio, put her down. Ridge, your mother needs to wash your mouth out with soap and water."

My feet hit the ground so suddenly that I lose my footing. Another brother steps forward. "I'm the nice brother. Ignore my twin. I'm Galen." He holds out his hand.

I take it quickly as he begins to pull away. "I'm Beatrice."

His face splits into a huge grin. "Your popsicles are melting."

I blink, surprised.

"Stop flirting," Atilio says. "We've got shit to do." He grabs my hips and sits me down on a freezer lid. "You, don't move."

"Okay." I look into his brown eyes and see flecks of gold. *He has kind eyes,* I think as he pulls away.

I'm curious about what's going on here. Mr. Gleeson isn't afraid of them. So, they can't be robbing the store. Atilio and his brothers are bigger than me. They are over six feet tall. They all wear jeans and a T-shirt with leather jackets of different styles.

I know who each of the brothers are, even though this is the first time I've met them, or rather, the first time I've been in the same room with them.

I absentmindedly tear into another popsicle, sucking out all the melted liquid before pushing the last piece of ice up. I tilt my head and wrap my tongue around it before sucking it into my mouth. It's a little too long to fit, but I crunch it down.

"Those damn things should be illegal in your hands," Atilio says, rearranging his crotch. My eyes fly to his as my face flushes with heat. He gently removes the last one from my hands and smiles. "My brothers won't get shit done if they're busy watching these getting sucked into that pretty mouth."

My cheeks burn. "What are you doing here?" I ask, watching them start to read the labels on the crates in the back of the store. Anything to get their attention away from me and my mouth.

"Looking for something," Boone tells me, his dark eyes fixed on my legs in the shorts I wear. I'm surprised my mom let me out of the house in this outfit. It's tight and shows my curves in a way my mom wouldn't like.

Do the Redds like the way I look? I'm sure they're as curious about me, as I am about them.

"Found it!" a voice shouts.

"Don't drop it." Nico.

The sudden banging on the windows of the store freezes their movements. Mr. Gleeson gasps. "It's the sheriff." He goes pale.

Only one thing to do. I shuffle forward. "I suppose you have a truck in the back?"

"What of it?" Essex, the youngest, hisses and takes a step toward me.

Atilio holds out a hand. "Cut it out."

"If Mr. Gleeson doesn't open the front doors, the sheriff will drive around the back."

"She's right." Boone.

"Let me go out there with Mr. Gleeson and open up. I'll think of something to distract him. Just please don't leave until his car is gone." I wince. "My father will be furious if he finds out I helped you."

"We can't trust her!" Essex argues.

"I trusted you not to hurt me. I have no quarrel with you. Let me do this." I look at Atilio.

"Don't burn us," Atilio says.

"I won't." I look at each brother in turn, remembering which face goes with which name.

Mr. Gleeson takes my hand and pulls me through the store. "Are you sure, Beatrice?"

"You've always been kind to me, Mr. Gleeson, without asking for anything in return." I stop to wave to my uncle. "I'm doing this for you and them. They don't deserve the town treating them the way they do."

"Thank you." He slides the key into the lock. "If

you ever need anything, come to me, okay?" He meets my gaze briefly.

I nod as my uncle bursts into the store. "Sheriff," Mr. Gleeson stutters. He sounds angry, and yes, my uncle notices.

"Uncle David," I rush forward and hug him. Something I haven't done in a long time. I guess Mr. Gleeson isn't the only one acting strange. "I'm so glad to see you. I don't suppose you have a few minutes to give me a ride home. It's so hot out, and my mother wants some fresh, cold milk."

Shut up, Beatrice!

"Why was the door locked?"

"Oh, I was helping Mr. Gleeson lift some boxes in the back, and he's alone in here today. We're done now." I smile. "A ride home, please?"

He's quiet and looks between us. "Get the milk."

"Thanks!" I say happily and run to get another carton of milk. I can't even remember what happened to the one I was holding when Atilio grabbed me.

As I get another, I look behind me and see Essex watching me. I'm not sure what to make of him.

"Beatrice!" Uncle David calls. "I haven't got all day?" His voice comes closer as Essex fades from view.

"Got it." I turn down the aisle and find Uncle

David coming toward me with a panicked Mr. Gleeson trailing behind. "It was nice to see you again, Mr. Gleeson, I'll make sure to stop by more often."

Uncle David grunts and puts a strong hand on my shoulder. "You don't need to shop here anymore, Beatrice." He leads me out of the store and shoves me into the back of his patrol car. My heart races as the door slams shut. I tell myself I can survive this short ride.

I'm helping the Redds get out of town. I'm doing something rebellious. A first. My father will not be happy when he finds out. He won't be happy if anyone tells him what I wore into town either.

Uncle David gets behind the wheel and gives me a long look through the rearview mirror. His eyes make me want to squirm, but I don't. I can't go anywhere anyway.

Instead of heading home, he stops in front of the sheriff's office. I frown. "Why did we stop?"

"I work here. Enjoy the scenery. I'll be back...eventually." He climbs out and enters the office without looking back.

What! The! Hell!

I reach forward and slam the gate between the front and back of the car. I lean back in the seat and kick the door. I can't believe this is happening. My heart is racing as I realize I may be in more trouble than I thought. I must get out of here. Not only am I scared, but it's so hot. The air is stifling. In a panic, my hands slide along the inside of the door, trying to find a way out. I shout in frustration, then scream in terror as a hooded figure appears at the window. I put a hand over my mouth to muffle the scream.

The door opens. "Essex?" I mutter.

He glares. "Go! Now!"

I scuttle out of the car, dragging the stupid milk with me. I don't hang around to find out where Essex went. I crouch down and sneak past the sheriff's office, then dash along the street.

There will be so much trouble when Uncle David finds me gone. I hope no one saw Essex free me.

Sweat soaks my clothes as I run through my yard. My face is flushed, and I feel overheated. Entering the house through the kitchen door, I drop to my knees and roll onto my back. Panting, I give Evelyn—our maid—a thumbs up so she knows I'm okay. I'm in doubt, mind you, because my heart is pounding in my chest.

"What on earth happened, Beatrice? Have you been running in this heat?"

Tears fall. "Uncle David locked me in the back of

his police car. I couldn't get out. He left me there." I cry, not caring if Evelyn sees me.

"Oh, dear." She walks away and I hear the faucet turn on and a few seconds later turn off. She crouches down beside me and presses a cold, wet towel over my eyes and forehead. "Calm down and you'll cool off faster."

"I feel like such a baby."

"You are not. What your uncle did was cruel. He knows that confinement in small spaces scares you."

"He parked in front of the sheriff's office." I sit up and move so I'm leaning against a cabinet. "He left me there. It was so hot, and the air conditioning was off. I couldn't get out, Evelyn."

"He obviously came back and set you free."

I shake my head slowly, my eyes holding Evelyn's. "He doesn't know I'm gone yet. At least I don't think he does."

She frowns. "Then—"

I lean forward and put a hand over her mouth. I whisper, "Essex Redd showed up and opened the door."

Her eyes go wide. "Are you sure it was him? I can't tell the younger boys apart."

"I'm sure it was." Wasn't it? He didn't look like

someone who would help me. He'd rather stand there and watch me suffer.

"You mustn't mention his name to your parents. I'm not only thinking of him, but also of you."

"Don't worry, I won't mention the Redds at all."

"Good, now why don't you clean up while I pour you an iced tea."

"I'd like that, Evelyn."

As I get to my feet, the older woman pulls me into her arms. "At least you haven't seen the other boys in town. Your daddy would go crazy."

I flinch, which she catches. "I can't tell you. I promised."

"Beatrice, I fear for you if anyone finds out."

"It's okay." I put my arms around her. "I won't see them again, so don't worry.

Chapter Four - Atilio

As soon as my three youngest brothers enter the kitchen, my eyes narrow. They come to a stop. "Which genius opened the door of the cop car and let Beatrice out?" Evelyn had told me the girl thought it was Essex, but he would never do that. My eyes go to Galen.

So, I am surprised when Nico comes out from

behind the door and declares, "That genius was me." He grins. "The girl freaked out in the car. It was hot as hell." He shrugs and comes fully into the room. "I grabbed the sweatshirt Essex was wearing earlier and pulled up the hood. Nobody saw me but the girl." He grins. "And she thinks it was Essex."

"You idiot," Essex hisses. "Why the hell did you let her think it was me?"

"It wasn't intentional."

"No one sees or speaks to the girl again," I say. "She's off limits."

"Are you claiming her?" Ridge asks.

"She's the mayor's daughter, and her family runs Mount Sterling. So, no, I am not claiming her. She is young and naive. Stay the hell away from her."

"I was planning to," Essex admits.

"Regardless of this little conversation, I liked Beatrice. It can't be easy for her to have him as a father," Galen says. "She didn't blink an eye when we surrounded her. She helped us get away. She's cool."

Ridge puts an arm around his twin's neck. "My twin likes her." He grins.

"Enough! I don't tell you this often, but I will now. Stay away from her."

These idiots love to mess with me. The thing is, I've learned that if I'm not specific and cover all the bases, they're sneaky, and that doesn't change with age. That's what happens with five brothers.

Mom comes in from the back of the house and as I watch her, I wonder how she survived the six of us.

"What now?" she says.

I subtly shake my head at the idiots. "They set their sights on an unattainable girl, that's all. I told them to stay away."

"Hmm."

"You didn't have to tell me." Essex glares. "Her father killed ours."

Mom gasps knowing who he refers to, a hand to her chest. I jump up and go to her, but Essex is there first. "I'm sorry, but it's true."

"No." She pats Essex's cheeks. "Do not blame Beatrice for her father's misdeeds. Evelyn Park works in the Lincoln Mansion. She adores Beatrice. I won't hear a bad word about her." Mama still has that 'look' that shuts my brother up like nothing else can. "Now leave Atilio alone and clean up the mess you tried to hide in the garage."

Once we're alone, Mom adds, "You should find yourself a nice girl. Someone to take care of you. You took on a lot when your father died. It worries me."

"I found a nice girl today," I add, remembering how Beatrice Lincoln felt when I held her close.

Mom gives me a somber look. "Take your own advice and stay away from the girl. If you go after Beatrice, you will only bring yourself grief. Her family will bring a lot of trouble that none of us can handle."

"I understand that. I was teasing." I get up from the table and kiss Mom on the cheek. She stands and pulls me into her arms. "You're a good son, Atilio."

Mom rarely gets emotional, but when she does, it hits me. I kiss her cheek before pulling away. "I'm going to help them clean up." I pause in the doorway and turn to face her. "Beatrice, why is she so unhappy?"

I surprise her, and worry lines appear on her face. "Atilio," she whispers.

"Please, Mom, tell me."

"She will be married and pregnant within a year, all arranged. The sweet, innocent child is not free to live the life she wants… Please do not look in her direction."

I hold mom's eyes for a while. I want to reassure her that I'll never see Beatrice again, but that's impossible when the girl piques my interest. She showed no fear when I took her in my arms. And the way she ate those popsicles should be illegal. I doubt I'll be the only one having wet dreams about her tonight.

"Don't worry, Mom," I say before heading outside. As I do so, one of my brothers leans against the wall near the kitchen window. I frown, "You heard everything?"

He starts walking toward the garage. "Yeah, I heard. I hope you are planning on listening to Mom." He stomps off.

I grimace and watch Essex go.

Available Now!

OTHER BOOKS BY AUTHOR

Hawke's Ridge

Maddox · Colton (2026)

Den Hollows

One of Six · Two of Six (2026)

Den of Filth (New MC Series 2025)

Reckless Wilder (2026)

Fifth Realm Series (Romantasy)

Quiver of Chaos · Wings & Arrows (2026)

Standalone Romantasy

Persephone Unchained

Tallulah James Mystery

Dead and a Murder or Two · Dead and the Wedding Crashers · Dead and a Deadly Deed · Dead and a Best Friend

Boston Bay Vikings

Camden · Bennett · Ethan · Sutton · Carter · Bryson · Ivan · Theo · Noah · Knox · Jericho · Roman

Boston Bay Vikings Minor League

Lake · Rhodes · Nikoli · Dario · Madden · Bradford

Single Titles

Butterflies and Darkness · Come Back to Me · Indecent Villain · Lawful · Love Stryker · Tears in the Rain · Whispers of Yesterday

Holiday Season

Holiday Kisses in the Snow · Jingle Bells

Romantic Suspense Series

Twenty Eight Days · The Next Victim (2025)

Blossom Creek

Christmas at Emelia's · A Rake in Blossom Creek · Heatwave in Blossom Creek · Secret Love in Blossom Creek · Mischief in Blossom Creek · Runaway Bride in Blossom Creek · Naughty & Nice in Blossom Creek

Bad Boy Rockers

My Brother's Girl · Past Sins · My Best Friend's Sister · Never Let Go · Saving Jace · Silent Night (Novella)

Kincaid Sisters

Meant to be Mine · You Were Always Mine · Will You be Mine

McKenzie Brothers

Playing with the Boss · A McKenzie Wedding (Novella) · Playing with Fire · Playing with Desire · Playing with Trouble · Playing with their Hearts · A McKenzie Christmas (Novella)

De La Fuente Family (McKenzie Spinoff)

Love in Montana · Love in Purgatory · Love in Bloom · Love in Country · Love in Flame · Love in Game · Love in Education

McKenzie Cousins

(McKenzie Spinoff)

Baby Makes Three · A Business Decision · Secret Kisses · Kissing Cousins · If Only · Princess & the Puck · A Bakers Delight · A Cowboy for Christmas · A Secret Affair · One Christmas · The Pregnant Professor · It Started with a Kiss

Novella's

Educate Me · One Dance · Pure

ABOUT THE AUTHOR

While Lexi is the author of the chick lit series, Tallulah James Mystery, and the fantasy/romance series, The Fifth Realm, she is also the author of over seventy novels. Based in Ireland, this British author has been writing since 2013.

Follow on social media:

Website: http://lexibuchanan.net
Email: authorlexibuchanan@gmail.com

facebook.com/lexibuchananauthor
x.com/AuthorLexi
instagram.com/authorlexib
bookbub.com/author/lexi-buchanan
amazon.com/Lexi-Buchanan/e/B009SPA94U